William, Her Guiding Star

Louise Behiel

This book is dedicated to *Lucy,* my 12 pound canine dictator, master, and companion who passed in October of 2023. She was small but mighty and her loss was harder than I ever imagined.

I love you, Lucy.

Now and Forever

Run and play with your brother, Jake.

CONTENTS

CHAPTER ONE

Agnes Harrison stood at the attic window of her family's Mayfair home. The streets below were quiet, considering the hour. She bent and peered through the telescope lens, looking up at the sky. This new apparatus was better than her older one, but she was sure she could see forever with proper magnification.

She jotted notes in the notebook of her discoveries and then stopped. Put her pencil down and looked through the eyepiece.

What did birds feel flying above everyone on Earth? Would a man ever soar like that? What an intriguing thought! She couldn't imagine how it would happen. Newton had proved the Law of Gravity, which caused anything dropped to fall to the ground.

It would be incredible to float above London, the countryside, and see for miles. Sadly, not in her lifetime, but someday, she was certain. As long as humans kept exploring, studying, and learning, they would break the known laws of science and get a person into the sky.

Hot air balloons! We're doing those right now, although rarely. They carried only a few people and some of them had crashed, but the experience of floating above the earth in the silence had to be remarkable.

Ripping open her notebook, she grabbed her pencil and made a note to herself in big, bold letters. 'Make an appointment for a ride in a hot-air balloon.' She double stroked beneath the words. It was necessary for her research. It would help her learn more about space, flying, and being lighter than air.

"Agnes? Agnes, are you up there?" her mother called from the base of the attic stairs.

She closed the notebook, centered the pencil on it, and went to the top of the door. "Yes, mama. I'm here. Do you need something?"

"Your father and I are starting our plans for the Christmas season, and we wondered if you would join us. We will invite some of his fellow Parliamentarians to our Christmas ball and some younger people, too."

Agnes refrained from rolling her eyes. They didn't understand she didn't want to meet more young men. It seemed pointless. Most were interested in gambling, racing horses, and having relations with as many women as possible. None of which appealed to her.

She'd studied games of chance for a while. It was an exciting exercise in the mathematical laws of probabilities. But soon, nobody would play with her. And since the quality Gaming Hells didn't allow females, she lost interest.

At balls, her parents' friends no longer welcomed her at a card table. Without intending to, she counted cards and calculated odds, and messed up the game because of her inability to keep a straight face.

She could not ignore what she knew when sitting there. When she tired of people's frustration with her, she stayed away from the salons where people were gambling.

One man offered her coin to teach him her system. But a person with no fluency for numbers was not able to learn how to profitably gamble. For him, it would always be the luck of the draw, since he lacked the ability to see the cards, calculate probabilities, and use that information to guide his bets.

Even worse, she concluded that knowing the odds wouldn't affect his bet because he was after the thrill rather than winning. It was a bitter lesson when she realized many players didn't care if they won or lost. They were only chasing the excitement.

Which made no sense.

Men created another problem for her. When she first came out, a rake had propositioned her. When he started flirting, he winked. She asked if he had something in his eye. He said no and laughed.

Then he offered to take her to the terrace for some fresh air.

"Are you feeling overheated?"

He smiled at her. "Yes. The ballroom is rather warm."

Unlike most of her female peers, she knew about the human reproduction system and his goal. She considered her response and should have known better, but she couldn't help herself.

She looked him in the eye and asked, "Is it the crowd making you overheat or your thoughts about the women?"

He stumbled and mumbled and murmured an apology, then excused himself, almost tripping over his feet, getting away from her. No other man ever tried to take her for a walk on the terrace.

Agnes would far rather be in the basement working with her test tubes and chemicals or the attic, looking at the sky, than dealing with the heat and odors of a ball, whether at her parents' home or somewhere else.

The women were always polite, talking with cold voices and tones. The politeness that screams, "You don't fit. You're laughable. Go away."

When she realized they were right, the gossip and the comments no longer hurt. Instead, she was proud the ton accepted she didn't belong, nor did she want to be where she saw no value.

For any woman to be satisfied by putting some man in the parson's mousetrap and drag him down the aisle to say 'I do' seemed ridiculous. Given the men she had met and their lack of curiosity, she would rather stay at home and work with her experiments or watch the sky.

It was easier than conversing about the weather because there were two answers in England: it's lovely, or it's raining. And yet, she knew people who could talk all day about it. What a waste of time and energy.

"Mother, you know how I feel about balls. And I don't have a good eye for decorating or the skills to organize events like this, but I'll try. However, I don't have time to attend. I need to use my telescope and document the night skies. A comet is coming soon and I want to see it.

"Agnes, we agreed we wouldn't request your presence at many social affairs, but when they are in our house, you would be present and accounted for, dressed in your finest, and as available as possible." Her mother looked her in the eye. "Isn't that true?"

Agnes sighed. "Yes, we have that agreement, and you have been most generous in keeping your side of it. But I want to study the skies. Scientific research demands consistency, meaning it is best to watch it every single night at the same hour to see the changes.

"If I'd known you planned to use your pin money to buy a new telescope, I would not have asked your father to increase it. But I did, and he did. And now you have something else to take all your time."

Agnes squirmed. Her mother was right. She had not explained she needed additional funds to purchase this equipment.

"For one night, you will adhere to the letter and intent of our agreement and attend the Christmas ball after greeting guests in the receiving line. You'll dance when you're asked, sit with us for supper, socialize, visit, and be nice to people.

"Mother, I don't do well making small talk, and I shall remain a wallflower, as usual."

"Perhaps this time will be different. I pray this event includes a young man who sees your worth and beauty. He'll recognize what you bring to the world. And he'll know that you are an exceptional woman."

Agnes doubted such a being existed. She had never met one this far and had been introduced to legions of males. A spinster of twenty-five, she had hoped her parents would cease trying to partner her up with some peer of the ton and leave her on the shelf. But not today.

She sighed. "I agreed, and I'll be there. I'm certain this also means you'll want to go to the modiste for a new dress. Promise me this is only one night."

Her mother smiled at her. "Fear not, my daughter. We're hosting it in London and will have everyone to the house. With the weather so bad, very few families are going to the country."

Thank heavens. She had all of her equipment set up here. She preferred to remain in the city, rather than their estate, after moving everything around and setting up her new telescope.

Away from London, with its lights, smog, and smoke in the air, she could see a lot more. But staying here meant more research time. She would study the sky in this year of our Lord, eighteen hundred and seventeen. Except for one night when she would ignore her studies and keep her parents happy.

A single ball. How bad could it be?

T he home of Louis, his oldest triplet brother, and his wife was being refurbished. Recently added was a knight's suit of armor, to appease Eliza's six-year-old niece, who was convinced there were knights in all the homes in London, regardless of what she'd been told.

The two females had searched for his sibling and sought his help and protection. Helping them had led to the formation of Triple E Investigations, the agency formed by the triplets, who had discovered a knack for sleuthing. It had given them a focus for their time, rather than attending social events and looking for willing widows, and they all enjoyed the work.

But William found being around his brother Louis and his wife Eliza to be tedious. They were in love and easy with their affection for each other that it became uncomfortable. He doubted he would ever find a woman to share as they did. Mind you, he wasn't looking. He lived a good life with a loving family and had an opportunity to make a difference for others.

A relationship with a member of the weaker sex seemed impossible, considering the time required to escort a lady to balls, soirees, and card parties. Such a commitment was asking too much of him and his busy schedule.

After knocking, he stepped inside. Before getting very far, Wilson, the butler, said, "Mister William, how nice to see you again." The servant closed the door and asked, "Are you looking for Lord Evans?"

"Is he around?" He leaned close. "And decent for company?"

The stoic man nodded. "Always, sir. He's at his desk reviewing letters and reports with his secretary."

"No need to show me the way, Wilson. I've been there a few times already." He handed the butler his greatcoat and gloves, but before he got to his brother's study, the door opened and Louis stepped out.

"It's good to see you." He wrapped the youngest triplet in a manly hug. "Thank you for coming right away."

"When the boss summons, I respond." William walked to the fireplace, rubbing his hands together to warm them.

"Not true. I'm but one of the Triple E Investigators."

"Yes, but your house is the company's official address, which means requests come to you, making the world assume you are in charge, and Henry and I are but your minions."

"We know better."

William chuckled. "I don't care what people think as long as I get my share of the profits." He poured a brandy, then settled in the chair before the fire.

"Which is why I sent you a message. We've got a request for another job. And I'm hoping you will take it."

"Why wouldn't I?"

"It just arrived. The Earl of Harrison's safe was broken into. A few things were moved around."

"Harrison? That name sounds familiar," William said, trying to remember where he'd heard it.

"That's why I want to discuss it with you, since you have an acquaintance with their daughter, Agnes."

Oh my God. If there was one woman he never wanted to see or speak to again, it was her. She lived on knowledge, information, and education and was against anyone who refused to join her there.

The last time they met, it had been humiliating. She had questioned his intelligence in front of a group of his friends. He had rejoined telling her, "At least I am not unkind or cruel, my lady." He bowed from the waist, turned on his heel and left, making it a point of honor to avoid being in the same room with the woman.

Others agreed. He wasn't certain she intended to be mean, but she didn't understand how others felt. She had no patience with anyone uninterested in higher studies, and she made no secret of her feelings, telling all and sundry that focusing only on finding a husband was stupid.

In her opinion, all people should be concerned about the state of society and the amount of knowledge, or lack thereof, in the world. Agnes believed women had the same responsibility as men for the study and implementation of science. She could not understand that not everyone, male or female, wanted to learn.

Juliette, the wife of his eldest brother, the duke, was a trained physician who was not allowed hospital privileges because of her gender, which he found unfair, since she was a gifted doctor. But his sister-in-law had entered the field because she was passionate about it, not because she was supposed to. It made a difference, which Agnes couldn't or wouldn't see.

The earl's daughter had a keen intellect and a sharp mind. But she was a spinster and an ape-leader, with no hope of marriage, love, or children. From that perspective, he could feel sorry for her. But from no other, because he'd met no one who could cut another to ribbons as quickly as her. But despite his misgivings, she caused his cock to tingle, even though she was unattainable and, worse, undesirable.

"I don't think it's in the best interests of the agency for me to take that request, Louis. Let Henry handle it."

"He accepted a job for the Earl of Baystone yesterday and is unavailable. If you can't take it, I'll tell Harrison we have to pass. He wants this resolved right away. I lack the manpower, if you aren't available." He studied his brother for a moment.

"Mrs. J. is still in Bath, and I don't expect her before the New Year. According to the earl, that is too late. He's afraid of another robbery. Remember, he's a high-ranking parliamentarian who has documents from both the house and the Prime Minister."

"Anything of national importance?"

"Could be. He is adamant this theft is related to his political position and his access to information. It isn't one of his staff since few of them can read and wouldn't know what they're looking at."

Neither would he. It was his family's dark secret that he could not make sense of the printed word—the letters jumped around, flitted, moved, and danced with each other, but never remained still long enough for him to understand them. His brothers covered for him, as did the rest of the family. Regardless, it always spelled defective. Different. Freak.

"The Earl doesn't want you to read the papers. He wants you to find who's stealing them or who's looking for them because someone opened his safe and looked through everything inside, then picked the lock on his desk. When we stop it, and I know you can, our job is done. Better yet, our finances are set for this year and most of the next because he will remit an enormous sum of money for this answer."

William glanced at his brother, who wasn't given to exaggeration. "How much?"

"Enough. He fears national safety may be at risk and he'll pay to ensure that such a travesty doesn't happen."

"He could solve the problem by leaving important documents at his parliamentary office and working there," William said, playing with the quill on the desk.

"We know he could. But he's not going to. Very few of the sitting lords work in their assigned offices. Instead, they use their comfortable study at home, where liquor and tea service are handy."

"Because that matters more than national security."

"Harrison will continue to risk England's safety even though he could put a stop to it." Louis took the quill from his brother's hand. "It seems ridiculous to you and I, but we don't have to sit in the house nor work in those small offices provided to the Lords."

"Allwyn refuses to spend any more time there than he has to. He says it's not productive. People are always interrupting and wanting his attention.

"I know, and I understand his point of view. He is one of, if not the most influential, men in the country, between his title and wealth. But I doubt that's true for the earl." Louis shrugged a shoulder. "I am researching his finances, although the report will take a few days," his brother said, fingers tapping on the surface of the desk.

"Good information to have." Something was wrong with this request. "Wait a minute! If somebody has accessed the documents already, why is he worried about it happening again? They know what was in the safe."

"He fears they will steal them next time."

"Seems unlikely, but...." He shrugged. "I'm still not sure I should take this job."

Louis rubbed his chin. "Why don't we do this? You go to their house today and check out the environment. Talk to the servants. See what you discover. When Henry returns, I'll send him to finish the investigation and we'll find something else for you. There will be many requests to keep you busy."

"Are you sure he'll take over for me? I can put up with the situation for the short term. Anything more than that might be asking for trouble."

"I'll change the assignments when Henry returns, if you stay on this job until then. But if for any reason he's delayed, you must remain on this investigation."

"Fair enough. How long will it take to resolve the theft of a few animals?"

"Great. Now let's chat about what Harrison thinks, what his worries are, and what his message said. Then you'll meet with him and ask for more information." Louis studied his brother's reaction. "Is there a problem?"

"No, assuming I have your assurance I won't have to put up with Lady Agnes for an extended period, I'll start things." Hand up, palm toward his brother. "I'm only starting it. It will be up to you or Henry to finish this off. And I'm only agreeing to do it for a few days, because this could be important to the agency. But that's the limit of my tolerance for that woman."

William shot his cuffs and straightened his lapels. He could put up with almost anything for a day or two. Even a few encounters with Agnes. But only if he had to. And only with the promise that his brother would take over if he hadn't solved the thefts before Henry returned.

Three hours later, the youngest triplet knocked on the Harrison's door in Mayfair. He didn't want to accept this job, but had little choice given the importance to England and the financial security it would provide for Triple E Investigations.

After handing his calling card to the butler, he was escorted to the earl's study, where the middle-aged, balding man welcomed him with both a glass of whisky and a comfortable seat.

The room was typical. Across from the door, a fireplace with a large hearth and a bright fire provided a cozy ambiance while warming it. Intricately detailed carvings on the mantlepiece were created by the finest craftsman. On either side, floor to ceiling windows fronted with cream covers and navy drapes, allowed in natural light. An oak desk sat near and at an angle from the fireplace, with two tall leather chairs facing it and a larger one behind it.

Richly polished wood paneling on the walls, which were adorned with a Rembrandt and an old tapestry. The others were covered with bookshelves and rugs were placed for comfort and warmth. A well-stocked liquor tray sat on a side board. A circle of gray armchairs and a navy settee surrounded a small, low table.

"I'm not sure what your brother told you, but I'll give you the details." Harrison sipped his drink. "Someone has been in my safe and left things out of place. I am a regimented man and I organize my reports and file them in a specific order. This morning, they were disorganized and disordered, making me certain somebody's been in it. The problem is, I don't know who."

William heard nothing that surprised him. It was common knowledge that Harrison was fussy about papers and information. He disliked confusion and disorder. He believed there was a right way to do anything, and he knew it.

The latter reminded him of Agnes. But a trait seen as a strength in a man was labeled shrewishness in a woman. Her failing was the meanness in how she delivered her comments, but he determined to be gentler in his judgment of her.

"What complicates this is our annual seasonal party in a little more than a week."

"How many are you expecting?" William asked.

"My countess and daughter are making those plans. I provided a list of notable lords and their wives to include, but they've added to those names."

"In the midst of the possible thievery of national secrets, you and your wife are hosting a ball for an unknown number of people any of whom could be the thief or paying the man to search through your desk and your safe." William studied him. "Do I have that right?" The earl had no reaction to his question.

"Yes. Well, once you're married, you will understand how it is when women get an idea in their heads. There is no changing it. And I didn't try too hard because this party is an annual function and crush. My peers in Parliament expect it from us."

The man's arrogance was beyond belief. How could anyone protect national secrets during a Christmas ball? "Can your study be locked?"

"I have always left the room open for those who wanted to relax in here, away from the crowd." He studied William for a moment. "I don't intend to change that tradition this year. It's up to you and your men to guard my office from a distance."

Unbelievable. He wouldn't lock it. "Do you have government documents here right now?"

"Yes. Of course. There is much to be done during the sitting of the House of Lords and the only way I can keep up is to work here, often late into the night."

"I understand. My brother Allwyn does the same thing. It is not a crime, and it speaks to your dedication to guide the country that you devote many hours to the house's agenda." William sipped his drink as he considered the options. "Would I be able to bring another man to guard the office? He'd make sure nobody opens your safe or your desk."

"This room is open for our guests," the earl chuckled. "Sometimes it provides an opportunity for an assignation. But more often than not, it's for someone like my daughter to come in, close and lock the door, and have a few minutes' respite from the heat, noise, and the crowd. I will deny no one that chance. No, I don't want a stranger in here for the evening."

The man didn't make it easy to defend his precious papers. But William had promised and would do his best. "Who else knows the combination to the safe?" he asked the earl.

"But ... You ... What are you suggesting? Do you think someone in my family is opening it? Trying to break into my desk drawers?"

"My apologies, my lord. I didn't mean to cast aspersions on your relatives. Is it possible that anybody, staff, tradesmen, or whoever is in the house might have inadvertently seen you open it or come across the combination? We have to start somewhere, and that's the obvious place."

The earl glared at him. "Let me assure you that no one knows. I have never shared it with my wife, my daughter, or my secretary. The person who got into the safe could figure it out. It is your job to determine who, how, and why, not mine."

"Again, my lord, I'm sorry if I offended. I'm trying to find the best place to start my investigation. Since you're certain the problem cannot lie with your wife or Agnes, I know to look elsewhere." He raised his hand. "In situations like this, it is often a family member who's looking for coin or something to embarrass the parent. I wanted to be sure that wasn't the case."

"My younger son is a pastor in a small parish near Bath. He hasn't been home in several months. My heir is painfully honest. He would never consider going into my safe."

"What about your daughter?" He knew asking questions about Agnes would raise the ire of the earl. But sometimes when people were angry, they said things they wouldn't say when calm. Besides that, Agnes was an intelligent woman. If anyone around here could figure out the safe's combination, it would be her.

"On my honor, I stand behind my wife and daughter. And both sons. None of them has any interest in any of these documents, which are tedious bills we will vote on in the near future. But there is one that is about the activities of Napoleon and the safety of Europe. It cannot get into the wrong hands."

"They sequestered him on Saint Helena and can't escape."

"That's true, but if a dedicated army attacked our defenses, it is possible they could free him."

"Who would dare such a thing?"

"Only men on a suicide mission, but their plans are still important. And some of that information is in the documents in my safe."

As Harrison explained the situation and his reasons for concern, William's reservations fell away. This could become a matter of another war, and he would not let Agnes keep him from doing his duty to Crown and country.

"Then it's best I begin," Williams said, rising to his feet. "I'd like to question your servants." He held up his hand toward the client. "I know you are adamant it wasn't any of them. But we first eliminate the right people. It will serve no good purpose if I ignore the staff and race around checking others only to discover it was an employee who received a payoff or has an axe to grind in your household, and is looking for money. Therefore, we'll start with them. A professional inquiry isn't rude or overbearing, but gets answers. Sometimes it's a matter of something being off in that person, which I can't articulate it but can sense. Then I dig deeper into his or her past to see what I shows up. If there's nothing, I'll assume my intuition was wrong. But if I'm correct, it saves a lot of time."

"Fine. I'll have the butler send them in individually. I presume you're attending the ball tomorrow night to watch the guests coming and going."

He hadn't planned on being present at a social event, but refrained from saying so. "I'd be happy to attend, my lord. Has His Grace accepted?"

"The Duke of Wolfstone? He's your brother, isn't he?"

"Yes, although I'm far down the line. He and my sister-in-law often accept such invitations and we must agree on what we shall say regarding my invitation, since I am not typically invited to social events with parliamentarians."

"Let me check with my wife. I think they declined."

"We should be sure about our story, whether he attends. Because others might have questions, a clear, consistent rationale for my presence will stop any gossip."

"Good point, young man. I can see why your firm is well regarded."

"We're new, but we are diligent in solving problems and issues that arise for those in the ton." William smiled at the earl, who was correct. Their reputation as an investigation agency was the best. It hadn't hurt that Bob had recommended them for all requests after he sold to them. But they had also worked hard to provide the services which people needed.

The man snapped his fingers. "I have the perfect reason for you to attend our Christmas ball, Mister Evans." The earl smiled. "You will be a guest of my daughter, Agnes."

William's stomach fell to his knees, and his heart nearly stopped. "Oh my, sir. I couldn't do that."

The older man, in full father mode, squinted his eyes at William and pressed his lips together. "Why ever not? Is there something wrong with Agnes?"

"No, my Lord. Nothing at all. Agnes is a beautiful, intelligent young woman who is well informed about a wide variety of topics. But we are not closely acquainted and I can't think of a reason to be here as her guest that won't set tongues to wagging."

"Nonsense, my boy. You ran into each other, perhaps at Hatchard's, and she invited you on the spur of the moment. Since Agnes is spontaneous, no one will question that story."

Anyone who knew William would laugh at the earl's ideas. He would never be caught dead in a bookstore. All those letters dancing around in front of him gave him a headache. "I'm not much for frequenting bookstores, my lord."

"If not, Hatchards, I don't doubt you and Agnes will discover a suitable place to have crossed paths." He called for the butler to find Agnes and bring her immediately.

William didn't like the idea of being Agnes' guest. Some people knew how he felt about the lady. It was not a likely situation to explain his invitation.

As he finished his drink, Agnes joined them. "Father. You wanted to see me?"

The woman pushed her spectacles higher on the bridge of her nose while tilting her head. Her eyes, framed by the eyeglasses, were a light, honey brown. The subtle scrunching of her nose, as if seeking clearer vision, softened her appearance. Her brunette hair, pulled tightly from her face, was in a tidy chignon at her neck, belied that softness, as did her simple, dark dress, which was at least three years out of date.

"Yes, I did, daughter." He pointed to William. "Do you know this young man?"

"We have unfor... we have met, Father. Why?"

"I am hiring him to do some work for me, which necessitates his attendance at the Christmas ball. If anyone should ask, we explain that he is here at your invitation, after running into each other a couple of days ago."

"You expect people to believe that I asked William Evans, and he accepted?" She shook her head. "That might push credibility a little too far."

CHAPTER TWO

Agnes Harrison looked at the man standing in front of her. Tall, with dark hair and blue eyes, he attracted female attention wherever he went. Perhaps it was the dimple in his left cheek, but women, young and old, fawned over him. She had noticed his thinking process, logical and orderly, which was more than could be said for many men of the ton.

When she first came out, they spoke a few times, and she was delighted he conversed on topics other than the weather and others in attendance. But over the years, their acquaintance had soured, and their meetings had not been pleasant. His change started when he joined a group where she was chatting about mathematical studies and referenced two books. No one had read them, but this man laughed at her recommendation.

When she asked what he found humorous, he replied with his own question, "Why would anyone waste their time reading a book about the properties of numbers?" He had shaken his head in disbelief.

"Because it helps to enrich your mind and teaches you to think critically."

"I don't need to read a tome to develop that ability." He looked at the others and into her eyes and said, as he bowed slightly. "If you will excuse me, there is someone I wish to speak with." He'd made his opinion of her very clear to her and the group, which immediately broke up.

Humiliated, she'd seethed in anger and frustration. How dare he speak to her in that tone? Who did he think he was? His relationship to a Duke didn't give him the right to treat her like the dirt under his Hessians. It was rude.

Subsequent meetings were more of the same and part of her discomfort at ton social events.

Agnes looked at her father. "This is not a good idea. Lord Evans and I are not friends. I doubt anyone would assume a man of his standing would socialize or languish in any of the places I frequent." She turned to William. "Tell me, sir, have you ever been in a bookstore?"

"Indeed, I have. Miss Harrison. But I must admit it's been some years. Both my mother and my tutor brought me when I was in leading strings. I've not had much excuse to visit Hatchards since then."

"I presume you keep busy reading the penny press and haven't time for intellectual pursuits and educational study."

"No, not at all. I have never read it, but that's primarily because I'm solving problems, helping people, and ensuring those I care about are safe."

The absolute gall of the men to suggest that his investigations were of any importance to anyone. Who was he kidding? William Evans had a well-deserved notoriety as a rake and a scoundrel. No, he never trifled with a debutante's reputation, but it was common knowledge he would sleep with any willing widow. He would travel for days to a country party where debauchery and gambling were on the menu. Why, he and his triplet brothers Louis and Henry were called the Terrible Threesome, not to their faces, of course, but behind their backs. And yet, a single woman sought his attention.

The man was not unattractive. She'd give him that. Tall enough to be seen over the crowd. His broad shoulders gave the appearance of strength, especially since he didn't wear padding. His looks mirrored his closest brothers, but the deep dimple in his left cheek was unique and separated him from the other two. A square jaw and full lips completed an appealing picture, if a person was of that sort of mindset. But of course, she wasn't.

"Yes. Well, as you have seen, Father, he and I have nothing in common. He admits he's never read a book, and I can barely keep my nose out of one."

The man in question asked, "Do you have some reservation about people who don't enjoy books, Lady Harrison? In your pursuit of higher knowledge, you are perhaps unique among the ton. Most certainly amongst the women I have met, with a single exception. That having been said, I agree that a meeting at a bookstore would not pass anyone's review. My family would consider that a Banbury tale because they are aware I don't favor such shops. But if she stumbled as she was coming out of Hatchard's with several heavy tomes in hand and because I was right there, I gallantly caught her before she fell. After righting her, I picked up her volumes and returned them to her. In gratitude for my chivalry, she invited me to the ball."

Steam built between Agnes' ears. She wanted to scream at him for suggesting she was clumsy, even if it was occasionally true. But his story had more believability than saying they met inside the store. No one would question his version of events. And it was nothing more than good manners to invite him to the Christmas ball.

She sighed, hating being bested by another. But his was a believable idea that would satisfy everyone's questions. He would come, make his bows to the receiving line, dance with a few women, and then leave.

"I agree with you, Mr. Evans. That approach would work. I am not an ungraceful female, but anyone can trip. So, it wouldn't be an extraordinary suggestion, especially since the ton believes you are enough of a gentleman to save me from falling. Your story would stand up to scrutiny."

"Why, thank you, Miss Harrison. That's the first pleasant word about yours truly I've heard from you."

The earl looked between them, from one to the other. "Daughter, do you and this man have some history? Is there something I need to know?"

Agnes did not want her father to be involved in the ongoing war between William and her. Their exchange of words, usually difficult, showed the depth of his social skills, and caught her off guard, leaving her without a response. In the middle of the night, she'd awaken with a perfect rejoinder to his comments, but never when he was present. She found herself flustered when he directed his attention to her. His blue-eyed gaze did strange things to her stomach. If only he hadn't been so maddening and such a troublesome person to be around.

But for one ball, Lord Evans would be in her home. She would never convince her father otherwise. What harm could it do? For a single night, she could tolerate anything. She'd keep her distance, as everyone expected, if they gave the matter two thoughts.

"If there's nothing else, I was helping mother." She looked at William. "There is much to do when organizing a ball and often depends on mathematics, to be sure everything is balanced and equally distributed."

"How lovely for you, yet another place to use your mathematical knowledge." He winked. "You should convince your parents to host more balls to help them with planning." His sarcasm was not lost on her.

She held her tongue, despite wanting to chastise him for his snide comments. He didn't understand or appreciate her work and her extended studies? Like society, who disapproved of women who used their minds? "I do not have time for that, since I recently purchased a new telescope and have been studying the sky every night."

"And how does that benefit people?" he asked.

"Eventually, knowledge of the skies, combined with mathematics, will enable us to fly." Surely even a moron like him could understand the importance of such an advance.

"Pardon me? You honestly expect a man to travel above the ground, the same as birds?"

His thinking was very limited, which was surprising given that his sister-in-law was a pre-eminent physician, despite being female. Why couldn't he see that changes were coming?

"Not today or tomorrow, and probably not in our lifetime. But science will eventually move men and woman from one place to another above the ground. I'm not sure how or when, but I don't doubt it." She didn't add that she believed man would walk on the moon and other planets, too. That was far beyond his rigid imagination and thinking ability.

"People float in hot air balloons now. But they can't go a great distance and are exposed to the wind and elements. They can only do that if the weather is good, the temperature is decent, and there's no lightning."

William studied her. "Are you suggesting there will be another method of flying?"

"Science has only scraped the surface of knowledge. Research will show us how to move hundreds of people around the world in hours rather than months."

William's brows notched and his forehead creased. He squinted his eyes as he looked at her. "You honestly assume it will become possible to transport travelers from England to the colonies in less than a day? Good heavens, woman, steam has taken the trip from months to weeks. It can't happen any quicker."

What a limiting point of view. Maybe it was better he didn't involve himself in science. He could set research back by years. "Of course, it won't with that attitude. We all must consider beyond what we see and look for what we want. I want to live in a world where people can travel around the globe overnight. Or to Glasgow in an hour."

"What you're describing would mean a change to everything in our lives. There would be no stability, nor constancy, for any of us."

"No, what I am suggesting is that the accumulation of knowledge required to make such things is not only possible, but common. When it happens, the world will be used to the idea and accept such travel as normal." She heard the remonstrance in her voice but didn't care.

William shook his head as he watched her. "I'm uncertain whether to applaud your vision or label you a bedlamite. Such ideas are unheard of."

"Perhaps, if you read more, you might learn more." A look passed over his face and clouded his eyes. Sadness or despair marked his expression, but quickly disappeared. He'd shut her out. He was hiding something, and she vowed to discover his secret.

William watched Agnes walk away, her hips swaying. It wasn't often his inability to read left him aware of what he missed.

But his shortcoming denied him access to many things she considered commonplace.

Imagine expecting science to create a way for men to circle the globe in hours, rather than months. After listening to his brother and friends in the London Railroad Society talk about the future of transportation, he knew that faster travel increased profits and changed lives. Trust Agnes' intelligence and her ability to recognize possibilities to leave even those gentlemen behind.

No one had ever suggested a shipload of people might travel around the world in hours. With enough time, he'd bet she would discuss putting men on the moon. Once again, he was frustrated by a desire to learn more about such ideas, which would never happen.

Without reading skills, he could not research to determine if she was right or wrong in her view of the future. Nor was he able to study the possibilities, although he'd love to.

What she was describing made no sense, but she believed every word. He didn't like her manner of expressing her opinions. To think in such a grand way but lack the ability to share her thoughts without making others defensive was as much of a handicap to her as his inability to read.

The earl coughed. "My daughter has some extraordinary ideas. Allowing her to pursue them was the safest path to keep her healthy and well. I don't know where she got the ridiculous idea of people in the air moving around the Earth in hours. But I've learned there is no point in arguing with her." He chuckled. "I have never won an argument with her about the future. It is a sad combination for a woman to be that intelligent and totally unafraid to speak her mind."

"In my limited experience, Agnes has never been shy about expressing her opinions.

"You've interacted with her."

"A few times."

The earl scowled. "I presume you were a gentleman."

How to explain that the man's daughter irritated him, unlike any other woman. "Yes, but she and I have had words at different events."

"I'm not surprised. I can't name a single person who sees beyond her peccadilloes and understands that we mere mortals cannot think like her."

William shook his head. Her brain worked in ways that exceeded the comprehension of this mortal and most of the rest of the world.

"My daughter could make a big difference to society. But men won't associate with a woman who knows as much or more than they do. Were she a male, she would have finished college in her early teens. Her thirst for knowledge and for research are heavy task masters, but she loves every minute of it."

Agnes was smarter than most others. "Our family has a similar situation with my sister-in-law, The Duchess of Wolfstone, also known as Doctor Evans. After her parents died, she applied to the school of medicine in Scotland, attending classes as a man. She graduated, but the medical society does not allow women members, disallowing her to practice in a hospital."

"I have heard some stories about her."

"She's an excellent physician. Brought my youngest brother, Philip, back from unconsciousness. She considers the body and people's lives differently than most other doctors." He studied the earl, looking for a reaction. "Agnes thinks the same way about science."

"I expect you to dance with her tomorrow. It will lend credence to our reason for your presence."

"Even if I have to go to the attic to find her?"

"I have told her she must remain in the ballroom and no trips upstairs to look at the stars. If she sneaks out, I intend to cut her allowance and take away her telescope." The aristocrat slapped William's back. "Needless to say, she'll be nearby all evening."

"Dancing with your daughter provides another opportunity and vantage point to watch the crowd and perhaps observe anything out of the ordinary."

"Exactly." The earl motioned for him to follow. "I'll put you in the gold salon and have individual servants come to you. When you've interviewed them, let me know."

"Thank you, sir."

Starting with the butler, William spoke to each staff member. Very few were literate and even fewer understood what happened in the House. After chatting with the last tweeny, he agreed with Harrison. None of them knew anything about his safe or the documents locked inside. Many of them never entered Harrison's study for fear of reprimand or losing their position. The girl said, "Since me mam would be upset with me if I lost my job, sir, I don't never go near the front rooms. I stay in the back, where my duties are."

William wouldn't expect a thief to admit to his activities, but he believed those he'd questioned. Their conversations had been open and forthright, and he had sensed no subterfuge.

The butler asked if he wanted tea before speaking to the yard and the stable hands.

"Thank you, but I would prefer to speak to them first."

"The earl suggested you meet them behind the kitchen, since they are not used to being in here."

"Of course."

An hour later, he had spoken to all those working outside. None knew the location of the study or paid attention to the activities of those in the house, except as it affected their work. None of them could read. John Coachman drove Harrison to Parliament when they were in London, but he didn't know more than that.

Returning inside, William was directed to the earl, who was standing near the fireplace. "As expected, I don't believe any of your staff had anything to do with the break-in to the safe." He looked at his client, wondering how he'd react to the next conversation, which would be more difficult. "Does your wife have the combination?"

The earl's head snapped back, and his face reddened. "Of course not. Why would you ask such an inane question?"

"Some men share this type of information with their spouse."

He turned away from William. "I don't. I have told no one."

"Without meaning to be rude, what happens to the items in your safe if you passed?"

"The combination is with my solicitor."

"And your son?"

"Heavens no. He lacks the experience to handle these matters. Perhaps when he's older."

"How about Agnes?"

"My daughter? Are you a bedlamite? She has no interest or concern about the contents of my safe; hell, she doesn't know if I'm home most of the time. She has her studies, her telescope, and her lab."

"I still want to talk to her."

The earl scowled at him. "I do not care for your implications, young man."

"Nothing untoward, let me assure you, sir, except for a high regard for your daughter's intelligence and abilities. Of all the people I've ever met, your daughter is the only person who might break into your safe other than to solve an intellectual puzzle." He held up his hand. "She has no reason for such an action, but if her curiosity is caught, I don't doubt she would figure out the combination."

Harrison looked at him in disbelief, then shook his head, hands fisted, pressing against his sides. "I am certain she has never tried to get into the safe."

"Can you tell me where she is? I'd like to talk to her." He smiled and ducked his chin. "Besides, our story is likely to be more believable if we are comfortable with each other, which takes a bit of time."

With a small nod, he agreed. "A maid will join you and my daughter."

William left the study, climbed the stairs, knocked, and waited.

The housemaid, who was behind him, said, "If the lady is working, she won't hear you knock, my lord. Best step inside and call to her. I'll follow and wait."

"Thank you." He opened the door and stepped into an atypical attic. It was clean and spacious, although a long table cut the room in half. In the middle of the space, his quarry was bent over the eyepiece of an enormous telescope, which was pointed toward the sky through an open window on the roof.

Glancing from the equipment, Agnes scribbled notes in her journal, then looked back at the lens. He watched her for several minutes before he interrupted.

"Excuse me, Lady Harrison."

"Who on earth?" she asked as she jumped up, looking around. "Oh. What can I do for you?"

"I thought we should chat about why I'm coming to the Christmas ball."

Behind him, Agnes saw her maid standing at the door. "I don't know what else there is to discuss. We've said how we met, and I invited you."

"I agree. The basics are covered. But we should add more details about that meeting."

"Why on earth would we need to do that?"

"As it stands right now, we're saying you dropped your books. I picked them up and handed them to you, and you thanked me. Then invited me to your family's Christmas Ball."

"Oh, I see your point. We must have made small talk and spent a moment or two together before I would invite you." Agnes wasn't sure what to say. What on earth would she discuss with this man she didn't like and shared nothing in common with, despite him saving her from an accident? Even though she found him annoyingly attractive. "Do you have any ideas?"

"We should come up with a scenario that is comfortable for both of us to mention, if we're asked."

"Do you expect anyone to ask?" Beyond discussing the weather and questioning some lord's financial situation, the ton discussed nothing of import. But logically, his request made sense. "Yes, I am asking for your opinion. This is a social matter, and you are more versed in such circumstances than I."

He looked dazed. "You want my ideas?"

"I do."

Pointing to the telescope, he crossed the attic to stand at her side. "What can you see through it? When I look up, the sky is blue or covered with clouds."

"Gaze through it. There is more than you expect."

"Are you certain I should?"

"Yes, you'll learn what has fascinated me."

He stood beside her and leaned down, his eye against the eyepiece.

"If it's out of focus, turn this knob one way or the other and the images will clear."

He did as instructed and jerked his head away, glancing at her for information. "What am I seeing?"

"The moon, a couple of planets, and, of course, the sun."

He straightened and asked, "They are all visible during the day?"

"Yes."

He fitted his eye to the eyepiece again. "This is amazing. I've occasionally seen the moon in the daytime, but not often and never a planet."

She wasn't sure of the importance of her observations, but assumed they would add to the knowledge of the objects out there and their paths. Someday, somewhere, somebody with a much bigger telescope would determine the distance between the stellar bodies.

Her mouth dried and her heartbeat sped up. Having an attractive man looking into her equipment did weird things to her.

He turned to her. "What happens if you move the instrument? Can you see something different?"

She understood his curiosity. "Of course. Turn this crank."

He straightened and saw the lever she pointed to and moved it a half circle, then resumed his position.

"I'm closer to the sun."

"Yes, but refrain from going any nearer because it might hurt your eyes. In time, we will be able to track the stars and tell how old they are."

"Do they have an age? They aren't eternal?"

"I assume not. The science of archaeology tells us that the earth has a history. It started long ago, although we don't know when or how. But many people are finding bones and artifacts from the past."

He stood up to his full height, looked at her, and said, "Now that you've explained it, I must agree. I can't fathom a reason a star wouldn't have a beginning, the same as the earth."

Surprise twisted her insides. "You attended a talk by an archaeologist?"

"Several. I find it quite interesting. It raises many questions about history, both concerning the world and England. Consider the pyramids. I understand modern tools and abilities couldn't duplicate them, which begs the question how were they were built." He smiled at her. "It's a curious mystery."

"I've never been too interested in archaeology, but your curiosity makes me wonder if I missed something."

"I did not intend to suggest one is better than another, Lady Agnes. Nor to disparage your studies of the sky or mathematics in favor of the history of the Earth. We each have unique interests and questions about science and life."

She considered his comments as she gazed into his blue eyes. This was a different point of view than he'd shared with her. Do other people know this about him, or was he opening a part of himself to her?

"An in-depth study of one or two subjects is all a person can accomplish in their lifetime. Any more is not possible. There's too much to learn."

She nodded, surprised he understood.

"It must be satisfying to go deeply into a single subject." He pointed to the telescope. "I never considered your studies in this way before. You have built on a foundation of science and math to lead you into astronomy."

His forthrightness amazed Agnes. Few people comprehended the relationship between the topics of her interest. Working on the three together, she easily lost a day or two or even a week trying to solve a problem.

"What books have you read on archaeology?" she asked.

His face hardened and his gaze cooled to freezing. She felt as if she were talking to a different man.

"None, Lady Agnes." He looked at the maid and back at her. "I came here to talk to you about your father's safe and how often you've been in it and why."

His feelings were suddenly shuttered, which was disconcerting but interesting. His reaction made her curious about what was going on with William Evans. Why had he changed from interested and charming to cold and distant?

"Miss Harrison? The safe?"

"It holds boring papers and not much else. I watched Father open it one day and wondered about the combination. When he was next away from home, I pushed a chair to the wall, opened the picture, and played with the numbers on the dial."

"How old were you?"

"Oh heavens, I can't remember. Seven or eight, maybe. Perhaps nine? I'm not sure. It was a long time ago."

"And you've been able to open it ever since.

"The only things inside are from Parliament, and I have no interest in them. I don't go in and out of it. I haven't opened it in years... shortly after I first discovered the combination."

"Are you saying you only went into it once?"

She laughed. "No. Since whenever I looked, it was boring and disappointing and a waste of my time, I gave up snooping."

"Can you still get into it?" William asked.

Agnes shrugged. "I suppose, if I was curious about the contents."

"If he hasn't changed it, would you remember the numbers?"

"Of course. He used his birthday."

"You are able to open it anytime you desire."

"Are you accusing me of something? Has somebody been in father's safe? I can assure you it wasn't me. I don't have the time nor the interest to read boring documents from the house."

"No, I can't see you going into it to look at reports. A map of the sky, mathematical theorems, formulas, for sure. But papers from Parliament would bore you."

"Shall we discuss why I invited you to the Christmas party?"

William smiled at her. "I think we just have. If one of your books was on astronomy and we talked about it, then after a civil, friendly chat, it would be natural to invite me to the ball. And offer me an opportunity to look at the night sky through your telescope."

"You are right. Mr. Evans. How astute of you to invent a conversation." Her stomach clenched, and her chest tightened in disappointment. She thought they were having a meaningful dialogue about her work.

Apparently not.

CHAPTER THREE

William returned to the earl.

"Did you reassure yourself about my daughter's access to my safe?"

"Agnes and I discussed it. As a child, she discovered that the combination is the numbers of your birthday, but she stopped opening it because it contained boring documents, rather than anything interesting."

The man spluttered and stammered as he stood. He poured himself a glass of brandy and almost choked on the first sip. After his cough subsided, he turned to William. "Is that what she said?"

"She was curious, and when you were away, she pushed a chair to the wall, moved the picture and began testing combinations of numbers. According to Agnes, it took no time to get inside, once she approached it logically."

He collapsed into his seat because his knees had given out. "I believe you, but I am shocked she's known it all these years."

"I suggest you change it as soon as possible." William held up a hand to the man. "Not because I'm worried about your daughter, but since she has figured it out, someone else could do the same. Especially using your birthday for the combination."

The earl was pale. "Given this surprise, please talk to my wife. Perhaps she has been in and out of it, too."

"I will ask her, but again, I am confident Agnes is not responsible for your recent concerns."

"Thank heavens for that." Harrison shook his head. "If someone wanted something from me, all they'd have to do is nab my daughter and force her to open the safe." He shrugged. "Unbelievable."

"After I meet with your wife, we can discuss additional security measures."

William found the countess in her sitting room, reviewing the ball's menu with the cook. After being invited inside, he introduced himself and asked for a moment of privacy.

Once they were alone, he settled across from her and explained the reason for his interruption. "Are you aware that your husband's safe was opened, his desk was broken into, and someone has rifled through his papers?"

"Oh, dear." She shook her head and pursed her lips. "He hasn't mentioned it. Such a worry, I'm sure. He works long hours in his study."

"Do you know the combination?"

"No, I don't. But if I had to guess, my husband would use numbers that are easy to remember."

"What do you mean?"

"He is much too organized to choose a random set. He'd prefer something like his birthday."

"Not yours?"

She laughed. "Heavens, no. If his secretary didn't remind him, he would forget that date." She leaned close and whispered, "The young man keeps him on track with such things. Gifts, too, I imagine."

"But you've never opened his safe."

"Of course not. Why would I want to review documents from the House? Dry, stuffy, prose that uses a lot of words to say very little."

Unable to stop himself, he chuckled. "I will keep your secret, my lady."

"You had better, young man. What did you think of Agnes' telescope?"

It wasn't surprising in a well-run household that the mistress knew what was going on, including his visit to the attic. "It is quite astounding. I saw stars and the moon."

"It is fascinating enough that my daughter could spend all day with the darned thing. I'm hoping our ball gives her something else to consider."

William nodded, unsure of what to say since he didn't agree. Agnes would show her future children how to use a telescope and try to interest them in higher mathematics.

"Thank you for your time, my lady. I look forward to having your company over the next few days."

He retraced his steps and relayed this latest information to the earl. They agreed that neither woman was likely the culprit, but his research raised a different question: since the man was predictable, anyone might have figured out the combination to the safe. The desk was a lesser concern, because even a child with the right pick or blunt force could get inside.

"I suggest you appoint a trustworthy servant to sit in your study at night. Another should stay during the day, when you're not here."

"Is that necessary?"

"Yes, else I wouldn't have suggested it. Someone is accessing your papers, but we do not know who. Since they are important, we must eliminate the risk."

"Fine, my secretary will work in here if I'm not at my desk and the butler can assign a footman overnight."

"Excellent," William said, extending his hand. "While asking questions away from the house, I'll return every day and again for the ball. We'll see if anyone shows any interest in the study while your residence is busy, which will provide a better sense of the source of the threat." He started for the door, then turned back. "Should someone who has no business in here enter, please retain them and send a messenger. I am at your disposal for the duration of this investigation."

"I just remembered that my secretary is returning home tonight. His father is not well, and he needs to pay his respects. While he's away, I expect you to occupy my office."

William did not want to sit here for days, but having offered to be available, he had no reason to refuse, especially since it was another case from the peerage, which would build their reputation. "Of course, my lord."

Agnes fisted her hands behind her skirt, trying not to fidget as she greeted guests in the receiving line. The evening, clear and cool, delighted her mother, for it was a perfect night to celebrate the upcoming season.

As the queue of people crept through the front door, Agnes saw William, wearing cream-colored satin knee breeches, a white waistcoat and stockings and a black tailcoat with an elaborately tied cravat. His short curls touched the collar of his coat. Finally, he stood before her and her face warmed when he bowed, kissed her hand, and said, "Thank you for the invitation, my lady. I look forward to sharing a dance." His dimple flashed, and she acknowledged the warmth in his eyes. He was an attractive man. Glancing around, the other women were noticing the same thing.

She murmured her agreement and nodded. No one seemed interested in his attendance. Anyone who overheard his greeting would not wonder why she had invited him. Their chat had made this interaction easy. They would deal with questions in the same way.

While welcoming the next person, she acknowledged to herself that he'd been right. Talking about her telescope and astronomy had relaxed her and helped them come up with a good story. She'd give him the benefit of the doubt about their conversation, despite her disappointment that a pleasurable interchange with a gentleman was for another purpose.

Silly woman. She had forgotten their roles and their considerable differences.

As the line dwindled, her parents motioned to her and moved into the ballroom. Her father circulated, talking to his cronies from the lords. Her mother crossed to some female friends, but Agnes remained where she was, at the foot of the stairs, observing their guests, looking for an unobtrusive place to stand, where she'd be out of sight and not feel like a duck out of water. She hated these social occasions. They made her breath hitch and her skin itch.

Before she selected a safe spot, William was beside her, handing her a flute of champagne.

"I thought you might enjoy some wine before the dancing starts."

He continued to surprise her with his kindness. "Thank you for a lovely idea." Her gloved hand slid over his warm one as she accepted the delicate glass. Sipping the cool drink, she relaxed, glad to have someone beside her but lost for words, as usual.

"Is the Christmas ball always well attended?" he asked, surveying the crowd.

"Yes, it has become a highlight of the season for those families who can't get to their country homes for the holidays."

"The weather has been unpredictable in recent weeks. I understand why many choose to remain in the city. Between the risk of snow and the poor roads, safety takes precedence."

"Which means my parents' ball is a crush, which is a good thing."

"Is it always this well attended?" he asked, surveying the crowd.

"Yes, it has become a highlight of the season for those families who can't get to their country homes for the holidays."

"Is there something else to say about the seasonal changes?"

"I thought we were talking about the attendance."

He smiled. "We were, I suppose, but somehow it morphed into a strange conversation."

"You don't care to discuss the weather, Lord Evans? How very unusual of you."

"Lady Harrison, I can make small talk with the best of people, but I prefer more important topics."

"Really? Like what?"

"If you were upstairs, what would you see through your telescope?"

Her body came alive as she looked up the stairs longingly, but she remained aware of her promise. "Right now, stars across the sky and a little later, the moon."

"How many?"

"No one knows for sure, but with a stronger instrument, thousands are visible."

"Really?"

She nodded, comfortable with this conversation. "Not with mine. Its lenses are not strong enough to see that far."

"Are more powerful ones available?"

"They are terribly dear and require a sturdy floor for the weight." She sighed as disappointment swamped her, remembering her search for a better instrument. "They're huge and need a big opening in the roof." She'd never have one, since the house floors wouldn't support it.

"Your attic has a window under the eaves."

She nodded, surprised he had paid that much attention. "It doesn't directly face the sky, but is at an angle." She held up her hand. "Don't misunderstand me, I am grateful for the space and the place for my studies. But I would love to gaze straight up at the heavens."

"I'm sure that will happen for you, my lady." He saluted her with his champagne flute. "I hope I can look through your next instrument."

No person had ever shared her interest in her telescope. This man was asking to examine the sky, with her following one. Maybe he wasn't as bad as she'd thought, at least in this circumstance. It was comforting to stand with someone and converse. Several guests had noticed them, given the heads tipped in their direction and conversation behind fans. But this time, she was comfortable, thanks to the gentleman beside her.

Looking at the couples dancing, her unease built and almost choked her. She was standing here, conspicuously chatting, rather than positioned in a quiet corner of the room. Agnes hated balls and music was part of the reason. While her brain was always in top-notch form, her feet, both of them left, were failures. Worried about tripping over her partner or stepping on their toes, she couldn't enjoy the orchestra. Her stomach tightened and twisted with fear she'd make a fool of herself when they took to the floor for their dance.

Her last dancing master, one on a long list, had departed, cursing under his breath about her lack of skills. Her mother had berated her for being stubborn, since no person could be as unmusical as she was. She ached to move gracefully to the music, but her body betrayed her every time.

"I know it's not a waltz, but may I have the pleasure of this dance?"

She couldn't imagine anything she'd like less. "Uhm, no, not right now."
She grimaced, then looked up at him, forcing her lips to lift in a smile. "I
would prefer to wait a little while."

"Oh, of course. You have names on your card. My apologies for being
gauche."

"No. Not at all." In a heartbeat and given his kindness, she decided to
trust him, and leaned closer. "I am not a skilled dancer, and dancing in
sets terrifies me. I forget the steps or who I'm supposed to be with, then I
confuse the movements and trip everyone up."

"It can't be as bad as you fear, but I will respect your wishes. However,
the first waltz is mine." He took her card, signed his name, and made no
comment about the empty lines. He was proving himself a more decent
person than she assumed.

All her tension disappeared. She was grateful for his understanding.

He leaned closer. "Now that I've claimed our dance, I'm off to check out
the study and see if anyone entered while enjoying our conversation."

Watching his straight back and strong gait, she felt more in charity with
him than she'd dreamed possible. He seemed almost human tonight. And
friendly. Dragging her gaze from his retreating form to the ballroom, she
realized he was more attractive than many men in attendance. How had
she missed that observation?

After he disappeared, Agnes strolled the perimeter of the room,
watching sets come together for the cotillion. Finding an inconspicuous
spot, she turned to the dance floor. The steps didn't seem that difficult,
but even though she had memorized their order, her feet wouldn't move
to that list, and never in time with the music.

She hoped she'd remember the count when waltzing with William, since
it was simpler, and she might be able to follow him without making them
conspicuous. Unless her past repeated itself. Again.

Embarrassing memories of trips and trodden toes warmed her cheeks.

She shook away her uncomfortable reminiscences. There was no point
mulling over ancient history. She was not a desirable dance partner, which
is why she escaped as many balls as possible. There was nothing more
tedious than standing on the side or sitting with the dowagers and her

mother as dancers formed beautiful patterns to the music. She would rather read a penny dreadful or a gossip rag.

But watching as William returned to the ballroom, she wondered if tonight might be different. A waltz. She crossed her fingers, hoping she wouldn't make a fool of herself.

William spent a fair bit of time in the study, waiting for nothing. No one even jiggled the doorknob. He placed markers which would show if anyone entered through the hallway. After an hour, he returned.

Agnes was across the ballroom, near her mother, hiding. Which, given the ton's opinion of her, might be for the best, since the modern world had no room for smart women—especially when they were interested in topics considered the exclusive domain of men. It must be hard for females like her and Juliette to know their minds are better than most males, but be chastised and made fun of for their ability. And yet if they were gifted on the harp, or the pianoforte, and played for personal pleasure, they would be lauded. The more he thought about the situation, the more frustrating it seemed. And he had been as bad as anyone.

He crossed the floor as the violinists tested their instruments. He stopped, extended his hand to Agnes, and said, "I believe this is our dance."

She nodded, but her gaze froze as the women tittered and giggled. Obviously, this was a rare occurrence. But he had promised, and he kept his word, regardless of the cost.

In the center of the room, William took her gloved hand and placed his other low on her back. She was shaking, her glove damp.

"Are you unwell, Agnes?"

Her face pale, she swallowed and gripped his hand tight enough to hurt.

"Take a deep breath and relax." He leaned close and whispered to her, "Don't worry about holding on to me. I've got you. I won't let you fall."

She looked over both her shoulders, then turned to him. "That may be your experience, but I have tripped some of the best dancing masters in London."

William pressed his lips together, so he didn't laugh. The lady genius was admitting to something she didn't do well. He never expected to see the day. "Fear not. I won't let you down." He smiled at her. "Take another deep breath and listen to the music."

When the orchestra started to play, he led her in the first few steps of the waltz. "Relax, Agnes. This is not painful."

"Easy for you to say," she responded, her face white, her hand squeezing even tighter.

Her body was rigid and a mite far from his.

Listening, as they moved around the floor, he leaned close and asked, "Are you counting?"

"How else am I supposed to remember what step to take?"

"Don't count Agnes. Music is based on mathematics. Hear the rhythm of the numbers from the orchestra. Success at the waltz comes from absorbing them."

She took another deep breath and cocked her head. Step by step, she relaxed, coming closer to him. Their footwork became smooth, matching the tempo of the music, rather than a march. After a moment, he said, "It's time to twirl. Just feel the rhythm." And he led her in a grand turn and felt her leaning into him, allowing him to lead her to new places.

Afterward, as they moved into the swirl of the crowd, she opened her eyes and smiled at him. "That was easy. Counting never crossed my mind."

"Remember Agnes, it's all numbers. And when you relate life to them, you can do anything."

She looked up at him, her gaze warm with gratitude, and whispered. "Thank you." They made several more silent turns around the room. Agnes's smile beaming her delight.

When the music stopped, he bowed, she curtsied, and they began to cross the floor, but she crooked her finger for him to bend down towards her and said, "I have never enjoyed a dance more. I am grateful, My Lord.

His heart warmed. "It was my pleasure, Lady Agnes. Perhaps we can do it again another time."

After leaving her with her mother, he returned to the study, where he examined the markers he'd placed earlier. No one had entered the room.

He checked the dusting of flour on the windowsill, which was untouched, showing no entries from the outside.

As soon as he had a moment with Lord Harrison, William would ask him to open his safe and verify its contents. That answer would tell him if his simple security measures had worked and if the earl was telling him the truth or not.

But his host wouldn't be available for several hours. After double checking the locks on the windows, he closed the study door and walked to the gaming room.

As always, the number of people betting on the turn of a card and the amounts on the table were shocking.

The numbers and symbols on the cards moved too much for him to take a chance on playing, because he only saw a blur. He couldn't identify the suit or numeral, which made gambling difficult. He didn't miss it, since he'd never tried his hands at those games. But if someone forbid him from a game of billiards, he would make quick work of them.

Besides, he didn't have money to waste on cards. He and his brothers were working to establish their new business. Allwyn was generous with their quarterly allowances. But what man wanted to live on the largesse of his older brother? More importantly, he was ready to move out of his bachelor accommodation, wanting more space and some privacy.

He didn't need a grand residence like Louis. But his triplet sibling was married with a family, while he was single with no intention of marrying soon. As a result, he preferred a tidy little house, somewhere in Mayfair or, more likely, Marylebone. His own space, where he didn't have to contend with the comings and goings of the other tenants, which were becoming tiresome.

He chuckled at his egalitarian ideas, because in most families, the second and subsequent sons lived on minor estates owned by the peer. Allwyn would happily have him oversee a country landholding. And his life would be decent.

But there was one problem. Because of his reading issues, he couldn't manage an estate. He'd have to rely on the steward, which was a road paved to hell, albeit with good intentions. No, running a large property was not for him. That's why Triple E Investigations was such a godsend.

His job didn't necessitate understanding the written word. He listened, paid attention, and asked intelligent questions. Best of all, he had a great memory and easily recalled what was said to him. He didn't make notes but relied on his mind.

It had taken him years to realize he wasn't a dunderhead, he just couldn't read. His brain didn't process the letters. Other people may not understand, but he had learned to live with it and to rely on his recollection and senses to keep him on the right track.

This far, it had worked. He turned from the gaming salon and walked into the ballroom as Agnes returned.

She came to him, looked around his shoulder, and asked. "Have you been at the tables?"

"Heavens no. I don't gamble. I have better things to do with my time and coins than take a chance on the whims of lady luck and a possibly marked deck of cards." He shook his head. "I can honestly say I've never spent a pence on a card game. And I have no intention of starting today."

"That is most exemplary, William." Agnes said. "I have never made the acquaintance of a man who doesn't gamble."

"Including your father? He doesn't strike me as one who would rely on lady luck."

"No, except if he wants to have an inauspicious conversation with someone at the table. Then he'll open his waistcoat, loosen his cravat, bring out his coins, and ask to be dealt in."

"I suppose the interrogation begins slowly?"

"You know my father." Agnes looked at him for a moment. "Did you discover what you were seeking in the study?"

"Yes, I did." He would not explain the real reason for leaving the ballroom.

"And what, pray tell, were you hoping to find?"

Drat the woman and her curiosity. He leaned close and softened his voice. "Between us, I was looking for some peace and quiet. The noise, the smell of perfume and cologne, along with the constant chatter, can become rather disconcerting to my nerves. And so, you caught me. I snuck away to have a few minutes of rest."

Agnes touched her throat and tentatively smiled. She stared at him as if he was from the moon. "I thought I was the only person in the world who felt that way."

William grinned at her and her naivete. "I can promise you are not the only one. My brother, Allwyn, is a genius at moving through a crowd like this and talking to people and appearing to have a wonderful time. But at the end of the night, rest assured, he's made a couple of business contacts. He's offered an opinion on a bill in the House or the importance of female physicians in England or the antics of his little boy. But even he is glad to get home."

"He sounds like a family man. There aren't many of those in the ton." Her brows furrowed. "I don't think I've met the duchess."

"She seldom comes to these functions. As a practicing physician, she's kept busy."

"She's a doctor? Did I understand that correctly?" Agnes squinted her eyes, and her face scrunched in confusion.

"Yes. Her credentials are, of course, not sanctioned by England's Medical Society and therefore she uses her skills and talents to help anyone who needs them."

"How interesting. A female physician. The idea had never crossed my mind. But now that you mention it. I'm surprised women are not clamoring for the opportunity."

"We never know what we want until someone shows us it's possible." That was true for each of his married brothers and their wives.

"You are right, Mister Evans. I will remember that in the future."

William smiled at her. She was a softer female than she presented in society. Underneath her shell was a caring, questioning, cautious young woman who wasn't sure how to be amongst her peers. He identified with her hesitation, because he'd lived it.

"I hear the orchestra preparing for another waltz. Please do me the honor of sharing this second dance with me." He grinned. "Society will be scandalized, but we know it is practice."

"Society is scandalized by many things in my family, and this wouldn't be the first. It would be my pleasure," she said, placing her hand on his arm. "Shall we?"

CHAPTER FOUR

During their second waltz, Agnes admitted to herself that there was more to William than she'd thought. His respect for his sister-in-law and her studies spoke highly of him. Even more astonishing was his understanding of the connection between music and mathematics. Being held in his arms as they swirled around the floor was as intoxicating as finding a new star. As the music ended, it was natural to invite him to join her and her parents for supper.

Delighted when he accepted, she led him to their table.

He bowed to the earl and countess. "Agnes graciously invited me to dine with you. I hope that matches your pleasure."

"Of course," answered his host. "Please, be seated."

The foursome exchanged dinner pleasantries, chatting about the crush at the ball and how lucky they were that the weather had held. Despite the topic of conversation, Agnes was relaxed and enjoying herself.

"I noticed the two of you waltzing," said the countess. "My daughter rarely enjoys it, but your turns around the floor would decry that opinion."

"Mr. Williams is a most proficient dancer who makes anyone look more than adequate."

"Hush," William responded. "You will put me to the blush with your flattery. Dancing with you was my pleasure."

She whispered softly enough that only he heard her, "But only when I learned to think of music as numbers." It warmed her heart to have a normal conversation with a peer and not act like a blooming idiot.

"I'm sure there is much to discuss about this evening on the morrow," said the earl.

"There's little to add to this discussion," William replied. "Everything seems in order."

For the rest of the meal, the topics were typical nonsense, but she took part in a limited fashion. It seemed a miracle that this man, this attractive man had put her at ease. The scientist in her wanted to make notes of her observations and attempt to replicate the experience with another male. But she was too nervous, given her humiliation during her past forays into society. Instead of following scientific inquiry, Agnes relaxed and joined the discussion.

Her parents liked William, and she admitted she was proud to sit next to him. Despite her reservations, she was at a ball, with stars in her eyes, enjoying the conversation and the company.

After dinner, he excused himself and left.

She felt strangely bereft, which came from the absence of a friendly face, rather than anything more personal. Yes, that was undoubtedly the reason.

She had discovered an ally, perhaps even a friend, who understood her, which was difficult, given that he had been mean to her in the past. She rose. "Please excuse me." She smiled at her parents. "I am fatigued and thought to retire." After bobbing a quick courtesy, she hurried across the dance floor and up to her quarters. As her maid helped her change to sleeping garments, Agnes hummed the tune from the first waltz. As soon as the woman left, she danced around her bedroom, smiling from ear to ear.

Tonight, she'd waltzed. William was a genius, suggesting she follow the tempo and pace of the music as if they were numbers. Eventually, she let the image of the numerals slide and responded to the melody. It was heavenly.

What an astounding idea. Agnes had never joined mathematics and music and applied it to moving around the dance floor. At first, uncertain about his suggestion, it worked and was amazing. She could flow with the orchestra's rhythm rather than counting the steps.

The most attractive man at the ball gave her an incredible gift—a pleasure unbeknownst to her before tonight. There would be gossip about their two dances, but she was happy to weather the storm to enjoy sharing those times with him.

William returned to his bachelor quarters, glad to be out of the maelstrom of the Harrison's ball. Inside, he opened the buttons on his jacket and waistcoat, then pulled his cravat free.

"Here now, let me get that for you," Robbins, his valet, said, hurrying to his side. "How was your evening?"

"Interesting, but nothing out of the ordinary." Unless he counted sharing two dances with Agnes Harrison. The first began as he expected. She was stiff and challenging to lead around the floor. As soon as he suggested she think of the flow of numbers, as opposed to the steps, she softened in his arms, and her timing became impeccable.

She was delectable to hold, compact but soft and curved in all the right places, but not overblown. He'd forced his fingers to remain on her back, rather than slide lower. And in a couple of turns, he had held her tightly enough to know that her dress was naturally filled with delightful softness.

Who would have guessed? How many other people were amazed or amused at the workings of her mind and missed the woman's form?

In the first steps of the waltz, he'd noticed her lips were plump and pink, making him wonder about other parts of her. Her skin was flawless—smooth and creamy. Her dark eyes were fringed with long lashes, which fanned her cheeks when she concentrated.

It had been a lovely evening, but was unlikely to be repeated, since Agnes rarely attended balls.

He fell asleep, remembering their waltz and the feel of her against him and in his arms.

As planned, William arrived at the Harrison's home the next day.

"The earl is not yet available, but he instructed me to invite you inside."

Once he handed his greatcoat to the butler, the man asked, "Would you care to join Lady Agnes at her noon meal?"

"Yes." then followed him to the dining room.

Looking around, he noticed greenery no longer hung from the railings, and the decorations were simplified.

"Your father suggested Lord Evans might join you while he awaits the earl."

"Oh." She nodded. "Please, have a seat. Would you care for service?"

He bowed over her hand and kissed her knuckles. "Thank you. Since I broke my fast early this morning, after a bruising ride on Rotten Row, lunch would not be amiss." Agnes was lovely. A couple of curls framed her face and drew his attention to her big brown eyes. She wasn't wearing her glasses and her dress was of the latest fashion.

Once he was seated, he asked, "Did you rest well, my lady?" This woman was an attractive blend of the student who didn't care about her appearance to the one who took his breath away. The second waltz had set the ton on fire with gossip, but it mattered not. The pleasure in Alice's eyes when she felt the movement of the music was beyond measure.

"Yes." She leaned toward him. "Thank you again for your suggestion on the dance floor. I have never enjoyed waltzing until then."

He had to force his gaze to her face, rather than her delectable bits that seemed on offer. "I'd heard the connection before."

"It is ironic. I knew the facts but never linked them in relationship to dancing. I doubt I would have ever done it on my own."

"Unlikely, Lady Agnes. You would have reached that conclusion at some time." But he was pleased it had happened because of his comments. Her delight softened something inside him.

"You are most kind to say that." Then she turned her attention back to her meal.

"Did you look at the stars last night?"

"No, I retired after you left, Lord Evans."

He waited until his lunch was served, then leaned close to her. "I don't mean to be forward, but I would be most amenable if you'd call me William when we are private. There are many of us brothers and I sometimes fail to respond to it."

She smiled. "Certainly, but only if you use my first name when we are alone."

He nodded and took a bite of food, then said, "The stars were bright, but I'm sure you were exhausted after such a successful evening." He expected her to have gone to the attic and studied the sky, especially since it was a clear night. And then slept much of today.

"It was a crush." She smiled at him. "Mother was thrilled."

"She has every reason to be pleased. People will discuss the ball for months to come. She set a tasteful example of how to decorate and entertain."

As they talked, William heard activity outside the dining room. "Are your parents planning another event?" he asked, tipping his head to the hall.

"No, but mother has a big family, and there are three of us children, filling the house with relatives for the next few weeks."

"They host frequent gatherings over the holidays?"

She lifted one shoulder as she considered his question. "I suppose they do. We remain in the city for the holiday as often as not. Father works over the break, meeting with peers who are here." She shrugged. "If I expected to go to the country for Christmas, I wouldn't have unboxed my new telescope. It is much easier to transport in the box."

"You were expecting to be here over the turn of the calendar."

Nodding, she grinned at him, then leaned close. "I was. Besides all the business reasons my father has to stay here, mother loves to host the ball."

"It showed." Before he said anything else, the earl joined them.

He kissed Agnes' cheek and nodded to William. "Good morning." He sat at the head of the table. "I hope you don't mind if I have lunch before we discuss your findings."

"Of course not. After I've finished, I'll check on the security measures in your study. They weren't disturbed when I left last night."

She addressed her father. "Lord Evans asked me several questions about your safe yesterday. Is there a problem?"

He glanced at his client and shrugged, not surprised.

"Nothing serious, daughter. Don't fret about it."

She rested her hands on her lap and looked him in the eye. "I only worry about things if I am not given the facts. Then I cannot stop myself from solving the question."

William agreed. Her mind would not let go of a problem until she'd found an answer.

The earl sighed. "Someone opened my safe and handled the documents inside. At the same time, they broke into my desk."

"As I told Lord Evans yesterday, I have known how the combination for years, but it has been almost that long since I bothered." She shook her head. "It is as easy to get into, but again, there's nothing to cause me to do it."

"I never suspected you to be the culprit, Agnes, however, William and I agreed he should question every household member. He even spoke to your mother."

"I would bet my new telescope that she has never been in your safe, but could provide the combination if asked."

He coughed to cover his chuckle. The lady understood her parents.

"Yes, well, your observation is correct. I will change the numbers."

"That's a good idea." William finished his meal and rose. "Please excuse me. I'll examine the study while you finish your lunch."

Agnes' gaze followed him out of the room. He moved as if comfortable in his body. When she returned her attention to the table, her father was watching her. He cocked one brow but remained silent, turning to his meal.

"Are you certain someone was in your safe?"

"Yes, because my papers were piled haphazardly."

"That would be a good indicator." He was as fastidious about his things as she was about her experiments. "Have you considered how comparable is our approach to work, father?"

He frowned. "What do you mean?"

"You and I are both fussy. You know someone has been in your safe, and I can tell if anyone handling my information has affected my results." She smiled at his look of incredulity. "Is it horrendous to see the familial connections between us?"

"Of course not, daughter. But it is a new thought for me to mull over." He took a bite of his poached fish. "How about your mother? Any similarities with her?"

"Now that you mention it," she said, "She and I are both skilled at organizing large events. For her, they are parties, while mine are experiments looking for solutions to mathematical and astronomical problems."

Her father studied her for a moment, then nodded. "After due consideration, I think you're right. Is there anything else you inherited from us?"

Agnes considered his question. He was not supportive of her opinions or ways, calling them ridiculous and against nature.

"My desire to walk my path from you. And mother shared her understanding of people, which I'm learning."

He coughed and gulped some water. "I have no idea what you're talking about, daughter."

"Consider this, father. You spend hours every day trying to change the laws of England, to better fit what you think they should be. You use legal language to do it in the House of Parliament, but it is still about changing the world."

He deliberately placed his fork on the side of his plate, wiped his mouth, and studied her. "And how does my behavior match yours, pray tell?"

"They are the same, but our methods are different. I speak my mind, trying to educate others, regardless of the situation, while you write laws and memos and enlighten your peers about necessary changes to English society."

"Good Lord, girl. You consider them similar?"

"I think the goals are the same—to change the world."

Her father paled and then gulped down his wine. "Heaven help England, if you're right."

After lunch, Agnes went to the library, looking for more information about music and mathematics. She found one volume on the topic and sat down, determined to discover the finer points of this relationship, allowing her to follow the steps of a country dance.

As she studied, conversation from her father's study kept interfering with her concentration. Closing the book, she listened.

She wasn't close enough to make out the men's words.

Why would they interfere with her studies? That was new for her. Normally, she settled into a topic and the outside world ceased to exist. She heard and saw nothing. Her mother used to say she would miss a fire beside her if she was studying.

She recognized her father often had meetings in his study. The only thing different today was that William was with him rather than a stranger or a peer. Changing seats brought her a little closer to the wall between them.

Unable to hear what they were saying, the vibration of William's voice was clearer, and it pleased her. It was soothing. She was more relaxed, even amid learning a new topic, when she listened to him. How odd. Another issue that warranted examination.

William's discussion with Harrison added nothing to his research. As expected, items marking entry into the earl's stuffy from the hallway were disturbed, but a man had been inside overnight. The dust on the windowsill was unmarked.

"Do you have any ideas?" asked his client from his seat at the desk.

"Other than continuing to observe this room, there isn't much we can do. Once the House is back in session, we will watch your peers and see if any of them have a particular problem with the bill you're preparing.

"Stop," the earl said, palm extended. "Are you suggesting one of them could be responsible for the break-in to my safe?"

If the man thought that all men with titles were honest, he was in for a nasty shock. Some crimes committed by the top ten thousand were heinous. "When a person feels strongly about something, he acts in ways that serve his best interest, even if that means hiring someone to break into your safe. If he is determined to stall legislation, he adamantly opposes or wants to know how it will be worded to raise an appropriate rebuttal, then yes, a peer could be behind the problem. Anything is possible." He dropped into a chair in front of the earl's desk.

His host leaned across the surface, both arms resting on the polished wood. "But what about the French question? You seem convinced that the break-in is about a bill I will present or support in the House, but I believe it's more likely the result of some Frenchman wanting to discover the information we have about their plans to free Napoleon from Saint Helens."

William did not agree. He couldn't swear to his opinion, but he didn't think it was about the French question. "If that's the case, they will try again before the new year. After all, the only place you'll be working over the next week is here, and they would want to be informed about what you know and what's changing in your papers. However, if it's something to do with a bill, your home is safe until Parliament resumes."

The earl walked to the liquor tray and poured himself a drink and lifted the bottle to William, who agreed. "That is when the members will find out I was changing potential legislation." He handed the young man his scotch, then dropped into his chair.

After consideration, Lord Evans said, "They might wonder, but you can't present it to the House until they resume sitting, meaning there is no advantage checking your safe because your changes aren't conclusive. Far better to leave your study undisturbed until shortly before Parliament reconvenes. Then they can tell what you've done, how it will be presented, and its final form."

The earl nodded and raised his glass to William. "To change the subject a bit, I must say, you are good at this investigation business, young man. You have a devious mind, which I appreciate."

"Taken as a compliment, My Lord. Thank you." He sipped his drink. "My mother often made the same observation."

"Have you plans for the holidays?"

He tilted his head and raised his brows at the question. "Nothing specific. My family is in London, and we will have Christmas dinner together. And then, of course, delivering boxes on the twenty-sixth."

"We are staying here as well, and I would be more comfortable if you dropped in over the holidays. Perhaps every day, to see how things are going and if there is anything further has cropped up."

"I'm happy to do so, my lord. But you will be in and out of here and have a guard when it's empty, correct?"

"Yes, of course. But I would be reassured if someone with your experience and skills was around once or twice a day to ensure my study is untouched if you should be incorrect."

The earl leaned across his desk, lowered his voice, and said, "The more often you're here, the more normal it appears. And if our opponent becomes less vigilant and more complacent, he may try something. Right now, he is aware of unusual activities in this house, or he knows you are from Triple E Investigations and is therefore keeping his distance."

William shrugged and wagged his head back and forth. "I can't argue with your concerns and would be happy to drop by if it eases your worry. I would appreciate your schedule to avoid disrupting your family activities."

"My wife and I host our extended families for the holidays, including Christmas Day, and delivering boxes on the twenty-sixth. The celebrations begin tomorrow and continue until after the New Year. Because of all the people coming and going, you won't need an invitation. If you're here for dinner, we'll add another place. As for Boxing Day, having you with us would further normalize your presence."

The earl had a point. "But people will ask what is happening. What reason would I have for being here that often? I'm not an emissary for my brother, and you and I have never interacted until recently."

Harrison rubbed his thumb along his lower lip. "Yes, I agree. It's a valid question. How to explain your continued and repeated presence in our home?" He drummed his fingers on his desk, then shook his index finger at William and said, "I've got it. We will make it look as if you are courting Agnes." He held up his hand, palm up, "Don't misunderstand me. This is just an explanation for your being here."

He choked on his scotch. "Do you think that would work? I wouldn't want to hurt your daughter's feelings when the truth comes out."

"My daughter rarely knows the time or day of the week. Believe me, she is unlikely to see you as a potential suitor. She's expecting you to be around because you're investigating this situation and will assume this is more of the same. All you have to do is ensure you are regularly in this house." The earl looked at him for a minute. "Do you agree?"

"I'm happy to do whatever is necessary to resolve this mystery. Agnes knows about my investigation, but I don't want her to get the wrong idea and later be hurt."

"That won't happen. Your social path and that of my daughter rarely crossed in the past. Let me deal with her and her female feelings, should they come up."

William wasn't thrilled with this suggestion, which could pain Agnes, but didn't see any other choice. "Fair enough," he said. "Now, if you'll excuse me, I need to return home and complete my preparations for the holiday. Until tomorrow, in the afternoon, or later."

Harrison rose and extended his hand, shaking William's. "Thank you, young man. That would be excellent. I will expect you then. I appreciate your experience and dedication."

CHAPTER FIVE

When Agnes came downstairs in the morning, her middle buzzed and bubbled, seeing the house decorated for their family holiday. Spruce boughs covered tabletops and mantles. Some had candles affixed to them and others had berries or bright ribbons.

She breathed deeply, savoring the scent of pine. It evoked happiness for her and memories of good times.

Several of the doorways sported mistletoe, marked with a red bow to ensure they were obvious. A large centerpiece with white wax pillars standing tall in gold holders graced the dining room table. On the sideboard, bows added to the festive atmosphere.

"Mama, you have outdone yourself again." Agnes circled her hand. "Everything is beautiful, and I love the scent of fresh pine. It reminds me the holidays are imminent."

Her mother sipped her tea, then said, "It is a good thing, since they are upon us. There are two gifts I've yet to select, so I'm to Bond Street this afternoon. Would you like to join me?"

As she served herself breakfast from the sideboard, Agnes considered her mother's invitation and nodded. "I would. I want to visit Hatchards and look for a new book."

"Another one, just before Christmas? Remember, we're having company every day for the next few weeks and there is lots to do." She shook her head. "Will you have a moment to read?"

She sat down and placed her napkin on her lap. "Not to worry. I'm sure I'll find the time to get lost between the covers." Her mother was always concerned about how much time she spent reading or studying.

"There is no doubt about that," she said, wagging her finger at her daughter. "You haven't forgotten your brother, wife, and children are joining us, have you?"

"Of course not. I can't wait to play with the little rapscallions. They are a delight." She studied her parent for a moment. "May I ask you a question about our family?"

"Yes," but her voice was soft and her eyes narrowed.

"I'm wondering about Peter. Why did he study as a barrister? He is the heir. Most men in his position live on a quarterly allowance and enjoy life."

"It's your father's decision, my dear. He cannot abide inactivity and it will be years until he comes into his inheritance. Father is of the opinion that the new earl should know the rights and responsibilities of the title, the land, and the investments. He believes England is better served by men in the Lords who understand the law. He made it worth Peter's time to study the subject at Oxford. Your brother loved it and has never looked back."

Agnes glanced at her mother from the corner of her eye, then said, "Grandfather would never have approved."

She nodded. "He agreed with very little, except his opinions. I hate to speak ill of the dead, but I have never met a more odious man. Fortunately for us, the current earl has a more modern outlook," she added with a grin.

"He told me repeatedly that I was an abomination because I liked to read and study rather than stitch or paint."

"Your father spoke to him about his attitudes toward you, to no avail, unfortunately. He felt females should conform to the mold he considered suitable."

Agnes did not know anyone had spoken up for her, although she would have been very young at the time of those conversations. "I am glad papa is not as rigid in his ideas." She glanced at her mother to determine her mood. "I realized in the last day or two that our family is rather unique."

"I'm surprised it has taken you this long to notice, but then, you always have your nose stuck in a book, learning how the world works."

She wasn't sure how much to say before she'd hurt mother's feelings and cause harsh words. "Contemplation of our family made me realize our connections to each other, which are important to all of us and our differences from the ton."

"What do you mean?"

"Consider Peter's circumstance. He's working in a solicitor's office. Can you name one other heir to an earl who has a position?" She didn't want to be offensive, but she'd only recently put into words this unique situation.

Her mother reflected on her question. "No. But that doesn't signify. Your brother followed his father's advice and loves the practice of the law. You can't fault the man."

"I meant no disrespect to either of them. But it details how different our family is. I'm sure it has grandfather at sixes and sevens on the other side."

After another sip of tea, her mother said, "You mustn't talk of the departed like that, Agnes. It is disrespectful. There are a few places we don't march with the ton, but they are very limited. And arise from your father's take on life. Look at yourself. Few daughters could miss events or have a telescope in the attic."

"Agreed. But I've always felt I was the only one of your children out of step with society, and it turns out Peter is, as well. Only he doesn't seem to bother anyone." Other than his gender, she couldn't see the difference between them.

"Remember, it is nigh impossible for a woman to differ from ton expectations and marry well."

This was the problem, as Agnes saw it. Men had freedom, while rules and norms constrained women. "Why? Why can't a female follow her heart?" Males could do whatever they wanted.

Her mother patted her hand. "She can, but there are consequences to every choice, daughter. If a woman marries a man as poor as a church mouse, then it affects her life and that of her children. Because the idea of constant hunger and seeing your breath indoors is anathema to most people, they insist their daughters marry men of their station."

"But some of them are without funds. I'm certain you could name half a dozen peers who don't have two pence but maintain the facade of wealth. Girls are warned about them." And yet they are welcomed into society and treated as if they were wealthy.

Her mother considered her statement, then nodded. "Poverty exists everywhere, regardless of your station in life. But families try to protect their children, especially daughters, from such pain."

It was the first time they had discussed the situation. "When I look at my future, I don't see a husband or babies. I am a bluestocking. It would take an extraordinary man to overlook my failings and love me for myself. But a relationship would be incredibly difficult, given that I can think circles around most men." And most other people, if the truth be known. She couldn't imagine living with someone if their minds were dull and their conversation dispirited.

"What you never seemed to realize, Agnes, is that there are many ways of thinking. You can read a book, process its information and then test it with experiments or experience. But another might understand how a person is feeling by looking into their eyes. Others are skilled at painting or making music. People have a variety of talents and paths to approach life. You are very good at yours, but it is not the only route."

What an interesting thought. Different ways to think, all of them valid. She had never considered those differences before. "I've never heard you say such a thing, Mother."

"If I try to force my opinion on you, your stubbornness raises its head, and the conversation ends. I am surprised you are still sitting here. In the past, you would be in full retreat."

Although her mother's words stung a bit, Agnes couldn't argue. She had never had much patience with people who disagreed with her or saw things differently. It's what had happened between her and William, and in truth, with many of the members of the ton. Right now, she wasn't proud of her reaction to those differences. She'd have to learn how to accept others as they were, rather than judging them against her preferences. "I guess I am changing, mother. Slowly." Was that part of the difference in her interchanges with him? Perhaps it was her who was showing new behavior and not him. She was good with numbers and data, but feelings and conduct were beyond her.

"Waltzing with a certain young man helped you observe a different perspective about yourself and the world around you. For that, I will always be grateful to him. He has softened your edges, Agnes, and made you more patient, which can only help you in the future."

She hadn't considered others' opinions about her waltzes with William, except that they had caused many to gossip. But the dances had been worth the risk to her for the sheer pleasure of being in his arms and moving around the floor like everyone else, rather than somebody with two left feet.

Other than her parents' constant encouragement to accept society's invitations, the ton paid little attention to her and her activities, except to poke fun at her for her opinions. Her mother had always wanted her to be sociable, attending events and chatting with friends and acquaintances. But Agnes had no social connections in society, unless you counted the new relationship she had with William, although she was nervous about giving him that designation, since they were barely acquainted.

If possible, she'd like to know him better, but after his investigation was complete, they would rarely see each other. He was a social person, and she was not. He had an ease with people she had never developed. And he came from a family of the highest rank. All the upper ten thousand wanted to enjoy the light given off by such an elevated personage.

"You hold an exaggerated opinion of Mister Evans' effect on me. Dancing with him was pleasant, I admit, but that's all there was to it."

"Agnes, you can't deny your waltz with him was smoother and more rhythmic than any time you've danced."

"I agree, but it was because he told me to relate my mathematical knowledge to the notes. As soon as I followed his instructions, I felt the flow of the piece and mastered the steps."

Her mother shook her head. "Agnes, I declare. The very idea of thinking about mathematics while waltzing with an attractive man is beyond the pale. Why couldn't you enjoy the moment?"

"Without the numbers in my mind, I would have hated the dance. I would have stepped on his toes, tripped over my two left feet, or stumbled into another couple. He gifted me the combination, and it made an incredible difference in my appreciation of the waltz. Best of all, it will keep on giving." She wasn't sure she could apply the lesson to other dances, but she would try. Then maybe she could attend a few more balls, as her mother preferred, and not embarrass herself.

The next morning, William's first stop was Hatchard's bookstore. He wanted a book about astronomy. The idea had come to him late last night.

Inside, the clerk said, "There is only one in stock," handing it to William.

"This must be my lucky day." He handed the man a few coins, waited while they wrapped it, and left.

He stopped at a jewelry store to pick up a pin he'd ordered for his mother. While waiting for it to be packaged, he looked around the wide selection of stones, settings, and designs. The many choices for women's rings astonished him. He had never noticed it before.

After completing his other errands, William returned to his bachelor quarters, deposited his gift for Agnes, and had a quick bite to eat before changing for his afternoon calls. Earlier, he'd ordered flowers for the countess and hoped they were delivered before he arrived as a token of his appreciation to his hostess for her kindness.

The next item on his list was to stop at Wolfstone to talk to Allwyn about the holidays and his plans. Making his way to his brother's study, he noticed the house was being decorated for the holiday season.

One last look over his shoulders showed the servants rushing around, adding decorations in every conceivable place. He closed the door behind him, poured himself a drink, and dropped into a chair before the fire. "Are you having a yule log?"

"Of course. Are you worried we forgot that tradition?"

"No," he sipped his brandy, "but I wondered about changes to our traditions with a new duchess."

"I am the luckiest of men. My wife has no great desire to run the house and is delighted for mother to continue. Meanwhile, mama feels needed and appreciated while maintaining her prior responsibilities."

"Two happy women in the same home. You are a lucky fellow." As was his eldest triplet sibling, although differently.

"Louis told me you are working on an investigation for Harrison about someone getting into his safe. How is it going?"

"Slowly. I'm not even sure there is anything to investigate. If the questions came from anyone else, I would have assumed an over-anxious peer, but the earl is critically organized and not one to overreact to simple things."

"Do you think someone has broken into his house?"

"I do, but I have found nothing missing or misplaced after the first time, although the earl is adamant it will happen again."

"Harrison has a daughter, doesn't he? She seems nice enough, but she is an atypical society lady, as I recall."

"Agnes is not typical, but she's not the culprit," he explained, to protect the lady's name.

"I heard you waltzed with her twice the other night."

Depend on his brother to know all the details about a ball he and his wife hadn't attended. "Your sources are excellent. Who provided information about my dancing partners?" He didn't want anyone gossiping about Agnes.

"My source is immaterial, but I'm glad you're out and about, William. You've been rather absent from the social scene."

"I've been busy. Triple E takes a lot of my time, especially with Henry out of town and Louis enjoying married life." He preferred not to talk about his activities with his brother. Perhaps he should reconsider his opinion of his brother's tendency to collect information for personal or business use. Allwyn heard about everything in the ton and probably all of England.

He would not discuss his waltzes with Agnes. They were private moments between them. He couldn't name his feelings about them. Or his partner.

"What are your plans for Christmas and Boxing Day?"

"Harrison has asked me to frequent his house until after the new year, or the perpetrator is caught. I will be here, but also with them." It would be a very different holiday, since usually his family spent them together.

"Then we can expect you to open gifts?" That had become a lovely tradition, gift giving among themselves, then taking boxes to the poor the day after.

"Of course. I'll be here for dinner, after spending the afternoon with the Harrisons. I might return there after our meal, depending on what the earl desires." And what was going on? If things remained quiet at the earl's manor, he wouldn't stay late in the evening.

"Always keep the client happy."

"I know." William pushed himself up from the settee and reached into his pocket. "I bought mother a trinket and wanted you to have it wrapped." He handed him the brooch.

"Of course." He opened the lid and looked inside. "She will love it."

"Have you purchased Juliette's gift yet?" Allwyn had learned what his wife appreciated and gave it to her. But unlike other ladies of the ton, it wasn't jewelry, but more likely to be a new stethoscope or additional supplies for her clinic.

"Yes, but I am not talking about it. Since that woman is uncanny in her ability to ferret out information from the unlikeliest of sources, I'm saying nothing."

He laughed. "Sounds like a plan." He clapped his brother's shoulder. "Please remember me to mother and your lovely wife. I wouldn't want them to forget me right before Christmas."

"Of course."

On his way to the Harrison's, William considered the marriage of his eldest brother. Allwyn had vehemently denied any feelings for Juliette because of her profession. The possibility that she would see other men naked or the idea of a wife who was employed were two major stumbling blocks that caused him to struggle. But eventually he'd realized what he stood to lose if he maintained his ideas, admitted his love for her and came to terms with the work she did. But it hadn't been easy for him.

When he stopped in front of the Harrisons, William was pulled from his memories to the situation at hand. He handed his reins to the groom, and after the butler announced him, Harrison invited him to enter the study.

"What was the status this morning, my lord?"

"There were no problems overnight and when I checked the safe, everything was in order."

"That is good news. I presume someone was in the room all the time?"

"Yes, my secretary was here first thing and relieved the guard, then stayed until I sent him on his way an hour ago."

"Will the same man be standing watch tonight, or do you have another man?"

"I planned to use the same one. He can sleep through the day and work overnight, leaving less risk of him falling asleep on the job."

"Great idea." William checked the powder on the windowsill, which hadn't been disturbed. Everything else was in order.

As he finished his investigation, someone knocked on the door. "Excuse me, my lord, but your brother-in-law and his family have arrived."

"Put them in the large salon and send a maid for my daughter."

"If she's in the attic, I'll go with her. I wanted to take another look with her telescope."

The earl nodded. "Please join us when you've seen enough of the sky."

When the knock on the door interrupted her, Agnes looked up from her notes and diagrams. "Come in."

"Good afternoon," William said. "How are you?"

She smoothed her palms down her skirts, then pushed curls from her forehead. She wasn't sure how to behave in his company after their conversations and dances last night. Would he be the nice man, the one who was easy to talk with, or the other? "Fine, thank you. How are you?"

William rubbed his hands together and walked further into the attic. "I've been busy. Running errands, picking up a Christmas gift for my mother, and visiting my brother, Allwyn."

Agnes checked her notes and smiled. "I did some of the same this morning, but my day doesn't sound as lively as yours." She looked at the maid. "You may wait outside. We won't be long."

"What are you seeing in the skies today?" he asked, stepping beside her.

His hair was tousled, and his cheeks were in high color, but he was as appealing as last night. "Similar as before, but you're welcome to look." She glanced at him, glad he was here, yet she had an empty feeling in the pit of her stomach and butterflies were dancing in that space.

"I'd love to, if you don't mind."

Agnes stepped aside to give William room to stand by the telescope and looked over his shoulder. He leaned closer, adjusted the dials, and commented, "I can't see the moon today."

"It will be visible tonight," she said. He seemed interested in the sky and what he was seeing. She bounced from foot to foot and wanted to sing, although she couldn't carry a tune. It was the first time someone else enjoyed something scientific she treasured.

"It is amazing to comprehend, isn't it?" he asked as he raised away from the eyepiece and turned to her. His gaze caught hers. Then he leaned closer, so very near, and watched her.

Agnes did not enjoy waiting. She rose on her toes and kissed him gently. William's hands bracketed her face, and he tipped her head and tongued the seam of her lips. She liked the feeling, but he withdrew an inch, smiled at her, and whispered, "Open for me. I want to taste you."

Then he claimed her mouth again. This time she opened for him and was too shocked to register what was happening, only able to savor the moment as his tongue slid against hers.

One arm wrapped around her back and tucked her close to him, and then his other moved to the rise of her bottom, holding her in place while kissing her.

The sensory impressions stole her breath and nearly overwhelmed her. She wanted more. More of his taste, his nearness, and of being in his arms. Never had she realized the pleasure of being held by a man. The right one.

William pulled his mouth from hers. He was breathing heavily, and his cheeks were flushed, and he glanced at the open door.

"Do I need to apologize?"

"For what? I reached for you," she said.

He chuckled. "I guess you were." He placed his forehead against hers and, with both arms around her back, held her close. "What am I to do with you, Agnes?"

Although this was Agnes's first kiss, she knew from reading a book she'd found hidden in the library that this was desire and that she wanted more, but was unaware of the next steps in the process. Did this make her a wanton? Were these feelings part of the reason girls focused on marriage? She stretched up on her toes to get close to him again.

William tapped her nose with his index finger and smiled. "I know where your mind has gone, and that is not happening, especially now." He looked at the door. "Your uncle and family have arrived, and the earl sent me to collect you. It would not be wise for us to take too long to arrive downstairs."

Although she liked them, she would far prefer to stay here with William and experiment.

"Can we agree my relatives have awful timing?"

He shook his head. "No. I can't guarantee my self-control if we were alone up here for much longer." He glanced at the door again. "Even with your maid in the hall."

"Precisely what I meant."

After Agnes tidied herself, they left the attic, Wiliam's hand heating the spot on her back where it rested. On the next floor, the stairs were wider, and they walked side by side, talking about the stars, how the moon would appear later tonight, and how she had discovered the enormity of the sky and the stories it told.

"It is an incredible canvas of light and dark contrasts, which become invisible during the day when the sun is shining."

"But not if it's cloudy."

She looked up at him and smiled. "Of course. But even then, sometimes there's a break in the cloud cover and I can see the blue sky above them, for just a moment. It is the most incredible experience to know that clouds are nothing more than a layer above the earth blocking out the sun.

"Each discovery excites you in different ways, my lady."

"Exactly." Learning about his kindness and his kisses had created new feelings and excitement, ones she wasn't sure how to name, but fully intended to further explore.

In the salon, he was introduced to her extended family. There were crustless sandwiches, biscuits, and hors d'oeuvres on the tables. The children played a board game. Harrison was tending bar and as soon as they entered, handed him a whisky and her a glass of Madeira.

After a sip of his drink, William excused himself and left the room.

Her aunt Jean tittered and said, "I suspect Agnes has a new beau."

"Mr. Evans is the brother of the Duke of Wolfstone. One of the triplets, don't you know?" explained the earl.

"We aren't courting," she corrected. "He is a dear friend who has discovered he loves looking at the sky through my telescope." Despite all her feelings, he was working for her father. She must remember that truth, regardless of everything he brought up in her.

"Is that what young people are calling it now? I suppose that's better than some excuses I used in my youth," her uncle said.

As everyone chuckled at his comment, William rushed into the room. "If I could speak privately with you for a moment, my lord." He stepped back and waited for her father. He leaned close and whispered something she couldn't hear, and they almost ran down the hall.

"What on earth happened?" asked her mother.

"I'm not sure. After a minute or two, when neither of them returned, her curiosity grew. She crossed the room and looked toward the study. "Excuse me, I'll check on the situation," Agnes said.

Following the men's voices, she stopped at the entry. One hand fisted her heart, and the other grabbed the doorpost. "Oh, my goodness." She had never seen such a scene. Blood was everywhere.

"Leave and close the door behind you," ordered her father.

"But what happened? Where did all this come from?" she asked, waving her arm in a circle.

He pointed towards the hall. "Get out and say nothing to anyone else."

Someone had been seriously injured or perhaps killed in here while they were in the drawing room. William was bent over, studying something on the floor behind the settee. "We should call a physician," she stated, maintaining her position.

He turned and looked at her and shook his head. "It's too late for that to do any good." His chin tipped towards the family salon. "You shouldn't be in here, Agnes. Go back and keep everyone in there. The children must not witness this mess."

Both men were right, but she hated leaving without having her questions answered. A person had died in here, perhaps while William was looking through her telescope. Or while they were kissing.

She backed out of the room, confused that such an important moment had occurred at the same time someone else's life ended. It was an eerie conjunction of significant moments. Of course, for the person on the floor behind the settee, it had been.... She didn't know what to call it. Who had killed another in their home? And why?

Inside the salon, her mother turned to her and asked, "Is there a problem?"

Agnes shook her head. She couldn't find the words to answer her. Nothing was normal, but there was no point going into it. Her father and William could explain better when they returned.

After returning to her seat, she sipped her Madeira and tried to make conversation. But she kept looking over her shoulder towards the salon door, waiting for the men to return.

CHAPTER SIX

William stood over the man who had been guarding the study. When his throat was cut, blood sprayed across the room. "Check your documents," he said to the earl. "He died protecting whatever is inside. Somebody wanted the contents."

Harrison's hand was shaking, and it took him three tries to get the combination right and the safe opened. "Again, they aren't piled as fastidiously as usual." He removed the papers and placed them on his desk, examining each for the projects he was working on, and said, "Everything is here, although I must go through each of these notes one at a time to see if anything is amiss, but a quick review suggests all is well."

William squatted beside the victim and looked over his shoulder at his client. "If you're right, this man died for nothing."

"What a tragic end to a trusted servant's life. I find it beyond the pale that anyone could murder another for no apparent reason. Whoever did this has been in my study before, has been in my safe before and knows there are no valuables and no coin to be had." He looked back at the man on the floor and shook his head. "Poor sod. While doing the job I paid him to do, he was murdered."

William rose and went to the window. The powder was untouched. "The murderer did not enter from outside. He had to come through there," he pointed to the hall door. "Either he entered the house elsewhere or he is a person in your employ."

"But you've questioned the servants already." Standing at his desk, the earl shook his head in frustration. "I can't believe there's a killer in their numbers."

"After my conversations with them, I agreed with you, but something isn't right here, and this man is dead. We must go forward assuming it's one of the staff and be on the lookout."

"How do you suggest we do that?" Harrison asked, tapping his index finger on the papers.

"We'll start with two men from Triple E Investigations. There will be no connection to you, or your work, and we won't be worried about their loyalty to anyone or anything but our company."

The earl stiffened away from his desk. "Is that necessary?"

"It is. We train them for these situations. I'm not willing to risk another of your servants. If we put two trained operators in your house twenty-four hours a day, we can protect your home and everyone in it." One thing was certain: whoever was snooping in Harrison's safe did not value a man's life. "I want them in here all the time."

Harrison spluttered. "I can't have strangers looking over my shoulder when I'm working on documents with national security implications. It would be unconscionable."

"Fair enough, as long as my men are in here when the room is empty. When you're inside, they'll stand guard at the door and window. Otherwise, they're in here."

He looked skeptical. "What if Agnes had been in here looking for something? Or your wife?"

"Oh, my heavens. Never for a moment had I considered my family might be at risk. That is beyond the pale."

"Agreed. Which is why we will always maintain a minimum of two men in your home."

"Would you be one of them?"

The question caught William unawares. It was actually a good idea. At least he'd be nearby if something happened. But he wanted a couple of guards in the study during the night. "As long as my presence won't raise too many questions with your family and friends, it makes sense for me to be here. But we still need two sentinels on duty overnight. I will not risk someone coming into this room when one of my men might be unaware and lose his life."

"You'll remain until this issue is resolved and we catch the break-in artist."

William gave Harrison's statement some consideration. It was a decent idea and would give him the right to roam randomly around the house looking for things that were out of place, but he'd just shared a passionate kiss with the man's daughter. Staying here would increase his temptation, which was already too high. But the case needed resolution and he must control himself. "Yes, I'll stay. I am obligated to attend Christmas morning and dinner at my brother's, but have no other plans. I will speak to my brother Louis, and we'll assign two of our investigators to be on site every night until we find the thief."

"And during the day?" the earl asked.

"I'm thinking about that. On one hand, a single man at the door when you're present should be sufficient. But I do not want an individual alone in here when you go to dinner or visit with your family."

"Here's an idea. My butler has been with us for decades. His brother also works for me. During the day, if I'm working in here, one of your agents is here. If I step out, then the other man stands watch with your investigator. And you'll be around, ensuring no one poses a risk to my family from another direction."

"That could work. One-on-one, any person can be defeated, but two men provide a necessary degree of safety."

"How soon will you move in?"

"After I'm finished here, I'll return home to pack a bag and speak to my brother. I should be back in a couple of hours." He would have to be firm with himself and the desire he felt for Agnes. He would never have guessed that her innocent kiss could start a fire in him that he was having trouble controlling.

Harrison shook his head. "I can't believe this is happening in my home." He glanced at the body lying on the floor. "Poor bastard doing his job to earn a few coins for his family, and this is what he gets."

"I don't think there's anything else for me to do in here. We should have him removed, and this room cleaned." William looked at the older man's face, which seemed to have aged in the past half hour, and said, "Unfortunately, you must continue to work in here despite his death. This is where your safe is and we need to watch it along with your desk."

"Yes, of course. No one will push me from my duties. I'll have the staff clean and paint immediately."

William admired the man's grit. He wasn't sure he could think in the same room where a trusted servant had been murdered. But Harrison was dedicated to his responsibilities as a member of the House of Lords and as an Englishman to protect the country, regardless of the personal cost.

While the earl instructed the butler to have the room cleaned and ready for morning, William walked around the main floor, checking the doors and windows. He did not want to make this home a fortress, but it might be necessary. Nearing the family salon, the squeals of the Harrison girls made him smile. Children and Christmas were always fun. And a pleasant change of atmosphere from the study.

He was examining the music room when Agnes joined him. "William, what are you looking for?"

"I am making sure no one is hiding in this room."

She peered from side to side, eyes wide. "Do you think someone might be in here?" she whispered.

"It's possible." He glanced at her. "Remain close to the door, just in case."

"What about you?" She looked at every corner of the room again. "Are you safe?"

"I am safer if I'm not worried about you," he said over his shoulder, as he checked behind the floor length dark blue drapes.

"Then I shall stay here."

"Thank you." He looked back to ensure her position as he stepped around the pianoforte.

She glanced into the hallway. "Will you search the entire house?"

He nodded. "We have to be certain that only the people who are supposed to be here are inside."

"You're ensuring the murderer is not hiding until he can get away." Her head swiveled from side to side. "That means you are worried it could be one of the servants."

"I'm not sure of anything at this moment, except I want everyone to be safe." He wasn't willing to risk the safety of anyone, starting with the woman watching him. Definitely, he would do a room by room search and pray that the murderer was not one step ahead of him.

Agnes remained in the doorway, but she looked up and down the hall. "Have you checked all the rooms between here and the front door?"

"I have, and they were all clear." He didn't even look at her as he answered her question.

"And what about father's study?"

"Your father has the servants taking care of the body and cleaning the room. It should be ready by morning."

"Except I know someone lost their life in there."

"Yes, Agnes, but we can't change the facts. I will do my best to protect everybody else."

"But what about after you leave? Don't most murders happen when everyone is sleeping?"

"As soon as I finish my search, I'm returning to my quarters to pack a bag. Your father has requested that I remain until I complete this investigation and find the murderer."

The idea of him spending the night sparked her interest. "Asked or insisted?"

He chuckled at her forthright question. "A little of both, but I was happy to agree. I'm adding some of my people for extra security to protect you and your family."

"You will stay here with us?" She tried to keep her voice neutral, to hide her excitement at the idea.

"For as long as it takes to find the person who murdered your servant and has been snooping into your father's vault." Finished his survey of the room, he came to stand in front of her.

"Were his papers disturbed again?"

William studied her, looking for something, but she had no intention of letting this go until she was satisfied with his answers.

"I think that is a question best asked of your father." His response was annoying, but not an answer. What was it with men who needed to protect women from information?

"I must conclude that his papers were disturbed, but you're unwilling to say that." She huffed for a minute. "I don't understand why you won't tell me the truth. You know I'll figure it out."

"Agreed, but I have a commitment to your father to maintain the confidentiality of the documents in his safe." He shook his head. "I am neither agreeing nor disagreeing, Agnes, but if you want further information, ask him. I lack both the expertise and the knowledge of what can and can't be shared."

"Are you saying you aren't certain what you may share with me? I am the man's daughter and am aware of everything that goes on in this house."

"Your father was specific that some documents were highly confidential. Such information would not be of the slightest interest to you."

"But I am his offspring." She wanted to stamp her foot in frustration. Drat the man.

"Be that as it may, I am not at liberty to discuss such things with you. Besides, I haven't looked at the papers. I can't tell you what's there or what he's got in his safe because I have no idea. My work is to protect the study. It is not to understand the documents."

"Then aren't you worried about overstepping your bounds by staying here? After all, we are not in there, and we don't go through his papers." She understood what he was saying but couldn't seem to help herself.

The look on his face was clear—he thought she was being unnecessarily difficult. But this entire situation was no longer an intellectual exercise. A man was dead because of the contents of the safe. She had the right to know what was that important.

"I am a guest. Nothing more or less." He shook his head. "Please join the others. I must finish my search of the house."

She huffed at his orders, wanting to decline, but did as he requested. She didn't have to like it, but she would drop her questions, for now.

When she returned to the salon, her mother arched her brows, silently asking what was happening. Agnes shook her head and shrugged. She had no answers. No, that wasn't quite true. Someone had been murdered, but she wouldn't mention such horror with her uncle and his family in the room. There was no need to terrify the children. Besides, when her father joined them, he could make the explanations. While she waited, she joined the youngsters in their game, but faced the door, to better keep track of everyone.

Sometimes later, the earl returned to the small party. After a couple of jovial comments about the demands of being in the House of Lords, he sat beside her mother and they leaned heads together, chatting. Given how her mother's complexion paled, Agnes assumed he had shared something about the events.

As soon as possible, she left the game the children were playing and joined her parents. In a very soft voice, she asked, "What is going on? Is William still here? Why do you want him to spend the next few days with us?"

Her mother looked at her father and sighed. "Best you answer her questions, Colin. You know how she is. She won't stop until she is satisfied."

"My curiosity makes me a brilliant scientist," she said. "But as mama noted, it causes me to be difficult to live with."

"William and some of his men are going to be in the house until the situation is resolved. We plan for there to always be at least two people in my study. Unless I am working in there, when one will stand guard at the door," her father said. "Safety is all that matters."

"What is of such significance that it needs to be heavily guarded?"

"The papers in my safe are bills and upcoming presentations to the House of Lords. There is nothing extraordinarily important in any of it. But someone assumes there is value in those documents. They seem to have leafed through them but have not taken anything." He shook his head. "Somehow, they think some information is worth murder."

"It must be a matter you're not aware of." She had to admit it sounded far-fetched.

Her father frowned at her. "Are you suggesting I'm unaware of the items in my safe?"

She realized she'd stepped on her father's toes and probably hurt his feelings. "No, my words didn't come out right. I meant to say that something in your documents is of paramount consequence to another, and you aren't aware of his motivation."

Her mother jerked her head back. "Agnes, that is the first time I have heard you apologize to someone for failing to communicate clearly. Well done, daughter."

She must have apologized to somebody, somewhere, at some point, although at the moment no one came to mind. She couldn't be so thoughtless in her words that she didn't realize she was being offensive.

"Thank you for clarifying, Agnes. It is possible you're correct, but I have no idea who that could be or why anything might be important to that person."

"And significant enough to kill another for it." Agnes's mother shivered. "It is beyond consideration that someone should die in our home for reasons we don't understand."

Before they said more, her uncle joined them. "Is something amiss, Colin?"

Her father rose to his feet and clapped his brother-in-law on the back. "Nothing to worry about. We had an issue with a servant, but I have dealt with it."

"I'm glad all is well. You look rather peaked. And Agnes is fidgety and set to jump out of her skin."

Her mother chuckled. "You know our daughter. If she is away from her experiments for too long, she becomes uncomfortable."

He laughed. "Of course, that makes sense."

She didn't appreciate blaming her desire for scientific study for her recent behavior, but it was a quick response and satisfied his curiosity.

Dinner was announced and soon after finishing their meal, her uncle said, "It is time we get the children home to bed. Thank you for a lovely evening. We will see you again on Christmas Day." He looked at Agnes. "Is your young man going to be here as well?"

"Oh, oh I... I...."

"Yes, Mr. Evans plans to spend part of the holiday with us. Of course, he will take the main meal with his family."

"Are you joining them?" he asked her.

"Uhm, we haven't discussed it." She wasn't sure what she should've said. There was no reason for her to join William at his mother's house. After all, he was working for her father, not paying court to her, but uncertain of what to say, she opted for silence.

Her uncle nodded. "Early days of courtship are always difficult." He glanced over at his wife. "When we were courting, a new set of rules had sprung up that nobody had shared. It was the oddest time." He laughed. "It's part of the reason we married as quickly as we did."

He looked at his family, who were donning their wraps. "Best decision I've ever made."

After her relatives left, Agnes and her parents turned to each other.

"Now, you will tell us both what is going on in our home," demanded her mother. "With no dodging or fabrications. I want to know the truth."

"Of course, dear. But prepare yourself. It's not a pretty sight." Her father led them to the study and opened the door, then stepped aside.

Mama looked inside and paled. "My heavens. What happened in here?" she asked, watching the servants scrub the carpet, the floors, and the wall.

"The guard we posted to protect this room was murdered and whoever did it left a terrible mess."

Her mother shook her head. "Poor man." Stepping away, she said, "Let's leave them to their work."

As they returned to the family salon, William met them in the hall. "I've gone through all the rooms, including the attic, and have found nothing amiss, meaning we lack any knowledge about how this villain got in. I'll speak to my brother about additional staff, starting tonight if possible. If not, then I and a servant are staying in the study overnight. Afterwards, I shall go to my quarters, pack a few things, and come back." He looked at her father. "Depending on how it goes, I might be late returning."

"We always have extra rooms ready for guests," said her mother. "We'll freshen one of those and advise the night footman. Cook will prepare a selection of items to soothe your hunger and place it in your room."

William kissed her hand. "Thank you, my lady. That is most generous of you and much appreciated." He turned to Agnes and her father. "Now I must be off. The sooner I leave, the sooner I return." He bowed to the earl and hurried down the hall, leaving them behind.

She felt strange, uncomfortable even, that William was departing. Would they be safe without him here? She knew neither of the two men standing here could protect her or her mother, which was not loyal but true. Worse, she was anticipating his return with pleasure. Having him in the house overnight seemed... sinful. Or delightful. The thought freed the butterflies in her stomach to flitter around and raise havoc. Another new experience.

CHAPTER SEVEN

William's discussion with his brother hadn't taken long. Since there was no one available to be the second guard in the study, he would take it. After rushing to his quarters and packing a few things, he raced back to the Harrison's home.

The butler assured him they had removed all evidence of the murder and directed him to his suite. He left his bag on a chair, wolfed down some sandwiches and biscuits on the tray, and returned to the main floor.

In the study, he replaced the footman filling in. Barely midnight, this would be a long night.

A couple of hours later, William heard movement in the hall. He put his ear to the wood, then from the other side, someone twisted the knob. He stepped back and yanked the door open. Agnes flew into the room and landed against his chest. Automatically, he wrapped his arms around her.

"What in the hell are you doing, roaming the house at this time of night, when a murder occurred in here earlier?" he whispered, looking up and down the hall.

"I wanted to be sure you returned and were safe."

"What am I to do with you?" William leaned his forehead against hers and sighed. "You must not take such risks again. Until we find this villain, you will stay in your room at night with the door locked and never move about the house alone."

"Don't be unkind. I worried about you and needed reassurance that you were well before I could sleep."

Agnes stood in the circle of his arms, tight against him, creating a reaction she was not aware of. He released her and stepped back, one of the hardest things he'd ever done. "As you can see, I am fine. Now, return to your room and lock the door."

"What if he's entered my suite while I'm here?" She asked, looking towards the stairs.

"You should've considered that before you came down here," he said a bit testily, since he didn't like her moving around the house alone at this time of night. "I can't leave John by himself."

The overnight footman stepped behind her. "I'll stand right here, Mr. Evans. I can hear the front door and keep watch in here while you escort Lady Harrison to her room."

"That is hardly appropriate," William said, then shrugged. "But there's no other choice." He nodded to the man. "Thank you." He extended his hand to Agnes. "Come along. I will accompany you to your quarters and search your suite to know you're safe."

Upstairs, leaving her in the open doorway, he stepped into her small, sparsely furnished sitting room, which had two desks, both covered with scribbled notes. Walking into her bedroom, the scent of her perfume hit him, reminding him of their waltz and holding her close as they circled the floor. Her delight at their success and then their kiss in the attic. He motioned her to come closer, propriety be damned. He needed to keep her in his line of sight, but the image of her standing, one hand on the jamb, set him on fire. In another circumstance, he'd take her in his arms and teach her the carnal delights he knew.

Five minutes later, confident her room was empty, he said to her, "Promise you won't come downstairs. I must be certain you're safe, Agnes, which means you remain in here."

"Will you worry about me?"

"Not if you stay in here with your doors locked. Then I can focus on guarding the study."

"Do you think he'll return tonight?"

"It's unlikely, but we have to be ready for anything." He stepped into the hallway. "Rest well."

He waited for her to lock the door behind him. Standing there, palm pressed to the wood, he held his breath. Leaving her alone was the last thing he wanted to do, but there was no other choice. He hoped she'd stay in her room, rather than venture out, because she was concerned for him. She had to be safe. And she would be, if she followed his directions. But there was something else—a feeling he was unwilling to identify, for it might open doors to places he didn't want to go.

Downstairs, nothing had changed. He snuffed the candles, leaving the room in darkness, and waited. Not even a leaf brushed against the windows.

Hours later, it looked like the beginning of a typical day, but yesterday had been normal until they discovered a body in the study. He would not make that mistake again.

The night footman covered a yawn when the butler replaced him in the morning. Shortly after, two of the investigators from Triple E showed up. Mrs. Johnson and Maitland, both experienced, had worked with them since the company started more than a year ago. They had been helpful to Louis when he searched for the man trying to kill Eliza, the woman he married.

"I thought you were away," he said to her.

"I was, but things wrapped up quick and I arrived late yesterday. The boss asked if I'd come over here to help."

"I'm glad you're back."

Reassured to have trusted agents standing guard and protecting the earl's family, William relaxed. After explaining their responsibilities, he retired to his room. It had been a long twenty-four hours and exhaustion dogged him.

His clothes were pressed and hung. His personal things were on the table behind the screen and a nightshirt lay on his pillow.

He changed into the strangling garment and crawled between the sheets. Hopefully, it wouldn't choke him, since he normally slept au naturel, but if something happened or someone came looking for him, this way, he'd be covered.

After a few hours of fitful sleep, he got out of bed and went downstairs. Mrs. Johnson and Maitland informed him that everything had been quiet. Satisfied that all was well, he followed the scents of the noon meal to the dining room, where the Harrisons were having lunch. "Mind if I join you?" he asked.

"Of course not. This is part of the plan. Consider our home yours and make yourself comfortable." Harrison looked at a footman. "Get the man some breakfast. I can't imagine he wants to start the day with baked fish in a lemon sauce."

Another servant poured his tea, and he was soon enjoying sausage, bacon, eggs, and toast.

Their congenial conversation made no reference to the events of last evening.

The earl returned to his study and his wife to her social planning in her sitting room, leaving him and Agnes in the company of several footmen and the butler hovering in the hall. She slowly ate her sweet, licking the pudding from her lips. He doubted she knew what she was doing to him, but he was glad the linen covered him, else he'd embarrass himself.

"Did you sleep well?" she asked.

"Yes. As soon as my head hit the pillow." She licked another spoon of dessert, and his libido jumped into high gear. He gulped down a glass of water and signaled for a second.

"Are you still worried about our safety?" Her soft voice was strained.

William wasn't sure where this conversation was going, but he would be as honest as possible. "Yes, but with an extra operative in place, we'll comb through the house again and remove the risk of any surprises anywhere. Then I'll be more comfortable."

"How can you be certain someone won't enter at night?"

"Your father and I will discuss that a little later. I think we should have a man at every doorway to ensure everyone's safety."

"If there are problems, we'll know they're from inside."

"Exactly." This woman was intelligent in very many ways. Few women would have reached that conclusion. Hell, few men would have made it either.

"Is that possible?" she asked, her voice low as she looked around the room.

"The purpose of an investigation is to discover the facts. I have no opinion on who or why this is happening. I have questions and look for answers."

"Evidence."

Again, she surprised him. "But until I find something certain, I won't conclude much of anything."

"I am impressed with your patience," Agnes said. "Were I in your position, I'd be spouting off all kinds of suppositions and ideas."

"That's a common reaction to a situation like this, but it does more harm than good."

"I lack the composure to wait and see what happens."

William burst into laughter. "I've noticed that." When he saw the quizzical expression on her face, he laughed even harder. "Oh, Agnes. You are priceless," he said, wiping his eyes.

"I'm sure I don't know what you mean, sir," she replied, her back stiff.

He reached across and took her hand. "You are the scientist of the two of us. Since you bought your first telescope, you've been studying the sky. After noting your observations in a notebook, you return to it again. You are in no hurry for the moon to move, or the stars to change. You observe and record."

"Well, of course. That is science," she replied, somewhat stiffly.

"Agnes, what you identify as scientific research is what I call investigation. They are similar, except for their topics of focus. I'm after the man who murdered one of your servants and you are looking for information about the movement of the stars, planets, and moon in the sky. We work in different areas, but the process is comparable."

She flinched as he spoke. "How astonishing. Research, to me, is unique to educational study. I've never likened it to something like an investigation."

"Imagine all the other things that people approach in the same way we're discussing. For example, some young women make notes about the eligible males of the ton, looking for characteristics they favor and men whose company they enjoy."

"Of course. Every girl is searching for a husband. Everyone knows that."

"But, my dear, you are jumping to conclusions without adequate information, because some of those females are categorizing peers to avoid as well as marry. And others are researching potential husbands for their friends."

"Really? How extraordinary! I never realized."

"Agnes, we are all trying to make our way in the world with the resources provided to us. You have a gifted mind, but not everyone is thusly blessed. People do their best with what they have at hand."

"But is marriage all that matters?"

"If you are a single female, a wedding is very important. For example, after your parents pass, what will you do, should your brothers refuse to allow you to live with them?"

"I can't imagine either of them making such a nasty decision."

"But in some families, that is the risk, giving a girl no choice but to marry. Some women want children and those also require marriage." He held up his hand to stop her. "I know a husband is not technically required, but a single woman is ostracized out of society unless she gives up the child at birth or works in a factory or as a maid."

Agnes studied him for a moment and nodded. "You are right, of course. I've never considered the plight of women in this way, but rather as a pastime to avoid the important study of science."

"But now you know differently. Many girls lack your options." He shrugged. "In most ton homes, there would be no discussion of a telescope in the attic, or scientific studies. You are blessed in your family, but not all are as lucky."

"I will remember that when thinking of others, even though I don't understand their research or their methods. And I won't argue with your conclusion because your hypothesis is correct. However, some of them are nattering ninnies with little consideration of anything other than the latest trouser-wearing title to walk in the door.”

Laughter burst out of him again. “Agreed. But that’s about them and their choices and doesn’t affect you. It’s no different from someone conducting research you think is irrelevant to the betterment of humanity.”

“But at least it affirms current knowledge,” she argued.

“As does theirs, Agnes.” He wiped his mouth and took her hand in his. “People are going to do what they choose. You don’t have to help them or fix them or re-direct them. You do your thing with your telescope and your experiments and leave them be.”

Her lips formed a pout. “But it seems childish.”

“Only to you, because you have options. To a woman without them, this is important. It might mean the difference between living and dying for some of them.”

She glanced at him. “I’ve never considered their risks before. Are you serious? Life or death?”

He nodded. “Please keep it in mind.”

“I’m not sure if I should, but the matter merits more thought.”

He patted her hand. “Good. I promise you’ll feel better as will they.” He smiled at her and rose. “Now kindly excuse me, because I have a house to search.”

Agnes watched William walk away and considered their conversation. She wasn’t certain she agreed, but she hadn’t argued with him either. When they talked, she found it difficult to concentrate on anything other than his mouth. Is this what kissing did to a woman’s mind?

Was that why very few wives were able to speak on any deep subjects? Come to think of it, there were few married women at the lectures she attended. Perhaps too much lovemaking caused their lack of interest, although she couldn't see a reason for that. A cause-and-effect relationship seemed improbable.

She looked down at the dessert she'd mauled while hardly tasting it, glad her parents had left, allowing her to chat with William. He fascinated her. His kiss had been extraordinary. But it was more than that. A thoughtful person, who had studied many topics and synthesized his knowledge in a way that affected the world. Or at least her. Everything he said made sense.

The sound of his voice was appealing and she could listen to him for hours because of his ability to take subjects and braid them together in ways she had never considered and explain the results in a way she understood. Not like she was a five-year-old still in the school room, but an adult woman with unique experiences. It was flattering and exciting, and she craved more.

There had been few opportunities in her life to chat about subjects with another who was as intelligent and as educated as she was. William brought all of that and made her feel good.

She couldn't wait to give him her Christmas gift, the book on astronomy. They could discuss the information while he read it. Perhaps she'd explain something, or they could use her telescope to see the items in the night sky that were mentioned in the tome. Rubbing her hands together with joy and anticipation, she was certain it would be her best holiday ever.

With that thought, Agnes jumped up from the table and hurried to her room. She wanted to be sure she wrapped her gift perfectly, to show how much time and attention she gave when preparing it for him.

Several hours later, she was in the attic studying the sky and making notes when the door opened, and William came inside. "Excuse our interruption, but Mrs. Johnson and I want to search these premises."

Although she'd never seen a female doing this work, she looked normal, in her mid to late thirties, with brown hair pulled into a bun on her neck.

After he introduced them, the woman said, with a slight nod of her head. "I am pleased to meet you, Lady Harrison."

"Likewise," Agnes replied. "Have you been an investigator for long?"

"Yes, it's been a while. I enjoy the work and it turns out there are many opportunities for female agents in these modern times."

"Have you worked on a murder investigation?"

William chuckled and turned to his co-worker. "As mentioned, Lady Harrison is direct and asks specific questions."

"I prefer such people, rather than those who say one thing and mean another, which I find incredibly difficult."

"Me as well," the younger woman replied. "I am happier when others are honest with me. It eliminates miscommunication and facilitates understanding."

Mrs. Johnson nodded. "I agree." Then she glanced at William. "We should make our way through the attic."

"Certainly." He smiled at Agnes. "We won't be long, and then you can get back to your notes."

They separated, going to opposite sides of the room. They looked around, over and inside and between every box, trunk, piece of furniture, and mannequin. Watching them, she marveled at their thoroughness and speed. It took no time to search the space, and she was quite certain if anything had been amiss, they would've discovered it. An extra level of safety, one she hadn't known she was missing, settled over her.

They returned to the stairs, and he whispered to his partner, who left, closing the door behind her. Then he turned to Agnes, "Do you have questions about our investigation?" he asked, walking toward her.

For a moment, she felt like prey. Then she giggled at her fanciful ideas. With his lithe movements, William might resemble a lion, but never when it involved her, nor in the attic.

"Did I say something humorous?" He stopped beside her.

"Not really, it was just a thought."

"Would you care to share it?" He moved a little closer.

She shook her head. "No. It was too ridiculous to repeat aloud."

"Is there anything else you'd like to ask?"

She bit on her bottom lip, shaking her head.

William groaned as he leaned toward her, licking the spot she had bitten.

She angled into him, wanting more, and he obliged, fitting his lips to hers as she ran her hands through his hair.

A moment later, he pulled away and sighed. "We must not, Agnes. You are a single woman, and I am a gentleman who will control my behavior near you. You deserve no less."

She wanted to step against him, wrap her arms around his waist, and kiss him again. Kissing him caused feelings she had never experienced or ever imagined.

"But we are alone, and no one comes up here."

"I have been hired by your father to protect the house, including you. And Mrs. Johnson is waiting for me. Another embrace means I am here longer than intended. Therefore, I will take my leave and finish searching the manor."

William turned around and walked to the door. His coat reached the top of his thighs, covering his back and bottom, but his tight trousers highlighted strong muscles. She told herself that studying the human form was another type of scientific inquiry, but the truth was she rather liked watching him.

Agnes enjoyed the view, even if he hadn't been willing to kiss her again. She did not know kissing was this pleasant, but then she'd never been kissed before.

There was something about the experience that baffled her. From a logical standpoint, it should mean nothing more than holding hands, and the idea of another person's tongue in her mouth should be repellent.

She chuckled. It was, if she thought about some people. But never with William. Why was that? What about the man that made these acts pleasant? Thrilling even.

When he leaned towards her, her temperature rose. The tips of her bosoms grew sensitive. Relieved when pressed close to him, her bosom felt fuller and heavier, and wanted more. But she wasn't sure what.

She sucked her bottom lip between her teeth and smiled. It was her good fortune he was staying here over the holidays and could answer all her questions. It was bound to be one of the most pleasant lessons of her life.

William adjusted his trousers before leaving the attic to keep his reaction to Agnes to himself. He trusted Mrs. J's ability to maintain a confidence, but there was no need to flaunt his lack of self-control. It would be ruinous for their agency were he to take advantage of the man's daughter while staying at his home.

What was it about Agnes that put him on tenterhooks? He had never liked the woman before starting this job. In fact, he had avoided her at social events. She had been the reason he tried to decline this case. And her father was a client. It would be ruinous to their agency for him to take advantage of the man's daughter while staying in his home to protect the family.

But watching her enthusiasm over her new telescope and her delight explaining the sky to him showed her in another light. She wasn't only an intelligent female who was uncomfortable in social situations, but a woman with passion and excitement. With no consideration, he reached out for both, and the result seared him. Now he was looking for opportunities to find her alone to steal a kiss. Every success made it harder to leave her. And yet he had no choice.

Seducing the client's daughter wasn't good for business, Agnes or him. This time Mrs. Johnson was waiting for him, but he must not start anything with the young woman. She was a maiden and would marry. Her husband deserved to claim her virginity and teach her about making love.

He needn't like his decision, but he had to follow through.

"How long has Lady Harrison been special to you?" asked Mrs. Johnson.

"She's not. We became friends because of our mutual interest in the sky. You saw her new telescope. It's quite the marvel of modern science."

"Yes, of course, it is only your intellectual pursuits that raise your temperature and muss your hair."

He smoothed his fingers over his head as the heat increased on his face. "She is a lady, and I wouldn't damage her reputation."

"I didn't mean to imply you would."

He coughed to cover his discomfort at being less than truthful. His associate deserved better from him, as did Agnes.

After searching the house, they agreed no one was onsite who should not have been.

They returned to the study just as Harrison was leaving. "I'm glad you're here. I am done for the day."

"We will take over from here, my lord," William assured him.

Inside, he and his two associates walked through everything that occurred, starting with the earl's belief about the first intrusion, through to the night of the murder and the subsequent searches.

"It makes no sense. It is unlikely that anyone outside of Parliament knows about the documents the earl is working on. Hell, most of the men in the lords have no idea about what he's reviewing," William said.

Mrs. Johnson agreed, then looked at Maitland. "Did you watch him put everything away?"

The agent nodded. "Because he is very particular about how he places things. I'm positive he is correct when he talks about the intruder."

"I agree. Our task is to figure out who is snooping and why. In the process, we must discover who murdered the footman guarding this room."

They discussed options and opportunities for a couple of hours and agreed that William would send men to snoop around. He would attend Spencewith's ball to ask questions and see if anything came to light. Tired of waiting for another strike, he wanted to put an end to this business as soon as possible and definitely before he took an intractable step with Agnes and forced them into a situation resolved only by marriage.

"You will both remain here until your replacements arrive?"

"Of course," Mrs. Johnson assured him.

As they discussed who to send where, the earl returned. "By the way, we are attending Spencewith's tonight. I presume you'll be in attendance as well, Lord Evans?"

"I wouldn't miss it." He looked at his team and said to the client. "I urge you to be very circumspect about telling anyone about the activities in your house."

"I won't say a word. How would it look if I couldn't protect confidential documents in my home?"

"Exactly. I will ask questions at the ball, but in a specific way. If there is information to be had, I'll find it."

"Excellent."

"Now, if you'll excuse me, I must run errands and prepare for tonight's entertainment."

William sent a message to his valet about the change in plans for tonight, then hurried to Louis' house and explained what they needed. They went through the list of investigators who could make the rounds, looking for tips. Some would frequent the taverns in Seven Dials. Others would go to the docks, while a third pair would visit the higher-class hells. In what seemed like no time, agents were on the prowl seeking a man or men who wanted information about parliament.

He was sick and tired of being on the defensive. They would take action and force the bastard into the open.

He spoke to his mother, brother, and sister-in-law for a few moments before returning to his old room. His valet had already arrived and had his evening clothes pressed and ready to wear.

"I'm sleeping for a few hours and then I'll dress for dinner and the ball."

After disrobing, he slid between the silk sheets and laid his head against the pillow. As his eyes closed, he again felt Agnes's hand against his cheek and sliding over his scalp and her lips against his. In moments, he had a raging cock stand and nowhere to put it. It wasn't enough his body responded to everything about the woman when he was in her presence. Now it was responding to thoughts of her. At this rate, he'd be a bedlamite in no time.

He punched the pillow and relaxed, waking after what seemed like too little sleep, dressed, and joined his family for a drink before dinner. Because he and Louis had agreed not to discuss business at these events but to enjoy the company, he teased his mother, cooed after his new nephew, and made disparaging remarks to Juliette about being married to his oldest brother.

When the duke invited him to the terrace for a cheroot, William assumed there was a personal matter to be discussed. But he was surprised. "Have you discovered anything about the break-ins to Harrison's safe?"

"I don't believe any of the family or servants to be involved. Louis and I assigned men to comb their sources to see if we can find answers."

"Are you aware of the information in the documents that Harrison has in his possession?"

"He said the majority were wording for bills or proposals coming up in the next sitting of the house."

"Did he say anything about foreign intelligence?"

What an uncomfortable conversation. William had to keep the confidentiality of his client, but his brother probably knew more about the situation than even Harrison.

"I take it from the look on your face that he's talked to you about a French movement to free Napoleon again." Allwyn studied him until he squirmed.

"I am very uncomfortable with this conversation, Your Grace," he said, using his brother's formal title to point out the difference in their positions. "I am certain you have extensive knowledge of the situation and the risks, but I must respect the confidentiality of my client."

"Well delivered, little brother," Allwyn replied, slapping him on the back. "Here is what I know." The duke had the ear of the Prince Regent, the major players in the House of Lords, and probably most of the heads of European nations. He was a powerful man whose reach extended far beyond London. If he was willing to talk, William was more than happy to listen.

Half an hour later, he was even more impressed with his brother's network of informants. He shared rumors of the proposed attack, as well as the reasons behind it. As his brother said, the plans made little sense and weren't likely to succeed, but the country had to be prepared, just in case their information could minimize the risk.

Behind them, the door opened, and Juliette called to them. "Have you two saved the world before you turn into icicles?"

Allwyn turned to his wife and smiled. "We're not quite frozen, but it's a near thing, my love."

"Then you can plan and plot later," she said with a smile. "Calliope and Jeremy have arrived, and dinner was announced."

Their brother-in-law was another man with a wide network of information sources. William would chat with him this evening, the moment the opportunity presented itself.

"Under no circumstances can we delay the meal. Cook would have our heads," Allwyn said, moving inside.

With that, their conversation ended and both he and his brother rejoined the others for a typical family time of teasing, laughter, and good fun.

Dinner finished, William joined his mother, siblings, and their spouses in carriages to the Spencewith's, whose Christmas ball was well attended. Only the highest ton received an invitation, and few declined. Rumor had it families changed their plans if invited, since it was important to attend and be seen in attendance.

Through the receiving line, the family followed Allwyn, Juliette, and their mother, Evelyn, into the ballroom. William looked for Agnes and her parents, but didn't see them. They split into smaller groups and made the rounds, greeting friends and chatting.

He continued to scan the crowd for the Harrisons, wondering if she would join them tonight. Not seeing them, he took a place near the stairs, where he could watch the receiving line.

The Harrison's, including their daughter, arrived fashionably late and proceeded to say hello, kiss cheeks, and shake hands with their host and his family.

Agnes was dressed in a flattering rose-colored gown with a high waist. He wasn't familiar with ladies' fashions, but assumed her dress was the most current design, but scowled as he realized how much of her bosom was on display. The woman should have worn a fichu. He would address the bare expanse at his first opportunity.

With one eye on Agnes, William spoke to a group near the Harrisons. While chatting, he watched for signs of nervousness or discomfort but saw nothing in his companions, the earl, or the men he was conversing with.

Five or ten minutes later, he was standing with his client. After complimenting both women, he turned to Agnes. "Might I enjoy your company during a waltz?" As before, he claimed both waltzes on her card, then smiled at her. "My mother would have my head if I didn't join her for dinner, so unfortunately, I'll have to leave the supper dance to some other lucky man."

Then he left, continuing to make small talk with the guests, always looking for someone who seemed uncomfortable or out of place. Or had French connections or an accent.

The music started and William made his way to the card room. It was unlikely anyone would be deep enough in his cups to say something inappropriate, but just in case, he would circulate in there. Perhaps someone was in the middle of a nasty streak of bad luck and sought an alternate income, or an unorthodox method to make good on his vowels.

He heard nothing and sensed no desperation from any of the players, but the night was early. He would repeat these rounds two or three times tonight, just in case there was something to be learned.

As the musicians prepared for the first waltz, William left the card salon and found Agnes, standing on the side of the ballroom, scanning the room.

"Are you looking for someone?" he asked, stepping beside her.

Her cheeks flushed a pretty pink, and she shook her head. "I knew you wouldn't forget, but I couldn't see where you'd gone."

"I've been doing the family thing, speaking to guests, and making sure the atmosphere is full of good cheer." He bowed over her hand. "I believe this is my dance, Lady Harrison."

She curtsied to him, smiled, and agreed. "It is, and I have been looking forward to it all evening."

He led her to the middle of the floor, put his arm around her back, and took her hand. "You are exceedingly lovely tonight, Agnes," he said, in the first steps of the waltz, "but I am not too enamored of your gown."

"What?" She frowned at him. "Is there a problem with it? My modiste assured me it was the highest stare of fashion."

"She is likely right, but I don't like it."

Shaking her head at him, she looked down. "Why not? It's one of the nicest gowns I've ever owned."

He tightened his arm around her waist and pulled her a little closer, then whispered, "From my point of view, I can almost see your nipples. Aren't you afraid some rake might get the wrong impression?"

Agnes threw back her head and laughed. When she could look at him and keep a straight face, she said, "There are many dresses cut lower than mine, Lord Evans. And I never worry about such things because rakes don't come close enough to get any ideas."

He tightened his hold on her waist. "And they better not, or they will have to deal with me."

CHAPTER EIGHT

U nless she misread the signs, William was jealous. Not of a real man, but some supposed rake, who might want to take advantage of her. How delightful.

Inside, some unbeknownst female element of her celebrated his reaction to her decolletage. She moved closer, ensuring her bosom nestled against his chest.

It felt wicked, but lovely. She never knew about such activities on the dance floor. But in the future, she would observe more carefully.

Was this interaction part of the game of finding a mate? Girls were told nothing about reproduction or sexual activity until the exchange of vows.

The friction and movement against her breasts gave her a moment of insight. This experience, this sensation, was one reason young women wanted to get married.

If she suggested to any of the debutantes that marriage was appealing because they were coming into their prime breeding years, they would ostracize her forever. But it seemed to be the truth of the matter.

And after the last week or ten days, she understood why.

As William spun her around the floor, she tightened her arm on his back and held on. She hadn't tripped, nor had she become dizzy in the turns. They had avoided each other's feet, and she had relished being in his arms and close to him.

The orchestra extended the last note for a heartbeat and then silence prevailed. She had danced with him without seeing the flow of numbers. She had followed the music and the lead of her partner through an entire dance, neither making a fool of herself nor embarrassing him.

Goodness gracious, what was happening to her? A few weeks ago, dancing was akin to a nightmare of tripping and looking foolish. Then, because of William's kindness, she danced while seeing the notes, and couldn't imagine anything better.

Tonight, she'd enjoyed more. The magic William wielded on her behalf was of no matter. She was grateful there was at least one dance where she didn't have to fear embarrassing herself or her partner.

Perhaps when his investigation finished, he could show her how to navigate the popular sets in ballrooms across London. But that was a wish for another day. Tonight, she appreciated his help and attention. And for teaching her things about people without even trying.

As he escorted her back to her mother, an attractive couple intercepted them. He introduced her to the Duke and Duchess of Castleridge, Jeremy and Calliope, his brother-in-law and sister.

She curtsied and joined a comfortable, easy conversation as they returned to the sidelines.

"William mentioned you're very interested in astronomy, Lady Agnes," Cally said.

"I find it fascinating that bodies move through space, and we can't observe them clearly, without the benefit of powerful telescopes. Right now, the sky is twinkling with stars, perhaps a planet or two, and the moon."

"But I can see most of those just by looking up."

"Of course. Forgive me for misspeaking, your Grace. What I meant is that a telescope makes more stars observable and the moon's appearance much clearer. And sometimes planets come into view and even comets. It is rare that any of those are visible to the naked eye, although it happens occasionally."

"How exciting to see things no one else knows is there. If I had the time, there is a small part of me that would be jealous of your study and discoveries. But our son takes up every spare moment."

"Congratulations. A baby is a wonderful addition." She looked around. "Are all of your family here tonight? I don't think I've had the pleasure of meeting all of them."

"Henry, the youngest of the triplets, is up north somewhere doing something," Cally said. "All but one of my brothers is in attendance."

"It has to be interesting to grow up with that many in your home, especially with three babes at once. And now that two of them are married, you are adding sisters to the mix. That must be fun, too."

"They are both delightful women who keep their husbands in check." Calliope leaned towards her and whispered, "which all my siblings require."

Shocked at the woman's comment, Agnes questioned, "Really? A duke and his brothers need to be managed?" Incredulity and curiosity tightened her voice.

"Especially dukes, since they sometimes assume they walk on water."

"Sweetheart are you disparaging those of us at the highest levels of the aristocracy?" her husband asked.

"Of course. Both you and Allwyn require reminders you are but mere mortals on the face of the earth, contrary to your own opinions."

"Unbelievable," he said. "And shocking. I must talk to your mother about your attitude toward the males in your family."

"Please do. She will clear up your outdated ideas in a heartbeat."

Jeremy laughed. "There's no doubt about that. I know better than to go to her with those comments, for she taught you such scandalous opinions."

Agnes watched their banter and smiled. Their comfort with each other, their ability to give-and-take in humor and in fun, warmed her heart. Glancing around, she wondered how many other couples had the same ease in their relationship? Perhaps companionship was another reason girls focused on marriage.

She was finding additional arguments for a young single woman to be looking for a husband. The sole-minded pursuit of a spouse had seemed trivial or boring, but maybe that need for a close compatriot was missing in her.

Perhaps her curiosity and intelligence had blinded her to some social realities. That idea had never crossed her mind before, but merited consideration. It was time for her to explore this situation as a potential failing in her, rather than other women.

Suddenly cold, she wondered if this long-held belief was wrong, where else might her logic have strayed? Her scientific pursuits were not in question. Her processes and observations were ironclad, however, her social interactions and activities, the ones her mother had encouraged, had gone amiss.

The marriage of her parents was far more typical than Calliope's. She remembered scraps of events and conversations and realized their relationship was her basis for her opinions about the wedded state. In her haste to lump them all together as the same, she'd made a horrid mistake. No two stars were identical. The same was true for marriages. In the Duke and Duchess of Castleridge, she saw another possibility. It appealed to her in more ways than she could count.

Looking around, she found William conversing with some lord. In the short time of their acquaintance, he had caused volcanic sized holes in her beliefs about society and the role of women. She wasn't convinced he was right, but she was determined to find out.

William couldn't tell what was running through Agnes' mind, but it was interesting. Her eyes were warm and... perhaps appreciative.

When he joined them, the women were deep in conversation. He turned to Jeremy and suggested they step outside for a cheroot and a drink.

They sauntered to a spot at the far end of the terrace, away from the other revelers.

Drinks in hand and cheroots lit, his brother-in-law said, "I presume there is a specific you want to discuss?"

William nodded. "There is, but I'm not sure how to get into it."

"To start, I have no information about the break-ins at Harrisons. Some of his documents are sensitive. I've been told they have something to do with some crazy French plot to free Napoleon from St. Helens. The rest are papers he's working on for the house and of little interest to anyone else."

"How do you know that? It's supposed to be top-secret."

"It is. Beyond the Prime Minister and a few of the senior ministers and Harrison, your brother and I are likely the only ones in the country who are aware of it."

William narrowed his eyes at his brother-in-law. "My question is, how come the two of you, who have no position in government outside of your seats in the House of Lords and no reason to have this knowledge, are cognizant of this much?"

Jeremy laughed. "The most important lesson I learned is that information is the most valuable commodity on earth. With it, all decisions are easier and more accurate. Sometimes it is irrelevant today but comes to have meaning in a week or two or a month or even a year down the road. Almost immediately arriving in London, I discovered it means power and coin, and I collected as much as I could."

"I've noticed, as you waxed poetic about your history, that you haven't answered my question, so let me repeat it. How did you discover this information?"

"I never name names. But I have a network of confidants, friends, and informants who pass along anything they deem of value."

"Can you share how it came to you?"

Jeremy dropped his cheroot and crushed it with his boot. He leaned his forearms on the railing and looked at William. "One source suggested it was a matter of national safety and security. But another considered it the result of deluded individuals trying to reclaim old glories for France."

William faced the duke. "Two people provided you with information about the documents in Harrison's safe. But they had different perspectives about the worth and meaning of it."

"Three, actually, but their consideration of its importance settled into those opinions."

"Is the Prime Minister familiar with your sources?"

Jeremy threw back his head and laughed. "Between you and me, he often comes to your brother or me or both of us to verify a tip from his intelligence agents. He knows what we do and isn't above using it when it serves him or the country."

William studied his brother-in-law. "The two of you are unbelievable." He slapped his hand on the brick wall. "I hope our investigation agency builds such a network."

"It takes time. People must learn they can trust you and will be fairly compensated for their information. Once that happens, they tell their friends who speak to theirs and on, in an ever-wider circle. Some of those who come to you will also be part of my group or your brother's. Then the challenge is to make sure we're not paying for three versions of the same thing from the same single source." Jeremy rose and stood beside him. "That's a problem for down the road. Right now, you're building your circle."

"What's your opinion?" William asked.

"Fools are raising money and interest to free Napoleon. Since they don't understand, it's impossible, I'm not too worried about it."

"And the Prime Minister?"

"He and your brother share that view."

"But someone has rifled Harrison safe, and a man was killed trying to protect it, which suggests somebody considers it important." William rubbed his left index finger along his forehead. "Unless, of course, this fanaticism has nothing to do with the break-in and a person is more interested in an upcoming bill to Parliament than Napoleon."

"What proposals or bills is Harrison working on?"

"I don't know. But I will rectify that in the morning. It is possible someone opposes or supports one. Now I have to find out who."

"Good luck with that." Jeremy shot his cuffs. "It's time we returned to the ladies. I'm sure my wife wants to dance with me."

As he followed the duke back to the ballroom, William realized the man had said nothing about bills being prepared for the House of Lords. Did he know something? Or was he giving him an opportunity to find the information for himself? He shrugged. Neither answer mattered. His only responsibility was to discover who was going through Harrison's safe, who murdered the guard, and to make sure he brought them to justice.

Through the evening, he noticed that his brother, Louis, danced with Agnes, and, of course, his family circled her and kept her engaged in conversation. Both raised her social cachet. Several other men asked her to dance, and he was pleased to see she did well. No tripping and no stumbling. She was getting her legs under her, and it was a pleasure to watch.

He spoke to others, trying to gauge their response to upcoming bills in the Lords or work by the committees or subcommittees. He learned nothing new but wouldn't yet strike any of them from his list of potential suspects.

When the orchestra prepared to play the next waltz, William secured Agnes's hand and led her to the floor. She moved into his arms with ease, almost as if she fit. Or belonged there.

He stopped those thoughts. He enjoyed kissing Agnes and dancing with her, but they lived different lives. She needed a partner who could match her in intelligence and willingness to research and study. He was not that man. Were they to get together, he would drive her to distraction in no time.

The woman respected education. He had a specific ability which lent itself to investigations, but not to Agnes' work. He was well aware of his limitations. A lifetime of tutors, professors, and fellow students had proven how dumb he was. He was lucky his brother had the idea to start the agency, which provided all three of them with an opportunity to make their own way in the world, without relying on the Duchy for allowances.

Their situation was the best of all worlds, but his did not include Agnes as anything more than a friend, a woman he was helping to see her strengths and weaknesses to take part more easily in society. Perhaps she would find a man deserving of her.

His heart twisted, but it was true. Otherwise, she spent her life alone and although he couldn't have her, he wasn't small minded enough to wish that on her. She deserved a husband who doted on her, children who loved her, and a home of her own, where she could study the stars and conduct experiments and satisfy her intellectual curiosity to her heart's content.

But, damn, it irritated him to think of her with another man. There was no reason for his reaction since he had no claim on her. Best he gets used to it, or any kind of relationship, even friendship, would be impossible.

As he led her around the room, Agnes tightened her hold.

"Is something amiss?" she asked him. "You seem distracted, or perhaps distant."

"My apologies. I was cataloguing the various responses to my questions and got lost in thought."

"I'm delighted you heard some answers," she said, "but the look on your face suggested a more personal concern. Or am I wrong?"

"How very observant. I started off considering tonight's conversations and drifted to other situations and implications. I apologize. How boorish for a man holding a beautiful woman to think of anyone or anything but her."

Her tinkling laughter raised his spirits. "You are still lost in thought, William, or you are thinking of another couple."

Her impish grin warmed his heart, and he relished her teasing. He tightened his arm around her back and leaned down close. "Any female who takes it upon herself to tease me risks being plastered against me for the rest of this dance. Mind your language, young lady."

"Are you making a threat or a promise?"

"It's your preference, Agnes."

"Then I shall take it as a vow. Which I intend to make you deliver."

He knew she would, and the certainty brought a smile to his face.

He returned her to his family and their friends and headed to the men's retiring room. On his way out, a servant stopped him and crooked his finger, urging William to follow him down the hall and into one of the rooms. The man wearing Harrison livery was average—in height, appearance, and language. Curious about his motives, he followed along.

Once inside, he closed the door behind him, when a searing pain in his head dropped him to his knees and then the floor. What the hell? The room slid into black, and the only sound was the distant orchestra, until it too faded.

On his side with his cheek on the carpet... a few minutes or a few hours later, head pounding, William heard two men talking in low voices. Lying still, the salon bright with candles, he slitted his eyes and looked around without moving.

"Why'd you hit him that hard?" asked the servant who led him here.

"You told me to be sure he didn't make any trouble and to keep him quiet." The second man glanced at William and pointed. "He's on the floor and silent. What more do you want?"

"That he can walk out of here on his own, stupid."

"He will, just as soon as ye got yer questions answered."

Since there was no time like the present to hear the rest of this scheme, he groaned. "What... what happened?"

Both men moved beside him. The one who coshed him over the head nudged him with his boot. "Sit up, ye wanker. I didn't cosh your noggin' that hard."

Unsure of what they wanted, he remained on the floor and moaned.

"Quit yer whining and get up before I give ye another smack to start you listening."

With no other option, he sat up, rubbing the spot they had hit him. "What happened?" he asked, looking around, then up. "Why did you hit me?"

"Because you're asking too damn many questions. The boss said to tell you to shut up and forget Harrison's safe, or the next time he hears about you making trouble, he's going to blow your head off."

The other man giggled. "Probably shoot you right where I coshed ye, mate."

William staggered to his feet. His head hurt, but he didn't want these fools to realize he felt better than he was acting. "Who's your boss?" He used his handkerchief and wiped the blood from his scalp.

"None of your business," the first replied. "Just remember what he said. Shut up with your questions or you'll pay."

"Will he send the two of you again? Since you did such a good job this time?"

"Maybe."

"Do you think this toff is right?" asked the man who hit him. "Will she pay to off this one?"

Who was the woman? Could this whole thing come from a woman? Perhaps a paramour who'd been given her congé by Harrison?

"Be quiet, stupid. We aren't saying anything to anyone. If we're paid to get rid of this bloke, he'll tell us."

"She's not exactly a fair bitch, though, is she? Might just give our coins to another couple of guys."

"Shut up!" He slapped his partner across the face, then turned his attention to William. "Mind what you were told. No more questions." He jerked his partner's arm and shoved him toward the entry before turning back. "Stay here for five minutes before you poke your head out. I'd hate to mess up the carpets with more of your blood." Then he pushed his friend out of the room, closing the door behind him.

William leaned his ear against the wood but heard nothing and twisted the knob, opening it less than a thumb's width.

Silence.

He pulled it open. The hall was deserted.

Slowly opening it wider, he stuck his head out and looked both ways. Since it seemed safe, he stepped out, closed the door, and walked away from the salon, checking every room.

No one.

At the end of the corridor, the servants' stairs led to the back of the house. With no other option, he descended, ending up near the kitchen. "Did two men come down here moments ago?" he asked a startled maid.

She shook her head. "No, sir. Are you lost? The main staircase are the other direction. Perhaps you are turned around." Her eyes got huge. "You are bleeding, my lord. Can I find someone to help you?"

He put up his hands. "No, thank you. I must have become confused after I tripped. I'll just return the way I came."

The orchestra was still playing, and the hum of the guests buzzed back here. Not much time had passed. Nodding his thanks to the maid, he returned upstairs and to the men's room. After rinsing the blood from his scalp, he returned to the ballroom. He did not know where those two had gone, but he'd learned something important. It wasn't a man wanting to see what was in the safe, but a woman—which put a different slant on the situation.

CHAPTER NINE

Agnes noticed William returning to the ballroom after being absent for a long time, not that she'd been watching. Or waiting for him.

At the base of the stairs, he looked around and as soon as he saw her, walked to her side. "What happened?" she asked.

"What do you mean?"

She leaned in close and took his hands. "There is a small smear of blood behind your ear. Tell me."

"It was nothing," he said, leaning toward her as if sharing a private moment with her.

Smiling, she turned her face to his. "It was something. If you choose not to say, that's your choice."

When a laugh rumbled out of him, she was reassured. It couldn't be too serious if he could chuckle.

"It's a long story, and I'll tell you when we arrive back home. In the meantime, I will step outside and use my handkerchief."

"If you're not here in a few minutes, I'll come looking for you, just in case you run into another problem." Silly man didn't realize how worrisome it was that he had a wound on his head, which could be dangerous. She would wait a moment, but not much longer.

"That won't happen, I promise." He looked around the room. "I will be right back. Be patient." Then he sauntered away, without a care in the world, though she knew better.

Watching him keep his silence meant he could keep a host of other confidences.

A woman hoping to marry should be as knowledgeable as possible about her prospective husband. Not that William was in this category. Not at all. But she wondered about his private life.

Glancing around the room, she speculated about these people, too. How many secrets were being held? Then she caught sight of her parents. Did they have things they kept from the world? Or from each other? From her?

All her realizations tonight were surprising, but only because they were new. She hadn't had the time nor a confidante to share them with.

William had shown that her disdain for the women of the ton was well known and people gossiped about them, even laughed at her. Recently, she'd realized her opinions weren't fair, nor were they realistic.

As she was musing about her learnings, he returned. "Thank you. I didn't realize I'd missed a spot."

"Will you tell me what happened now?"

He shook his head. "We'll talk about it later." He looked at the dance floor. "Let's enjoy this waltz and then perhaps you'll join my family and I for supper."

She extended her hand. "I hate not knowing things." It was the most irritating state in her life.

His lips lifted in a chuckle. "Your curiosity is a driving force, Agnes. I recognize that about you. But this is one time it remains unsatisfied until later."

He clasped her to him, and she relaxed into his arms. It felt like coming home, which was ridiculous. Her feelings must come from his kindness when helping her dance.

Just because she had learned much about herself tonight didn't mean she was developing a tendre for the man. Nor would she throw herself at him, despite where her heart took her meandering thoughts.

After the midnight supper, they, along with Allwyn and Juliette, stepped outside to recover from the heat of the ballroom.

"Your Grace, it is a pleasure to chat with you. Your brother-in-law has mentioned you often," Agnes said.

The duchess looked from her to William and back. "Is there anything I must renounce?"

"Absolutely not. He speaks of you in the most glowing terms. He explained that you're a physician. Is that correct?" They had stopped near the terrace wall, not far from the house.

"It is a two-edged sword. I am a graduate of a recognized and reputable medical school in Scotland. But because of my biology, I attended as a male and using my initials and I'm not allowed to join the medical society. But there are many needing care who pay no attention to my gender or prefer having a female tend to them. Especially in matters relating only to women, including childbirth."

This woman had accumulated a large amount of data and experience. She was one of the most fascinating people Agnes had met. "If I may be forward, did having a child transform your opinion or process when working with patients in that condition?" She put her hand over her mouth, realizing how inappropriate her question was. "Excuse me. I should not have asked that. My curiosity leads me to forget my manners occasionally."

"Nonsense. Every woman married or not should have information about birthing a babe. I do not understand society's standard that it is shameful." She leaned in closer. "Having a baby gave me insight into the fears, delights, and terror of bringing a person into this world. Medically, it changed little, except I know that something soothing to one can irritate another. As a result, I'm more careful as I approach each situation."

The duchess had lived through an experience and was using it as data to guide her work going forward. "How interesting. I've never thought of having a child as anything other than normal, since women do it all over the world. I never imagined it could be unique."

"Not only for each woman, but for each delivery."

If each event was unique, there would be very limited predictability. "That would make it more difficult to help a mother bring a baby into this world."

"There are some things that must happen. But even those have variance to them." Juliette looked at her, as if remembering she was speaking to a maiden, and said, "I understand you're interested in astronomy and mathematics."

Agnes nodded. "Yes, there is much to learn and little time to study. Sometimes I am overwhelmed with all the facts waiting to be discovered and how limited I am to contribute to that body of knowledge."

"Have you considered narrowing your field of interest? Perhaps the calculations of astronomy... or some other combination."

"William suggested the same thing, or something similar, and I must admit, starting a new scientific experiment is exciting. I become that caught up in my work that I stay in my laboratory for hours, sometimes days at a time, sleeping on a chair at my desk when I cannot hold my eyes open another moment."

"I remember that feeling very well. In my last year of study, there were very many areas I wanted to learn about. The fields, ranging from childbirth to injuries to consumption, were numerous and enticing."

"Did you end up selecting one or two?"

"I didn't. I realized that for me practising as an unlicensed physician, I would need to be a generalist. It is important for my patients that I possess broad knowledge of the body. Therefore, I took a wide range of courses covering a variety of topics and I learned from experience once I arrived in London." She leaned in close to Agnes and added, "It helps to be married to a man who never moans about my bill at the bookstore or the treatises I've ordered from Europe and Scotland."

Agnes looked at the imposing duke talking to William and chuckled. "You are a lucky lady. Most husbands would be irate about your book purchases, I'm sure." It was delightful to chat with another woman who shared her same vices.

"I find it amusing that men will grumble and fuss about the cost of dresses or jewels, but pay the bills, anyway. But let the discussion veer to a woman's intellectual pursuits and those same husbands become dictatorial and heavy-handed."

"My parents understand that my curiosity is as important to me as breathing. I am a bluestocking, for certain. But my studies keep me happy and allow me to feel I'm contributing, even in a small way." She smiled at her new friend. "Although I am convinced they would prefer me not to share such a spirited, informative conversation with a duchess."

Juliette looked around and nodded. "I have always wondered how many words about the weather are spoken during a ball like this."

Here was a female who shared some of her thoughts. "I am delighted to hear one in your position say such things, for I have often asked myself the same."

"Agnes, have you considered medical research? There is very much we don't know about the body, its functioning, and its strengths and weaknesses. A woman with your curiosity could make a substantial difference to the health of humanity."

"Thank you for your kind words, Your Grace. I have not, but it's no surprise. Anything more than a drop of blood and I am at risk of fainting. Whenever someone was injured at the estate, either the cook or the housekeeper would tend to them, while I made sure I was at the other end of the house." She shook her head. "Once I heard the sound of an arm being popped back into the shoulder joint." She shuddered. "It haunted my dreams for months."

"If you ever change your mind, please call on me. My husband is building a large treatment center, and we're including space for research. I am determined to hire as many females as possible. The quality of our work and our satisfied patients will eventually convince the medical society to give us entry."

"What a noble pursuit. Helping people while benefiting women. It is quite astounding."

"We must stick together, especially those who are interested in the sciences and studying. I am convinced that an individual woman's brain is as good as any man's. But without the proper education and opportunities, society will never realize it and continue to limit us to 'appropriate' activities, as defined by men."

"William and I discussed a similar topic. I realized I have been too harsh on those females only interested in marriage, for that is our cultural norm."

"It is and has been for centuries. Therefore, we must work to change them. Especially women like you and I who know differently and were given the opportunity and the skills to do other things."

Allwyn looked over his shoulder. "Our ladies seem to be getting on."

William glanced at them, then turned to his brother. "She isn't mine," he said, shaking his head. "Agnes is Harrison's only daughter, and my investigation is easier if it appears we are becoming better acquainted."

"You could have fooled me. You paid a lot of attention to her and her dance partners."

He leaned toward him. "There was a murder at her house a few days ago. Of course, I'm staying nearby. I won't risk another death while I am investigating."

"I understand you're being diligent, but my eyes tell me there's more to this than you are admitting, aware of it or not." He held up his hand. "You remind me of Jeremy before he realized he loved Calliope and Tony before he recognized his feelings for Charity."

"How about your behavior before you acknowledged how perfect Juliette is for you?"

Allwyn shook his head and laughed. "You are as bumble headed as I was. I'll give you credit for that." He looked at his wife, his eyes soft and his lips lifted in a small smile. "When I think what I might've missed because my understanding of cultural norms was skewed against my happiness, I have nightmares. My stupidity nearly cost me the only woman in the world who suits me perfectly." He shuddered. "I came so close." He turned his attention to his brother and slapped him on the back. "Don't do what we did and make it that damned hard on yourself. Acknowledge your feelings for her. As soon as you do that, you can start your life together."

He was uncertain how to respond, since he wasn't in love with Agnes. He appreciated her strength and intelligence and, in her own way, her kindness, but they would never suit. She was a genius who studied any topic that interested her, while he was a bumbling dummy with nothing other than skills. No, it was better for both of them if he kept that in mind.

"Suffice it to say, I disagree with you, so don't book St. George's just yet."

William looked around to be sure of their privacy, leaned his forearms on the railing, and glanced at his brother. "I think our villain is a woman."

Allwyn's eyebrows notched up. "What gives you that idea?"

"Earlier, I left the men's room, and a servant asked me to follow him. When I stepped into a salon, he coshed me on the head. When I came to, there were two men talking about the boss and several times they referred to 'her'. Whatever this is about, I've concluded it's possible a woman is responsible for everything that happened to Harrison."

"That opens a much different range of possibilities." His brother stared into the night. "Are you going to tell the earl about this discovery?"

"I'm not sure. It wouldn't be unusual for him to have had a series of mistresses. Any of them could be angry about being left behind. But I have heard nary a word about a recent mistress, which is where I'll start my next round of questioning."

"Nothing has come my way, either, but as a happily married man, they might not include me in the gossip about the demimonde. If I hear anything, I will advise you."

"Thanks. Best I get Agnes back to her parents before they think I've kidnapped her."

After leaving the terrace, she asked to be shown to several older women, widows, dowagers, and wives sitting in a tight group on one side of the ballroom.

Comfortable that she was safe, William circulated talking to many others. After most of the guests departed, he searched out the housekeeper. "It's common to hire extra staff for these busy nights. I am wondering about two men in particular." He described them to her as best he remembered, but she shook her head.

"I'm sorry. I don't recall anyone like that. Most of the hired people work the ballroom, where we can keep them under watch. Then our servants are on the upper floors. Whoever they were, they should never have been upstairs."

"Could you tell me how you verified who was brought in for the night?"

"We go through the same agency. They provide a list of those who will serve for us. We check them off as they report, to be sure no riffraff gets in." She scowled. "Apparently, someone failed to verify them correctly." She looked over her shoulder towards the kitchen. "I'll deal with that in the morning."

"William, what are you pestering Mrs. Hugbottom about?" the countess asked.

"Nothing earthshaking. I saw two servants upstairs who seemed out of place, and I wondered who they were."

"As I explained, we are careful about who we let into the house and nightly staff are not supposed to be above stairs."

"Did you follow them to see where they went? Does the butler need to check the silver?"

"I know nothing about that. I was just curious about those two men. It is quite possible they came in through the terrace or another door looking to make mischief."

"Then if you will excuse us, Mrs. Hugbottom and I have work to do tonight."

As he joined the family, he noted the questioning look on his mother's face as she glanced at Agnes. She always knew what was going on in the lives of her children. Tedious when he was younger, now it was cute, unless she was wrong. "I told you, mother, I'm working an investigation that has nothing to do with that young lady or any other female."

"I believe you, except she is the only woman you've danced with twice and accompanied to supper in years."

"Thank you for caring and for sharing, but if you'll excuse me, it's time I put my head on my pillow." He kissed her on the other cheek while hugging her close and left. He briefly considered stopping by Louis', but decided against it. The man was newly married and probably busy. Besides, if a woman was after Harrison and the documents in his safe, this was not a matter of national security but romance.

CHAPTER TEN

In the morning, William went to his brother's house. Louis was at breakfast when he arrived. "Help yourself."

"Thanks," he said, filling his plate with his favorite food—bacon, sausage, fruit, toast, and eggs. "Where's Eliza and Isabel?"

"My wife is in our room, probably breaking her fast with chocolate, and our daughter is likely with her governess already. She loves to read and hurries in the schoolroom as soon as her eyes were open or her nurse gives her permission."

"Sounds like a typical household." He carried his full plate to the table and sat beside his brother.

"I see you brought your appetite with you."

"Being coshed on the head will do that to a fellow."

"When did that happen? At the ball?" Louis glared at his younger sibling. "Why didn't you tell me last night?"

He spread his napkin on his lap. "You had already left, and that's where it occurred. Upstairs in one of the unused rooms."

His brother's brows notched. "Are you saying someone had the nerve to attack you at a crowded event?"

"Yes." He had recovered from the shock of the incident, but he agreed. It took balls to strike a man in a busy home.

Louis glared at him. "What the hell happened?"

William ran through the details, ending with him rubbing the spot on his head, which still hurt.

"It's unbelievable that they accosted you amid several hundred people!"

"I have the lump back here to prove it."

"What did they want?"

"Told me to stop asking questions about the break-in."

"That's no help. What do they fear you'll discover?"

"I'm not sure, but one of them referred to the boss as a woman." He watched for his brother's reaction.

"What? You're kidding!" Louis shook his head in disbelief.

"Puts a different slant on things, doesn't it?"

As his brother digested this latest information, William added. "I'll look at the betting books in the clubs, maybe go to some hells, and see what the money is saying."

Louis cut a piece of bacon, looking calmer now. "Perhaps we should station more men at Harrison's. If this is a pissed off woman, God knows what she'll do next." He looked at him. "A female doesn't kill a man over a bill in the lords. There must be something else."

"I'm sure there is, but Harrison wouldn't keep information about a mistress in his safe. I can't imagine him keeping anything to interest her. What peer keeps a souvenir of a paramour? And why would she want it?"

"This is ridiculous. We know there's nothing of any importance in it, except comments about French desperation. Are you sure they referenced the boss?"

"Yes. Might they have used the female words to confuse me? That's possible, but I doubt these two had adequate brain cells to manage more than the simplest jobs. I can't imagine them purposely using language to lead me astray."

"What could she be interested in?"

"A bill coming forward during the next session?"

"Still, it makes no sense. What woman cares enough about politics to kill?" Louis shook his head.

"I would be careful making that statement around the women in our lives. Mother, Calliope, and Juliette would ring a peal over you if they heard that."

He rubbed the back of his neck as the tips of his ears burned red. "As would my wife."

"Are you saying you learned nothing from the wedded men in our family and married a strong lady with opinions of her own?"

Louis struck his palm on his forehead. "It is a curse, I tell you. None of our female relatives are shy, simpering females who defer to their husbands."

"You're not complaining, are you?"

His brother laughed. "Never. I discovered the wonder of marriage to a woman with a good mind and personal opinions and enough confidence to share them. It is much more exciting than discussing the weather."

William put his hands up to block all the wedded bliss coming from his way. "Stop. I cannot stand anymore of your syrupy sweetness, which might gag a man before he's finished his meal."

"Have you given thought to a similar woman for yourself? I can't recommend a more intoxicating state."

"I haven't considered marriage, nor am I thinking about it in the near future."

"The way you danced with the Harrison chit would lead some to disagree with you."

"What is it with you and Allwyn? You're like two gossipy old widows who make a trip to St. George's out of a couple of dances. You, of all people, should remember that I live there because of our case. A lucrative one. Yes, I am kind to the woman. I admit I find her conversation uplifting. But that does not mean I will meet her at the cathedral."

"Funny, I recall saying the same thing when I met Eliza and Isabel. I was a single man enjoying my life with no intention of settling for the Parson's mousetrap anytime soon." He shrugged and grinned. "And yet, here I am. Happier than I've ever been and recommending marital bliss to everyone that has found the right partner."

"I am not in that situation. Agnes is a friend. Nothing more, other than the daughter of our client."

"Argue all you want, but you sound pathetic." Louis put up his hand. "Since neither of us will change our minds on this subject, suffice it to say I expect a big boon from you when I'm proven right."

"What?" William asked, eyes narrowed and brows notched. His brother would as likely ask for the sun and the moon and the stars, rather than something simple, like a bottle of excellent brandy.

"To be decided in the future."

"To be agreed on at a later date," he clarified.

Louis extended his hand, and they shook.

"Do you have any other ideas about our search?"

"None. The clubs and hells are a good place to start. Your next move will be determined by what you discover."

William pushed to his feet. "I'm off. I want to be at White's before the lunch crush, to check the betting book without a roomful of prying eyes."

"Send a messenger if you hear anything significant."

"Let's put more guards around the Harrison's house. Perhaps at each door, just to minimize the risk to the family. He'll pay whatever we ask, as long as we find the culprit."

"I'll post some men today."

William finished his meal and departed for the club, after putting up with more teasing from his brother. At White's, the doorman showed him to a table, and a footman delivered a cup of tea and offered a menu, which he declined.

He glanced at the paper, then made his way to the betting book. He flipped back several pages but found nothing unusual. The winner of a horserace, who would be married next, and the first person to have their quarterly allowance cut. All similar to the bets he had placed as a rowdy young man about town.

An hour later, an older gent, Baron Neufeld, joined him for tea. They had briefly conversed last night. "It was quite the crush, wasn't it?" he asked. "Everything was as expected for an event at the earl's home, although

I must say, those two footmen were dashed rude. Almost knocked my wife to the ground."

"Excuse me? A pair of servants?"

"The Baroness gets megrims and fresh air sometimes helps. We were returning to the house when they bounded by us. One of them hit my spouse in his rush to get by."

"That is horrible." William's heart rate sped up. "Do you know the time it happened or what they looked like?"

"Before supper. Couldn't really tell about their looks, it being dark, and all. But they were in a big hurry. Didn't even close the gate after running through it," the baron sniffed at their poor manners and shook his head in disgust. "Perhaps they should have someone check the silver. They ran as if the devil was hot on their heels. Since leaving it open encourages the riff raff to come inside the yard, I settled my Elizabeth on a bench and shut it myself. Can't risk undesirables getting in."

"Thank you for doing that. Keeps us all safer."

"The least I could do. I spoke to the duke last evening and was introduced to his duchess. They seem happy."

"They are." This was an interesting change of topic.

"Is she a good doctor? We've been seeing Baker for years, but I'm wondering if perhaps a female physician might do more for my wife's megrims."

"Juliette is brilliant. The London Hospital board was that impressed with the care she gave a patient, they sent an invitation to come on staff, until they realized her gender."

"Of course. Everyone knows females don't have the stomach for much of the problems that face doctors. But I wondered if she might help my wife, in case this is a female problem, if you get my drift."

"I can recommend my sister-in-law as the best physician I've ever seen. We only use her now."

"Excellent," the older man said, rising. "I'll see you around, Evans. Be sure to give my regards to your brother, His Grace."

"I will." William would bet that the men running across the yard were the two who accosted him, raising several questions. How long had they watched him? They had to be ready to approach him, leaving the men's room. This meant they knew him and the house well enough to lie in wait. They hadn't been lurking around when he came upstairs, but that proved nothing, since they were wearing servants' livery and wouldn't have stood out.

Additionally, they used the back stairs and were not seen by the other staff. Then they left and ran directly across the yard to the gate. They knew its location.

The entire event was well planned and orchestrated to warn him off this investigation.

He finished his newspaper and drank a pot of tea, but no one else approached him. Time to visit a few other clubs, to discover if anyone had information to add to the story. Later, he'd stop at the most popular gaming hells and listen for gossip.

He learned nothing new at his other stops. Frustrated, he returned to the Harrisons. Since men were in place both inside and outside the house, he hurried to the attic, eager to see Agnes today and hear her thoughts about last night's ball.

"You left early this morning," she said as he braced the door open.

"I had breakfast with Louis."

"He seems like a pleasant man."

"Haven't you heard, my dear? None of the Wolfstone men are nice. We are dangerous or daring, but that is much too bland a description for us." He moved behind the table, closer to her.

As expected, she laughed at his silliness. "In my opinion, you are the same." She looked down, then at him through her lashes. "Very much."

"Thank you, Agnes. I hold you in the same regard." With another woman, he would have thought she was flirting. If he hadn't been watching, he'd have missed the darkness that flashed through her eyes. "Did I say something wrong?"

"No, of course not." She shook her head, then turned her attention to her telescope. "There's not much happening in the sky today. It's almost a picture of yesterday."

Her tone was tight and strained. She was fighting tears. He crossed to her and rubbed her back. "Turn around and tell me what upset you."

She lifted away from the eyepiece, then shook her head. "Nothing. Nothing at all." She returned her attention to her telescope, but he heard her sniffle.

This time, he pulled her against him. "Come, sweetheart, what distressed you?"

She remained stiff in his arms, her eyes downcast. He tilted up her chin and finally caught her gaze. "You are on the verge of tears. We didn't have a long conversation and I upset you."

He considered their exchange and remembered nothing upsetting. He'd said she was nice—it couldn't be that. But he wouldn't try to force her to explain. Instead, he loosened his grip and rubbed her back. After a few moments, he asked, "Will you tell me what you're looking at this morning?"

Stepping away from him, she reached in a pocket for a handkerchief and wiped her nose. She adjusted the eyepiece and said, "I'm completing my daily observations. It is important that scientists be consistent in their research, especially for astronomy."

Since she was determined to ignore her tears, he could do no less. "Given how different the sky looks every time I've looked, that is a reasonable supposition. Are you learning anything?"

Facing him, she pressed her lips together, eyes narrowed. "Yes. Everything is new. Before I purchased this telescope, many details were lost to me."

Picking up her notebook, she flipped back several pages, finally tapping on an entry. "Do you see this?" She pushed it towards him.

It looked like the initial passage, since it was written on the top of the first page.

"When you read this," she returned to the last one, and tapped it, "and this, the repetitious nature of the travel of the moon in the sky, becomes obvious."

She shoved the notebook at him. "Here. Look at them for yourself," she ordered.

William's stomach fell to his feet and a raging headache began behind his eyes. He put up his hand and shook his head. "I believe you Agnes. There's no need for me to review your entries."

"No, I insist." She pushed it closer to him. "In fact, read them aloud and we can analyze my conclusions and determine if they're valid."

William tried to still the shaking of his fingers as he moved the book away from him. "I don't have time for astronomy this morning, Agnes." His mind raced for a reason to have brought him here if not to discuss the stars. "I wondered about your reaction to the ball. Did you enjoy yourself? You danced several times." He sounded like a bumbling fool. She likely considered him an idiot.

Brows notched, she looked at him. "The evening seemed to be a colossal success, but I am no expert on that subject. And yes, I had different partners, and every single one of them was a pleasure. I've never appreciated dancing more than I did last night." She squared her shoulders as she talked, but her voice was a monotone, and she clasped her hands together.

It wasn't exactly what he wanted to hear, although he was glad she enjoyed herself. "Uhm, that's good." He stepped back, looked around over both shoulders, and then said, "Very good. Now I must get return to work. Your father wants answers and standing here chatting with you about astronomy will not secure them."

Something dark flashed in her eyes as he turned away, but he wouldn't comment. She might take it as an opportunity to renew their conversation about her notes, and he wasn't going near that discussion.

What would she think of a man who couldn't read? Just as bad, what would her father make of an investigation agency with a dummy as one of the partners? Such knowledge would destroy their new partnership before it got off the ground, and he would not risk that. Regardless of the cost.

Agnes watched William walk out of the attic, her eyes filling with tears. She leaned down to study the sky through her telescope, but her vision blurred. She swiped at her cheeks with her palms, then blew her nose. He may be a nice man and a patient saint when teaching her about numbers and dancing. But best she never forget, he was a son of one of the leading ton families. They were never interested in her, even if they spent hours together. He proved her hypothesis that all men were the same. Below the surface, none of them were trustworthy. She wouldn't bare her feelings to him again.

He'd told her she was nice. What woman wants a back-handed compliment like that, especially from a man she considered more than a friend? One who kissed her silly and held her as if she was a fragile princess while they danced. It was praise reserved for associates or acquaintances. Even though she couldn't say the words first, her foolish heart had hoped they were closer than that.

Apparently not. He'd decreed her as nice.

She wouldn't make that mistake again. She'd learned her lesson twice this morning, starting with the backhanded compliment. And then his refusal to glance at her entries. He almost threw the notebook at her and couldn't get out of the attic quickly enough. Actions speak louder than words and his told her his opinion of her work. She had thought he appreciated and understood the importance of her studies, but apparently, she was wrong about that as well.

After wiping her nose again, she straightened her spine. She had gotten along just fine before she met William Evans, and she would do the same in the future, even if he wandered around the house and was underfoot all the time. The attic had been reserved for her work and she had given him free run of the space. That stopped now.

Her foolish heartbeat returned to normal. He no longer affected her or her moods. As a scientist, she would do what she did best. Having studied the man and arriving at fact-based conclusions, she was done with him and any possibility of any kind of relationship, including their friendship.

She had never assumed marriage and children were in her future, until a week ago, if she were honest. For some reason, he had broken through her boundaries and reserve and let her hope, for a moment or two, that something different was possible with him. Maybe more.

Now she knew better. She would not repeat that mistake. Not with him or any man. None of them were to be trusted.

She turned her attention to her telescope, putting him out of her mind.

Later, she changed for dinner. More family was visiting, and she wanted to look her best. To hell with William Evans and his opinions. She would enjoy this pre-Christmas celebration with her relatives, especially the children.

She liked the little ones, even though she didn't understand them. Her lack of knowledge and experience stopped tonight. She would become acquainted with her cousins and learn to communicate with them, treating the whole affair like a scientific undertaking, although she couldn't make notes until after the experiment.

The experiment was to determine if she was missing anything without having children. Her working hypothesis, going into this evening, was that her life as a scientist and researcher was fulfilling enough. The absence of a husband or babies in her situation would be of no mind and would not affect her happiness or her focus on her work.

Agnes joined her parents in the family salon.

"You are exceptionally lovely, darling," said her mother.

"Thank you. I have decided it's time I look my best whenever we have guests. It is important for me and my evolution as a scientist to better understand people, especially those around me. Tonight is the first night of my study."

"Depend on you, daughter, to turn relationships into research," said her father, his tone dry.

"It is the way I view the world. I see every change through a scientific lens." As she finished, the door opened. She expected the butler to announce their guests, but instead, William walked in. What was he doing here, joining them for dinner? She had been certain he'd return home for Christmas celebrations with his family or take his meal elsewhere.

"I'm glad you joined us. It's a huge imposition to stay here until this investigation is resolved, but I appreciate your dedication," her father said. Agnes fought to stave off an eye roll. For heaven's sake, she might have to put up with this man every evening until he discovered the person rifling documents in her father's safe and who had murdered the servant. Apparently, the world took no pity on female scientists trying to make their way into the social milieu, regardless of the level of discomfort.

He bowed to her parents, then turned to her and stopped in his tracks. "You are extraordinarily beautiful tonight, Agnes. I am delighted you're feeling better."

"Were you ill earlier?" asked her mother.

"No, not at all. We had a brief conversation about last night's ball, and he misconstrued some of my reactions."

He looked at her, a question in his eyes, and said, "Kindly accept my deepest apology for the confusion around our discussion, Agnes. I had no intention of hurting your feelings."

She waved away his comment. "As I explained to you, you didn't, and everything was fine. Please, let the matter drop."

"If that's your wish, I'm happy to oblige."

Before the conversation went any further, her mother's brother, wife, and four children, girls aged six and eight, and boys, twelve and thirteen, joined them. Her father introduced Lord Evans and a round of hellos followed, along with kisses, and under the chin chucks of the youngest, both the product of this second marriage for her formerly widowed uncle.

She watched the adults and acknowledge her father's extraordinary political skills, including William in family discussions and ensuring the comfort of everyone. Meanwhile, her mother and aunt had settled on the settee and chatted up a storm. Every time the two women got together, they separated themselves from the men and talked nonstop, despite the difference in their ages.

What would it be like to have a sister? Her brothers were older, and their different interests and intellectual pursuits made a close relationship unlikely. But perhaps a female sibling, especially an elder one, might have helped with her social conditioning. She would never know. The question was hypothetical at best, and ridiculous at worst.

Her cousins sat in the corner, watching their parents. This was the perfect time to become acquainted.

Agnes seated herself on the Ottoman facing them and smiled. "How are each of you?" A simple opening which should break the ice.

"Why do you care?" asked the eldest boy.

"You haven't spoken to us before. Why now?" questioned the second.

"Since the adults are talking to each other, I thought it might be an opportunity to chat."

The oldest looked around and leaned in closer. "You're saying that because there is no one more important to talk with, you'll favor us with your presence."

Taken aback by the boy's point of view and his comment, Agnes disagreed. "No, not at all. I realized that time is passing, and I am not well acquainted with any of you and sought this opportunity to change that."

"Elizabeth and I are fine," Hannah said.

The girls wore matching dresses, with cute pinafores covering them. Their hair hung down their back and reminded Agnes of herself at those ages. "I'm glad. Is your nurse still teaching you, or are you with a governess?"

Hannah giggled. "Nurse Hawkins takes care of us."

"Is there something the two of you enjoy doing with her?"

"They only do dumb things," said George, the oldest.

"Yes, they only play with dolls and stuffed bears and pretend they're mothers. It is boring, added Bartholomew, the second son.

Hannah fisted her hands on her hips and glared at her brother. "Well, they are more fun than frogs and worms and slimy fish. I can't imagine why anyone would handle those things."

"No one," said Elizabeth.

Agnes did not want this conversation to descend into a sibling argument, which evidently happened easily. Perhaps she was better off chatting with the boys. After all, they were some years older than the girls and had lost their mother at a young age. Their father had remarried, and the youngest were the result of that marriage.

Before she changed the direction of the conversation, the butler announced dinner. Since they were dining en famille, there was no formal procession to the table. The men led the way, chatting about Corn Laws.

The two women were talking about their plans for the holidays while Agnes and the children brought up the rear.

When she seated herself next to the girls, her mother's eyebrows arched high. Since she had no intention of explaining, she turned away and paid attention to them.

"We usually eat in the nursery," Hannah said.

"Yes, 'cause father doesn't appreciate mayhem at the table."

"Then we had best behave ourselves like proper little ladies tonight."

Elizabeth giggled. "Not you."

"No?" Agnes asked, wondering what they had heard about her.

"No, silly. You're a big lady."

Relief swamped her, and she smiled. "I guess I am, although my father, your uncle, still considers me his baby."

Both girls looked at him, gracing the head of the table like a king surveying his domain, and giggled.

Agnes grinned at them and nodded, but didn't share her thoughts about his appearance. They weren't old enough to understand her humor. He was a good man who sometimes took himself too seriously.

William was engaged in conversation with the two men.

"Why do you keep looking at that gentleman?" Hannah asked.

"Which one?" Agnes responded, to give herself a moment to come up with an intelligent answer.

"He's talking to father and uncle. You look at him, then away."

"I don't." But then she saw the looks on the girls' faces and realized she had to be truthful. "I wasn't aware of looking at him. He is a business friend of my father's and will be here for some time." She forced herself to focus on them, but the sound of his voice lured her attention back to him. There was something about him which drew her repeatedly, regardless that he didn't feel the same about her.

"Do you think he's attractive?" Hannah asked.

Agnes cocked her head and looked at him, then turned to them. "I suppose, in an older man sort of way."

"But you are an older woman. Do you like him?"

How should she answer that question without making a hash of things? "William is a good person, but he is the brother of a duke and is rather opinionated, if you must know the truth."

"Mother says all men are opin... opinionion... have opinions, even when they are wrong."

Agnes laughed. "Our mothers agree with that."

"Yours is pretty," Hannah breathed.

"She is, as is yours."

"We should ask them," crowed Elizabeth, looking at her mama.

She took the child's arm to get her attention. "We don't shout across the table. That is some of the mayhem your papa mentioned." It had been a hard lesson for her to learn, the few times she'd been invited to the dining room for a meal. Her father firmly believed children, especially girls, should eat above-stairs, out of the way.

"But mother always answers our questions."

"Of course she does, but we ask when we won't disturb the adults' conversations." She was still learning this lesson at social events with her peers.

"But it's 'portant'," Hannah said.

"It is, to you, sweetheart, but grownups see it differently. They believe their conversation is more important."

"I don't like that about big people," the girl declared, crossing her arms and pouting her lips.

William glanced at them and cocked one brow, as if to ask her how things were going.

Ignoring him and his questions, she turned to Hannah, speaking to her as a grown up and making the child laugh. Both girls wore smiles.

After dinner, everyone retired to the music room, where her aunt opened the pianoforte and played Christmas carols and the others sang along. Agnes did not have a pleasant singing voice, nor could she play an instrument, but she enjoyed the evening. Perhaps it was the sentiment of a family get-together. Or the children's sweet voices. Or listening to William's sorry attempts to carry a tune. The man had many talents, but not that one.

Afterward, they exchanged gifts and her relatives made ready to leave with promises to return for Christmas dinner.

In the doorway, someone had hung mistletoe, making the adults laugh. Her aunt kissed her uncle, and her parents bussed each other. William looked at her and smiled. "It's our turn, Agnes."

There wasn't a single thing she wanted to do less, but she wouldn't make a fuss in front of everyone and allowed him to lead her to the dangling Christmas decoration. He cupped her shoulders and held her still, as if he feared she'd run away. Finally, after looking into her eyes, he kissed both cheeks. The briefest kiss they'd shared. She didn't know whether to be relieved or upset, although anything more would be inappropriate with her family watching them.

This was expected between friends.

Agnes spun from him and scooped up Elizabeth and held her beneath the mistletoe and smacked the tip of her nose and her neck, making the girl giggle hysterically.

Then she kissed Hannah as well. But when she looked for the boys, Peter and George were nowhere to be found.

"Never mind them," her aunt said. "They're both at that age where kissing is disgusting, and they won't be caught dead doing it."

Everyone laughed, as expected. Her uncle called for them to get in the carriage and her relatives made their way out of the house, talking and laughing as a group.

When everything returned to normal, Agnes said her goodnights and retired to her room. She was exhausted. It had been an emotional day, but she had enjoyed becoming acquainted with her nieces. Her nephews had kept their distance, which wasn't offensive, since she had pushed them away for years. It was only fair they take time to trust her. But it would come, she was certain.

Agnes tossed and turned, unable to relax enough to go to sleep. The evening had been surprising. Her young female cousins were showing ideas and opinions of their own, which she found fascinating. She wondered about the development of children's minds, from infancy to the girls' ages.

And beyond, if truth be known. What made people so different? Was that part of the research that Her Grace, Juliette, had mentioned?

Finally, giving up on sleep, Agnes got out of bed, donned her wrapper and slippers and went downstairs to retrieve her book from the library. Perhaps a chapter or two would shut off her brain, and she could get some rest.

Only half a dozen steps from the bottom of the stairs, she was grabbed from behind and someone slapped a hand across her mouth.

Her heart stuttered, and she stumbled forward. The man's grip on her kept her from tumbling to the floor below.

"What are you doing in here?" he asked.

He overpowered her struggles to get away and walked her into her father's study. "I discovered this one sneaking around."

"Agnes, what are you doing downstairs?" William inquired.

Thank heavens he was here. He'd put a stop to this ruffian handling her.

"You know this woman, boss?"

"Of course." He tipped his head and smiled at her, signaling for her release. "I apologize, but we are watching for anyone in the house and my agent assumed the family had retired for the night." He took her by the hand, leading her toward him.

"Unable to sleep, I came downstairs," she turned to the man who had scared her on the stairs, "And was frightened near to death." She glared at him. "I didn't realize I wasn't allowed to walk around in my home overnight."

"Let me repeat my question, Agnes. Why would you come down here this late? Surely you knew there were men watching for intruders."

"I did but there was no point in tossing and turning, and since I couldn't sleep, I am on my way to retrieve my book." She glared at the man who'd grabbed her. "Until your friend scared me half to death."

"I'll accompany you, ensuring no more mistakes." With a hand on her back, he escorted her out the door.

Alone with William, his palm guiding her through the hall and room that were almost dark, caused her stomach to do strange things. As if there were butterflies in there.

"Do you see it?"

"Of course. It's right where I left it." She grabbed her book and looked at him, wondering if he felt the same thing she did. When he made no move to touch her, she ducked around him. "Thank you for your escort."

"Wait. You can't leave quite that quickly, Agnes."

"Why not? Am I a suspect?"

"No, you're standing under mistletoe." Then he walked toward her, like a cat stalking his prey.

"We have already done this once tonight and I am not doing it again," she put up her hands to ward him off.

"But we had an audience, and I couldn't kiss you as I wanted."

"How was that?" she asked, curiosity drawing her closer.

"Like this," he said, his lips against hers, his hands on her cheeks, his thumbs along her jaw.

"And this." He slanted her head, running his tongue on the seam of her mouth. When she gasped, he slipped inside.

His taste was an exotic, rich dessert. She shivered when he moved one hand to the back of her neck and made a playground of a sensitive place she hadn't known existed before this minute.

Their tongues explored, and she wanted more of something. He held her close, her breasts pressed against his chest, her buds tingling in reaction. She wrapped her arms around his waist, beneath his jacket, savoring his warmth.

His scent teased her. Sandalwood and citron would forever be a favorite.

He moved his hand from her neck to her cheeks, his thumbs sliding along her cheekbone as he slid his tongue away from her. He sealed his lips against hers before looking into her eyes.

"I seem to lack any control around you, Agnes. I don't have a clue why, since I've never had this problem before." He shook his head. "My reaction is made worse because you are the daughter of my client and I'm supposed to protect you, not ravish you.

She rather liked the ravishing part but recalled their conversation in the attic and gathered her wits around her. That man's kisses turned her brain to mush. She stepped away. "It's because I am very nice."

Then she returned to her room, dignity intact, despite missing his heat and his touch.

CHAPTER ELEVEN

Their kiss had been scorching hot. Despite all the reasons to keep his distance from her, he could not control himself around Agnes. He would have to do better in the future. They weren't a couple and wouldn't be. He must steel his resolve and limit their interactions to the simple ruse her father suggested.

Later, he another of their men replaced him and he retired to his room. But sleep eluded him and when it arrived, it wasn't restful, but filled with dreams and tossing and turning.

After giving up, he dressed and joined the earl for breakfast. They chatted about the family visit last evening and their plans for the day.

"I would like to speak to you in private this morning."

The man studied him for a minute, confusion marring his face. "Have you discovered something?"

"Perhaps."

"Well then, let's take our tea and talk in the study."

"A fresh service will be brought to you, my lord," said the butler.

William excused the two men standing watch, directing them to remain in the hall. He walked to the window and checked the flour on the windowsill, which remained undisturbed. A discreet knock preceded the delivery of their tea.

Once they were alone, the room descended into a tense silence, as if waiting for something to happen. After only a moment or two, the earl said, "You wanted to speak to me, young man."

William turned to face his client, uncertain of where to start. He didn't want to warn him about his information, but he needed to discover the truth. He added cream to his tea, stirred it, then settled into the chair in front of the desk.

"I had a moment of insight yesterday," he said to Harrison.

"How so?"

"We have talked to your staff and family, but there is an additional possibility for the person behind this break-in."

"Of course. We've talked about the peers in the House. Any of them might have an interest in my documents."

"Yes, but we agreed not to talk to them until you reconvened after the holidays. However, I thought of another group that needs investigation."

"Who is that? And why are you only coming up with them now?"

This would be the difficult part of the conversation. Men in the earl's position often took mistresses but didn't discuss those arrangements with others. "I have no explanation for my lapse, My Lord, however this has been an interesting group to consider."

"What are you talking about?" roared the earl. "Stop dilly dallying and state the facts."

William studied him for a moment and wondered why he was this angry? Would he be as anxious to begin the conversation when he heard the topic? If the man was furious, this could be the end of the case and their investigation, meaning it was important to him, the agency, and the earl. "Mistresses."

Harrison seemed to collapse into his chair. "I don't have one."

"Now or ever?"

His head whipped back, and he frowned, lips pressed together. "What do you think I am? An animal? I would never impose myself on my beautiful wife."

"You're saying you have had paramours in the past, but are currently without one?"

"Why is that important to this break-in?"

"I'm not sure, but answer the question, please."

"As a matter of fact, I don't. I gave her a parting gift earlier this month."

"How long had you been her protector?"

"I find these questions insulting and unnecessary. Of what impact would my choice of a mistress have upon your investigation?"

"I won't be certain until I have a list of their names and the time since you broke it off with them."

"There's not much to tell. I prefer stability and peace in all my endeavors, including my ...pleasure. I was Shelley's protector for over two years."

"Before that?"

"You can't expect me to remember every woman I've tumbled. It's not possible."

"No, but we know the difference between a quick tumble and offering protection."

The earl scowled. "Fine. Before Shelley was Adelia. She and I were together for twenty years."

Hard to believe he had been in a relationship with his paramour for two decades. Incredible.

"Why did it end?"

"It didn't. She wasn't well. I set her up in Bath, to take the waters regularly. Last I heard, she was getting worse."

"Have you been to see her since she moved?"

"Good god, no. Of course not. I gave her a pension and sent her on her way. Provided enough for her son to go to Eton and for her girls to have a decent governess. I can't abide stupid people around me, and those three were as bright as any. They needed an education, or they would get into trouble all the time."

Very interesting. The earl had a second family. "How old are these children?"

"I didn't keep track. The boy should be finished Eton, or close to it. The girls should be well married by now. But since I do not speak with their mother, I have no idea of their wellbeing."

"Would either of them have any interest in the contents of your safe?"

"For God's sake, no. Of course not. I doubt they know I have one, never mind what's in it."

"Can you think of any other female who might be interested in your private papers?"

"What a ludicrous suggestion. Women don't care about the topics enough to read them, and, more importantly, comprehend them."

"Agnes would, were she curious about them."

"That's true, but my daughter is an aberration in comparison to most females."

"You say that as if it's disgusting or undesirable." He couldn't imagine what her life must have been like if this was what her father really thought of her.

"No." He shook his head. "I didn't mean that. But we know a woman's responsibility is to marry well and bring either wealth, property, or power to her family. Agnes won't do any of the above. Instead of adding to the coffers of the estate, she requires a trust allowing her to live on her own until she dies, because God knows no man will have her."

William turned away from the earl and forced his hands to relax. He took a few deep breaths, closed his eyes for a moment, then exhaled before turning back to the client. "Agnes is a woman with her own style of learning. Nothing is beyond her mind if the teacher can tap into it." He shook his head. "She knew how to dance, but she couldn't feel the rhythm of the music until she visualized it as streams of numbers. As soon as she made that connection, she became an agile and lovely partner. I've danced with her several times, and she's never missed a step."

"You are being well compensated for your investigation, which includes paying attention to my daughter, therefore, don't pat yourself on the back too hard. When this case is over, you will return to your normal life and eventually into the parson's mousetrap with some typical, desirable society girl making her debut and looking good on your arm. If you wed as you should, she'll bring money into the family."

The whole conversation rather shocked William. For a man to speak thusly about his only daughter was disconcerting, in the least. His father would never use such words or tone when referring to Calliope, and if he did, his mother would have corrected him immediately. "I thought you had come to terms with Agnes's abilities."

"I have. But that doesn't mean I like them. She would rather die than be deprived of the opportunity to study, learn, and conduct her silly experiments. As a result, we gave our approval and the necessary space. I've explained to her brothers about her trust, allowing her to continue her studies as long as she wants. It is not large enough to bring a fortune hunter down on her but will keep her comfortable for her lifetime."

"What happens if she marries?"

"In the slim eventuality of such an occurrence, it converts to her dowry for she and her husband. But she must choose marriage or science. If she weds when she's older, I have made provision for some additional coin to be added to the fund."

"Who will administer her funds?" It was none of his business, but the man's opinion shocked him, given his daughter's intelligence.

"I have an excellent solicitor. My eldest son is also one. It's their responsibility to ensure she is protected."

The earl studied William. "You're very curious about Agnes, the arrangements for her life, and my thoughts about her."

"The females of my family are very independent women who have strong opinions on many topics. My sister-in-law, the Duchess of Wolfstone, is a well-educated, outstanding physician who was a godsend to my youngest brother, Philip. We were raised to cherish them and celebrate their uniqueness and, above all else, protect them from the slings and arrows of society."

"I do all of those things," the earl said. "No one will take advantage of her or speak poorly of her in my hearing. But I don't agree with her choices. It is abnormal for a woman to be more interested in science than marriage. Procreation of the species is a woman's only job on the face of the earth. When a female denies her natural drive and purpose, it shows a mistake, an insult to creation and the Creator. But she is my youngest, and I allow her to study and learn. After all, she doesn't hurt anyone. She spends enough money on her supplies and telescope and every other damn thing she buys to keep several merchants happy. And in the process, I have an energetic and healthy daughter, who has no idea how aberrant her thoughts, beliefs, and way of life are." The older man shook his head, "and I pray she never finds out. It is better for her to live in this strangeness. She does not have the requisite social skills and desires to become a good wife."

William didn't agree. Agnes would make some peer a wonderful spouse and would be a great mother to their children, like Juliette, who had her medical clinic and patients. Their son spent more time with his nurse than he did with her.

Calliope, on the other hand, preferred to tend to their baby herself, holding and cuddling him. Both newborns slept in a bassinet in their parents' room, rather than the nursery, as was the more common practice. The women respected each other's choices and were raising children in a way that suited them and their lifestyle.

Neither woman was behaving in the norm of society, where an infant was raised by his nurse and rarely saw the family. As he considered that truth, he realized that the method of rearing a child was a couple's choice.

Why wasn't there room for Agnes and her passions? If, like Juliette, she married a duke, no one would dare gainsay her choices. They would faun over her and seek her opinion and only speak of her with the highest regard, at least anywhere his relatives might hear what they were saying.

In many ways, he and Agnes were a matched pair. His inability to read, his stupidity, was a closely guarded secret among his siblings. Her intelligence and views of the world were hidden, as well as her parents could manage.

The big difference was his family accepted him as he was, whereas her father wished she were different.

"What brought you in here this morning, wanting to talk about my mistresses?"

"At the ball, a person I assumed was an upstairs servant led me into a salon on the second floor. When I stepped inside, someone coshed me over the head and knocked me out."

"In the middle of the evening? What happened then?"

He quickly explained the details of last evening. "What makes it very interesting is one of them referred to their boss as 'she'."

"Which is why you wanted to learn the names of any females I've protected."

"We will track them both down and question them. Are there any others I should add to the list, regardless of whether we think they may or may not have a motive for going through your safe?"

"In my youth, there were actresses and prostitutes, but I stopped that behavior once I realized the diseases they carry."

"Smart man. Some fellows never figure that out."

"If you've ever talked to a young buck worried about his cock falling off because he swived a hooker with a disease, you learn to keep it in your pants. That is why I preferred to have long-term relationships with my mistresses. If Adelia had not taken ill, I would not have replaced her. We would have grown into old age together and when she no longer served her purpose of companionship and sex, I would've pensioned her off."

"So other than your wife and your daughter, there are only two additional women I need to speak to. Can you provide their full names and their direction? With that information, I'll let you return to work. We will send an operative to Bath for that interview, and I shall remain here as planned."

"Give me a minute, young man." The earl unlocked his desk to retrieve a piece of paper and wrote the names of both women and their location. "I'm certain about Adelia's direction, since I pay for the house. This address," he tapped on the second one, "may or may not be accurate. She should have moved by now, and I have no idea if she's found another protector." He shrugged. "And unfortunately, I don't know her last name. It didn't come up in our conversations."

"I'll be able to find her. Thank you. I'm certain this was a difficult topic."

"No honorable man wants to talk about his mistresses in his family home. Nor does he want to move from them into a discussion about his only daughter. I trust you will keep both topics in the highest confidence."

"That goes without saying." William hurried from the room. Finally, he had something to work with. Someplace to start. This investigation had been frustrating because there were no breadcrumbs to follow. This lead might not be correct, but it pointed him in a different direction.

From the top of the stairs, Agnes watched William don his greatcoat and hurry outside. He hadn't mentioned leaving the house, but his schedule was unknown to her. She traced her lips with the tip of her finger and remembered the feel of his tongue as it slid over them. The pit of her stomach twisted and turned, the same feelings as last night when he really kissed her under the mistletoe.

Would he do it again? What would he think if she stepped close to him and kissed him? Would she have the courage to slide her tongue into his mouth? She would like to find out, despite still being angry with him. He only considered her a friend, and nice, but his kisses were divine. She might as well take advantage of this opportunity and learn as much as possible about romance and kissing, since it may never recur. Let him be confused by her behavior, rather than the other way around, for a change.

When she got to the attic, she looked at her space and felt nothing. Her new telescope had lost some of its glow. She bent to look into the eyepiece, adjusted the focus, and scanned the sky. For the first time, she didn't care about anything she saw. Nor did she pick up her pencil to write notes, nor did she adjust the telescope's coordinates.

She straightened up and rubbed her hand on the barrel of the instrument. The need for astronomical data had not changed. Her ability to observe and record her observations was the same. But as she looked at the door, she wished for someone to share her research with. A person who understood what she was talking about and its importance to her.

After a shuddery breath, she again bent over the eyepiece of the telescope. It would be wonderful to discuss her findings and hypotheses with another, but since that wasn't likely to happen, best she get on with the work at hand.

In this moment, it didn't seem like enough.

Although barely the lunch hour, Agnes straightened from writing her observations about the sky, put her hands on her hips and arched her back to loosen the stiffness.

She was exhausted. In the past, she'd often lost track of time, standing here for fifteen or eighteen hours. Today, three was her limit.

Her telescope sat in the only empty floor space in the attic. Every other square metre was covered with furniture, trunks, or boxes, making her surroundings dismal. Other than the open window for her instrument and her candles, the cavernous room was almost dark.

Funny, she had never noticed it before. But today, she couldn't remain any longer, for the atmosphere was unappealing. She closed her inkwell, sanded her notes, and left the attic, closing the door behind her, unsure when, or if, she'd return, because her surroundings mattered. Her pursuit of astronomy seemed less important, somehow.

With that last thought, she shook her head and muttered to herself. Nothing had changed and yet everything had. But she wasn't certain why she felt this way.

Her brain was the same, and her curiosity hadn't dried up, so what was the problem?

In her room, Agnes called for her maid and a bath, another anomaly, since bathing was in the morning, before going out in the evening, or last thing at night. She had no memories of leaving her work in the middle of the afternoon.

There was a first time for everything and today was that day.

As she relaxed in the tub, a soft knock interrupted her musings. A whispered conversation ensued between her maid and someone else. Then her mother walked in.

"Are you unwell, Agnes?"

"I'm fine. But I tired of studying the sky and thought a soak was just the thing I needed." She could not have stood her surroundings a moment longer, and she knew that the basement, where she'd conducted chemical experiments, would be worse.

"A relaxing bath?" Her mother rested the back of her hand on Agnes's forehead. "You don't seem warm. Is your tummy upset?"

"I told you, mama, I'm fine. I needed to relax."

"But it's the middle of the day." She shook her head and raised her shoulders, her brows notched. "You never take time away from your research, unless you're given no choice."

"Perhaps that's a behavior I will have to adjust." She wasn't sure why she wanted to change things, but today, leaving her telescope and having a warm scented bath in the middle of the afternoon seemed like heaven.

"Are you certain you are well?" her mother asked again. "This is unlike you."

"Yes. I am uncertain what's changed, but I looked around the attic and couldn't remain there another moment. As I came down the stairs, a hot soak was very appealing." She shrugged. "I can't explain it and my astronomical research will continue, but I'm done for today. I have decided to read a novel after I dress, then join you and father for dinner."

"How lovely, dear. It's rare we dine as a family when there are just three of us."

"Don't get too excited about the change, mama. I am not promising anything for tomorrow." She might wake up like her old self, completely focused on science, that everything else was of no consequence. Or not.

Her mother bent down and kissed the top of her head. "I look forward to your company. Now I'll leave you to your bath."

After the door closed, Agnes summoned her maid to wash her hair, then stepped out of the tub.

She put on a wrapper and sat at her dressing table as the woman worked through the tangles, then brushed it smooth. "I'm going to sit in front of the fire and let it dry while they clear the mess."

Sometime later, the servant interrupted her. "Excuse me, but we should style your hair."

She nodded and reluctantly left her cozy spot.

Tipping her head one way and then the other, she studied herself in the mirror. "Please do something a little fancier than usual," she asked. "Prettier than my chignon."

Her maid smiled. "Of course, Miss," then put the tongs to heat.

An hour later, Agnes beamed at her reflection. "You've done a great job. This is the right combination of pretty and tidy." She rose from the dressing table. "Can you find something to match my hair style?"

The woman nodded, then disappeared into her dressing room, and returned holding a lilac-colored gown over her arm. "Will this do for today?"

"Yes, it's perfect." She smiled at the servant. "I want to wear a new dress for dinner. Please be sure it is ready for me."

"Of course," she replied, as she helped Agnes out of her robe and into the layers of garments.

When everything was buttoned and placed, the maid smoothed her skirt one last time and stood back. "You are as pretty as an angel, miss."

She stepped in front of the looking glass and nodded. "I'm not sure about a heavenly being, but I look better than I thought possible." She smiled at her reflection and went downstairs to find a novel to read.

William double checked the direction provided by Harrison. He knocked on the door again and waited, but still, no one answered. He looked around, then stepped closer and twisted the knob. It silently opened, and he stepped inside.

A fine coating of dust covered the marble in the empty foyer. Without a painting, a side table or sconces on the wall made the space look desolate.

He closed the door behind him and walked through the main floor. Every room was bare. No furniture. No carpets. Nothing. In the kitchen, the counters had been wiped clean. The fireplace was devoid of ashes, but dust covered the shelves and surfaces.

William climbed to the second level, where he found the same thing. There was no sign of anyone residing here now or in the recent past, including Shelley.

Harrison claimed the woman was living here, last he heard, but there was no hint of an occupant in the house. It had been empty long enough that only his footprints disturbed the dust.

On the main floor, he found the staircase to the basement, where the wine cellar and coal bins were located. Lighting a candle from the sconce on the wall, he started down the stairs.

After a couple of steps, he stopped and glanced back at the way he'd come. He bent down and held the light as close to the treads as possible and confirmed his observation. They had recently been swept or cleaned.

He heard a soft noise below him, and he spun around. "Who's there?" he called, waiting.

Silence was his only answer, but he moved the candle to his left hand, in case someone was hiding. He crept down the stairs and across the landing, swiveling his head both ways, looking for anything unexpected.

There were several doors to his right and at the far end of this hall, he saw the house's coal bin. It was full, meaning the order for delivery had not been canceled.

He stopped and listened for any sound out of the norm. Again, nothing.

Slowly and carefully, he opened the first door, then swung it wide open, hoping to surprise anyone who might be inside. This room was empty, but dusty, suggesting it had been unused for months.

Behind the next one, shelves covered the walls. This would have been the wine cellar, but it was also bare. Before moving, William listened. Again, only silence.

He opened the last door but stopped in his tracks. A woman's body lay over a barrel, her neck twisted. He checked for a pulse but found nothing. The body was warm to the touch. She hadn't been dead for long. The hem of her light-colored dress was filthy, as if it had dragged on the stairs as she descended.

He left her remains and walked to the coal bin which stood beside another door, open. He ran through it and up a short flight of stairs and scanned the backyard. Nothing.

After looking around a second time, he went back to the house, closing and locking the lower entrance behind him and checked on the body and feeling for a pulse, just in case. No response.

The woman was dead.

He returned everything to the way he found it, and left, racing to Louis'. They ordered three men over there, one to stand outside every entry. He directed a message to Harrison, asking him to describe his former mistress. Then he made a quick stop in Mayfair, to see if his sister-in-law was home.

He threw his reins to a groomsman and raced inside, calling for Juliette as the door closed.

"Where's the fire?" His brother asked, striding from the study.

"I need your wife. Where is she?"

"I'm right here," she said, stepping from behind him. Her hair was messy and the buttons on her dress were mismatched.

"Sorry to interrupt, but where is my sister-in-law?"

Allwyn sighed. "Of course, you do." He narrowed his eyes, glaring at William. "Give us a minute." Then he closed the door.

He waited, shuffling from foot to foot.

A moment later, they stepped out. "What do you want?" his brother asked.

His sister-in-law's hair had been tidied and her buttons fixed. "I found a woman's body a couple of hours ago. I am wondering if you can tell me anything about the time or nature of her death, if you examine her before I call the Runners."

Juliette shrugged and wagged her head. "I'm not certain, but I'll try."

"Thank you. I've called for the carriage, and it will be outside in a moment."

"Let me get my bag."

Before she took two steps, her assistant, Pierre, joined them. "Are you going out?" he asked, her kit in hand.

"Yes, to see a woman."

"Let's go, then."

As they left, Allwyn coughed. When William turned, his older brother shook his finger at him. "You owe me—a lot." Then he returned to his study.

He chuckled. He'd interrupted a moment, but some things could be delayed, while others were critical.

After giving the coachman the direction, they set off at a fast clip.

CHAPTER TWELVE

At the house, William threw his reins to a man from their agency. "Has anybody come around?"

"No, sir. It's been quiet."

"Excellent." He hurried to the carriage, opened the door and helped Juliette to the ground. "Let's go this way." He extended his arm and lead her inside and down the stairs.

In the last room, the woman's body lay as he left it. She checked for a heartbeat, then said, "She's gone." The doctor looked up at him. "When did you find her?"

"I was here about two hours ago, maybe a little more, and she was like that when I arrived."

"Did you move her?"

"No. I felt for her pulse and noticed the odd angle of her head."

Juliette walked around the barrel, studying the body. "She has marks that show someone tried to strangle her, then broke her neck.

She leaned in close and touched the woman's cheek. "This is stiffening." She picked up her hand. "Her arm is not. My best guess is that she died just before you found her, but that is not exact."

"How did you come to that conclusion?"

"When people die, their face stiffens almost immediately. That condition moves down their bodies over the next six to ten hours. After a while, the body relaxes again."

"Interesting. If you're right, she would have been alive had I arrived earlier."

"We do not know that. There was a struggle." She held up the woman's hand. "Look here, she's ripped this nail back, which is common when struggling against another."

"As I walked downstairs, I heard a noise, but I wasn't sure if it was the house or something else. By the time I rounded the corner from the stairs into the hallway, there was nothing to see."

"This woman died at someone else's hands. But why?" Juliette looked around. "It's not like there's anything worth stealing in here."

"Nor in the rest of the residence," William added. "It is empty."

"Were you here to meet her?"

"A name was provided as a party to my current investigation and this direction, but I do not know if this woman is the named one, or someone different. "

Juliette moved the victim's skirt to the side. "She is carrying a reticule." She slid it off the woman's wrist and opened it. From the inside, she shook out a handkerchief, a few coins, and a crumpled piece of paper with this address written on it.

William took it. "Why would she have this direction, if she lived here at sometime?" Seeing Juliette's confusion, he explained, "She came in through the coal door, which suggests she knew its location, then went up the stairs, but didn't go any further."

"Someone embroidered her linen with the initials SP in the corner."

"I was told to ask for a woman by the name of Shelley. This might be her."

"How will you find out?"

William shrugged. "My contact knows her well. Hopefully, he can provide an identifying mark or two."

"I'll take her back to my clinic and keep her cool for a few hours while you track down her identity. I can't hold her for long, however."

He looked at his sister-in-law. "How are you going to move her remains?" She smiled at him. "Pierre knows how I work."

"I'm grateful you came along."

"This woman has a family who deserves to know she is deceased. And she needs you to discover who ended her life this early."

"I am not sure her relatives will want information about her demise."

"I agree," she sighed. "But we should still tell them."

They both turned to the sound of a wagon stopping on the street. "That must be my men." She looked around, then at William. "Is there a second way out of here?"

"Let me show you. It's back here." He led her beyond the coal bin to the stairs.

"This will make moving her much easier." Juliette stepped outside and waved to Pierre, who hurried to her side. They chatted for a few minutes and then he rushed away, returning with blankets.

She spread the first on the floor, beside the woman's body. "Place her in the center." The two men lifted her and positioned her as requested, then wrapped the edges of the cover around the body.

The doctor's assistant covered her with the other one.

"Take her feet and shoulders and carry her to the wagon.

They placed her in the box, then laid another, heavier blanket over her remains.

"Put her in the cold room at the clinic, and I'll be along."

"Should I send a man to help unload her?" William asked.

His sister-in-law shook her head. "No, thank you. I have men who can do that."

He nodded. "Then I'm off to discover if the lady has any identifying marks to determine if this is her."

He directed his agents to remain around the house and returned to the Harrisons for information to identify the victim.

The earl was in his study when William arrived. "Excuse me, my lord, but I have additional questions for you." He closed the door behind him and crossed to the desk.

"Did you find Shelley?"

"I'm not certain. Can you describe her?" Harrison should be able to provide specific details about the woman's appearance, even in less visible areas.

"Why? You spoke to her."

"I didn't, but I saw a female and would like to be sure it was the right one." The earl leaned away from William.

"Then you know she's young and beautiful."

"I do, but that applies to many women." He required more specific information about the victim.

Harrison's description matched the woman he'd found in the house. "Does she have any identifying marks?"

"Like scars or birthmarks?"

"Yes." This was what he needed to be sure about the identity of the body in Juliette's office.

"None that you will ever see."

"Please describe it to me."

"I won't. She is a courtesan but is entitled to her privacy."

He wanted to respect the earl's reticence to talk about a former mistress, but this was not the time for delicacy. He had to shock him into telling the truth. "I found a dead woman at the direction you gave me. From your description, it sounds like Shelley, but I can't be certain until she is correctly identified. Now tell me, does she have any identifying marks?"

The man scowled at him, then sighed. "She has a heart-shaped birthmark on her bottom, right side, low."

Finally, he was getting at the truth. He wasn't sure if it was the earl being a gentleman or trying to hide the identity of his mistress. "I will have a woman check for it. Is there anything else we should look for?"

"Not that I'm aware of."

"Thank you."

"What does this have to do with my safe?"

"I am not sure. But if this is Shelley, I find it odd that she was murdered as I went looking for her." He glanced at Harrison. "I don't believe in coincidences, meaning it is probable her death is tied to our investigation."

"I doubt that. She wasn't hired for her intelligence. She has other skills that more than compensate for that lack." He hesitated. "I meant she had...."

"I understand."

He left the house and rode hard to Juliette's clinic.

William paced across the waiting room. Was this woman Harrison's former mistress or someone at the wrong place and the wrong time which cost this woman her life?

He looked at the clock on the table and wanted to growl. It couldn't take more than five minutes to find a birthmark.

He continued pacing, checking his time piece every minute or two. Grinding his teeth and storming across the open space once more, impatience won, and he headed for the examining room. He had to know who was in there.

As he reached for the knob, the door opened from the other side, and he faced Juliette. She stood tall and glared at him. "I told you to wait out here for me."

"You did, and I was, but I couldn't fathom what was taking this long."

The doctor put her hand on his chest and pushed him back and out of her way, then closed it behind her. "Your victim has the mark you described in the location you suggested, leading me to conclude this is Shelley."

"Did you discover any other means of identifying her, beyond the initials on her handkerchief?"

"No. I haven't had time to look yet. But I saw the same ones near the waist on one of her petticoats."

William scrubbed his eyes in frustration. Why would a woman who used to live at that house have its direction on a paper in her reticule? Surely, she would remember a home she lived in for two years and wouldn't need to write it down. He paced across the waiting room and back and looked at Juliette, still blocking the entry to her surgery.

The answer hit him. She hadn't written the address down. She had been given her the note directing her to that house.

Someone wanted to talk to Shelley and staged the meeting at the residence where she had lived as Harrison's mistress, then murdered her. But why?

His mind twisted and whirled with ideas and suggestions. Slow down, William, he chided himself, and go back to the beginning. Think it through like a doctor diagnosed an illness. Or a good investigator solved a case.

He turned from his sister-in-law and paced across the room again. The dust was undisturbed on the main floor, meaning she used the coal doorway, rather than the one facing the street. She climbed the stairs but stopped at the top. That would explain why nothing was disturbed on the upper floors, but the treads were wiped clean.

William imagined her coming to the trade entrance of the house, fighting to open that door, and walking down those stairs into the dark, coal-dusted cellar. She had likely hoped to surprise the person who requested the meeting. Unfortunately, that man grabbed her from behind near the top of the stairs and dragged her into the room of her death.

What did he want from her? Had it to do with Bonaparte's freedom? Or something else? It had to be connected to her relationship with Harrison. But what?

The earl gave Shelley her conge weeks ago and hadn't seen or spoken to the woman since then.

Perhaps he was not being truthful about ending their affair, or the timing of it, but why would someone think she had information worth killing her for?

"I can see your mind racing in a hundred different directions," Juliette said, following him into the outer room. "I can't help you solve her murder, but I want her last name for my records. She'll have to be buried soon. Bodies don't do well in the fresh air for long."

William bussed her cheek. "Thank you. You've been an angel. A messenger will come with the woman's surname."

"Send it here, allowing us to enter it into the clinic files, but I'm for home if we're done."

His brother would be happy his wife was hurrying back, given what he had interrupted earlier. He gave her a lazy salute. "You'll get it as soon as I have it."

Agnes was determined to relax with a novel in the library. But the dratted book didn't hold her attention. She started at every sound and corrected her posture whenever the front door opened.

But she was still alone, despite spending three hours attempting to read a wretched story.

She rose and stormed across the room, studying the titles on the shelves. Many of them were books she'd bought when younger and trying to learn more about science. But at this moment, she could have swept them off the shelf and left them as fire starters, they held so little interest. She stalked around the library again and slid a finger between the drapes, opening one side marginally. The yard looked the same as it had a few minutes ago.

She was frustrated and grumpy. The cause of her strange mood eluded her. She sat with a paper and a quill and wrote at the top, 'What I'm Feeling.'

Then she made a list: bored, disappointed, no energy or enthusiasm, lack of care for astronomy, sad... and more negative feelings. She smoothed her hand over her new hairstyle and realized there were some positives in today's emotional buffet.

For the first time, she felt attractive. She wasn't a scientist in a beautiful dress, but a pretty woman wearing a flattering gown. She was glad that something other than science made her feel good. Her bath had been exquisite. Ordinarily, bathing was a necessary action, but today it had been pleasant and almost sensual. She loved the soap she'd used, and it soothed her sense of smell, even though she was oblivious to perfume.

The silk of her garments against her was heavenly and made her skin tingle while keeping her alert and aware. Her thick, heavy hair was light and nearly weightless, and yet beautiful and modern in its styling. The candles cast a soft glow that showed her in the best way.

A knock interrupted her list-writing. "Miss, dinner will be served shortly. Your mother invites you to join her for a glass of madeira before the meal."

"Of course. That's a lovely idea," she replied, following the butler to her mother's small salon. As she stepped into the room, she smiled. A plenitude of candles, which enhanced her appearance and her sense of beauty, brightened the cream and gold décor.

"Agnes, you are beautiful this evening." Her mother rose and crossed to her, then kissed her cheek. She leaned back and studied her. "There are no traces of cosmetics, but whatever you've done has been worth the time and energy."

It wasn't often her appearance was complimented. "Nothing special, except leave the attic earlier than usual and relax in a bath. My maid dressed my hair differently." Would anyone else notice the difference?

"Is there a reason for these changes, which you deem to be trivial?"

"Not really. I was looking through my telescope and realized that since I couldn't remain up there a moment longer, I came downstairs." She shrugged. "It wasn't anything momentous, just a desire for something different."

The butler poured and handed each woman a glass of wine. Her mother lifted hers to her daughter. "To the butterfly I have been waiting to see. Welcome, little one."

"Mama, stop it. You'll put me to the blush. I am the same person I have always been."

Despite her discomfort, she studied her over the rim of her wineglass. "You are, but you're not. There is something different tonight, Agnes. A glow and a confidence that brings out all your beauty, including the goodness of your soul."

"Thank you. Now, can we please discuss an interesting topic?"

"Fine. Let's do that. Besides looking through your telescope, watching the sky, and changing your entire daily routine, what did you do today?"

"Nothing. I got up, broke my fast and went to the attic." She shrugged. "There is no reason for my discontent, nor my boredom with astronomy." She sipped her wine and tipped her head as she considered the situation, then added, "It's as if a candle was smothered. One minute I was doing my usual routine and in the next I stepped away and left everything behind."

"Will you continue your studies tomorrow?"

"I can't say. I may awaken and return to the woman I was yesterday. Or not." She shrugged. "Since I'm unaware of the cause of this change, I am unable to predict the course of the future."

Her father walked through the open door and stopped on the threshold of the room. "Am I the lucky man who is sharing dinner with two beautiful women?" He kissed his wife on the cheek. "As always, your beauty makes my heart beat faster, my dear." Then he looked at her and said to her mother, "You will have to introduce me to this vision of loveliness, since I'm certain we haven't met before."

Agnes giggled at her father's silliness. "If you need an introduction to your only daughter at this time of my life, there's something wrong with you."

"Never say such a thing. My vision is perfect, and it sees a beautiful young woman."

"I doubt that. Both of you are looking through the eyes of parents at their only daughter and seeing only the best."

Her father kissed her hand, then poured himself a glass of wine.

"How was your day?" Agnes asked.

"Much like yesterday and every one since the break. Messages, documents, and meetings with those wanting political favors or assistance."

"It sounds very tedious to me, dear." Her mother smiled at her husband. "I cannot countenance how you stand it. The tedium of it would make me a bedlamite, with no doubt."

Her father laughed. "I regard your social activities in the same way. As always, we end up even in this discussion. It's a good thing I do what I do and leave you to do what you do, leaving us both content."

"And you both allow me to do as I choose to do, which keeps me happy."

"Dinner is served," the butler announced.

"Ladies, may I escort both of you to the table?" Harrison asked as he lifted both arms.

Agnes saw that the service was prepared for four. "Are we expecting a guest?"

"William was expected to join us, but he's got a fresh lead and is following up."

She hadn't changed her hair or worn a pretty dress for him, but she was disappointed he wasn't here, but since there was nothing to do about that or her strange restlessness, she took her place at the table.

As her mother was being seated, the front door opened, and she thought she heard his voice, then footsteps hurried down the hall.

"Please accept my apologies for my tardiness, but I have done been busy," William declared. "I'll freshen up and return momentarily."

"We're happy to wait dinner for you," offered her father.

A few minutes later, he sat across from her. "Thank you for waiting. This is the first meal we've enjoyed as a foursome since you've been entertaining your family for the holidays." He looked at her and stopped, his gaze moving over her face, hair, and neckline. "You look particularly lovely tonight, Lady Agnes," then, quickly remembering his manners, he turned to the end of the table. "You as well, Countess. The earl and I are lucky men to share dinner with ladies as beautiful as you."

"Thank you. Such a nice compliment. And yes, the holidays keep us busy with our extended family and friends," responded her mother.

"It is a good thing there are only we four. With two such lovely women, I am almost overwhelmed. If there were more of you, I'm sure my eyes would ache."

"We wouldn't want that to happen to a friend," Agnes said, pleased that he had noticed and commented on her effort to look her best. She had never taken such pain before, always preferring to remain with her work as long as possible before racing to join her parents. His appreciative smile made the sacrifice worthwhile.

Mama glanced from her to William and back again. "Of course not."

As they finished dessert, their guest turned to the earl. "Perhaps we might take our port in your study, my lord? There are a couple of things to discuss about my investigation."

"Why don't you join us in the salon? I'd like to know what's going on," Agnes suggested.

The earl studied the younger man for a moment, then shook his head. "There are some topics not suitable for females. I'll have to refuse your request, daughter. But if any of the new information is fitting for you, we will share it."

Her father was telling her that because she wasn't male, she was not fit to hear the latest details, even though she was one of the smartest people at the table. It was insulting. But like many other things in her life, there was nothing to be done about it and no point in fighting against it.

In the study, Harrison poured two glasses of port, and offered William the chair across from his desk. the earl sat behind it, sipped his drink, then asked, "What did you find out?"

"Based on your description, the dead woman is Shelley. Do you know her last name?"

The client shook his head. "I'm not certain. She might have said it was…." He raised his shoulders in frustration…. "Porter, perhaps, or Parker? It never seemed too important."

He wasn't surprised at the earl's reaction, although it was a statement of the man's values. "Do you remember where she was from?"

"I don't think she mentioned it, and if she did, she probably lied. The same is true for her last name. Why would she risk news of her amoral activities getting back to her family?"

Harrison's point of view was common in the ton, but it sounded harsh, since the lady in question was dead. "Then I guess we'll have to bury her in an unmarked pauper's grave."

"She doesn't deserve much else, does she? You're not suggesting that I have her buried in a respectable cemetery or crypt." The earl scowled at him. "She was my mistress and nothing more. When I ended our business relationship, it was over. I have no further responsibility for the woman or her life and frankly, I weary of talking about her. She lacked the brains to get into my safe or to understand the documents that were inside. And she wouldn't have dared discuss what I told her, not that it included anything important. She knew damn well that would be treason."

Harrison was right, but it was shocking to hear him talk about a woman of a two-year relationship in this fashion. He considered her a convenience, something he owned, until he threw it away. When that happened, she no longer crossed his mind, even though their separation had been less than a month ago.

"Your threats scared Shelley enough that she kept her mouth shut about anything you might've said to her."

"Do not misunderstand what I'm saying, young man. I don't discuss with anyone except the appropriate parties about the work I do in the house. There is no possibility I spilled a secret during pillow talk. I paid for her services to be available when I wanted her and where. There was no intention on either part that this service become something else. You've seen the chit. She's younger than my daughter. I appreciated her company for only one thing, and when we were done, we didn't snuggle or doze in bed. I got dressed and left because there were more important things waiting for me."

Harrison's perspective was common for a powerful man, yet William couldn't help but wonder how Shelley felt about their arrangement. Was she happy enough with the money he paid to stay home and wait for him whenever he dropped by? Or was it possible she sensed his disdain and his lack of respect and wanted to get even?

Most women of the demimonde accepted their position and their treatment. But if Shelley was an intelligent woman, someone with a wide curiosity and a great mind, who had fallen on hard times, how would she respond in this situation? If, God forbid, Agnes ever found herself in financial straits, with no one to turn to, she might look for a protector. But she would hate being treated like this.

The man was a fool if he thought all women were happy to be considered a cipher and never appreciated for anything more than their sex.

Fools abounded in the ton, most of them male. But he had shared their attitude and their ranks for the most part. Widows and actresses were good enough to swive but not to take to dinner or a ball. They were called by a variety of names and yet men still used them for their pleasure. He recalled an invitation to a party in the north with Louis and Henry. All three planned to enjoy themselves with women who were willing to share their beds.

As it happened, his eldest triplet sibling had stayed behind to complete some tasks for Allwyn and met Eliza as a result. But he and the middle triplet had continued to their destination and their plans. As he thought about it, he felt nearly sick to his stomach, for he couldn't remember the names or faces of all the women he'd been with.

How many fools were in the ton and had seats in the House of Lords? How many would shuffle women off to the side, labeling them either good or bad, because of the choices they made to survive, when men controlled the environment and never dealt the ladies a fair hand?

He now understood why Juliette, after the death of her parents, dressed in men's clothes and registered in medical school as a man. She would not accept the circumstances she found herself in and, therefore, changed them. It was an extraordinary act of courage. Far bigger than he had realized prior to this conversation. She was a brilliant doctor but was not allowed to practice medicine in hospitals because of her gender.

It made him furious to consider those she could save if men didn't stand in her way. And he respected Allwyn, even more, for building a clinic where women could help others.

No wonder it took his brother so long to acknowledge his love for Juliette. He, too, had been raised in the same social mores as Harrison. The good doctor was Alwyn's first challenge to those beliefs and values. It must have been difficult for him to reconcile the skills and abilities of the woman he loved with the standards of his society.

Even though their mother and sister were both incredibly strong women, who easily shared their opinions with the males around them, it wasn't the same as loving a female vastly different from society's norms.

Agnes was like Juliette. He had been as blind as his brother.

His feelings for her were confusing, but he wanted more than friendship with her. He'd have to figure it out before he kissed her again. Rising, he looked at Harrison. "Thank you for your time. If other questions come up during my investigation, I'll bring them to you, but for now, you've answered them all."

CHAPTER THIRTEEN

As her father and William walked away, Agnes was angrier than she could put into words. To be excluded because of her sex was not fair.

If there was a way to eavesdrop on their conversation, she would do it. But instead, she followed her mother into the family salon.

In the sitting room, she tapped her foot, watching the closed door. "Doesn't it irritate you, that society excludes us because we are female?"

"No, not at all. Men deal with difficult and disgusting subjects every day. I do not want such things in front of me, and I'm happy to let your father handle them."

"But if you're not given a chance to take part, they might discuss laws and rules that affect you without your opinion."

"Harrison watches out for my interests. He would never go along with something that harmed me."

"But if he's outvoted, then you and he are denied a choice." And would pay the price, whatever it is, like Her Grace, Dr. Juliette Evans. Shouldn't she have a say in who practiced medicine?

Her mother raised one shoulder and pressed her lips together. "I suppose you have a point, but your father is an influential man and his preferences carry weight with his peers."

"But what about protecting those who aren't married to prominent men?" She agreed with the assessment of her father's power, but few women had husbands who sat in the House of Lords. Those females were on their own.

"Agnes, you've just stated an important reason for a female to marry well. When you see a young chit wed to an older man, you are repulsed and disgusted. I applaud a smart woman securing the future for her and her children."

"Really? That's what you perceive?" That wasn't her perception, which leaned to seeing a girl giving up her life to some drooling, crotchety old peer for security.

"It is the way the world works. And it is one of many reasons the choice of a husband is so important. I understand you lack any desire for marriage, but that means you are without a male standing between you and everything else, looking out for your best interest."

"But why can't I look after my interests?" Heaven knows, she was brighter than almost every man she'd met. Trusting some of them to care for her and being reliant on them because of their sex seemed ludicrous. There were a few exceptions. His Grace, William's oldest brother, recognized his wife's worth. She couldn't see him deciding on her behalf without including her in the discussion. Would William be the same way? Could he be one of the rare men who saw the value of a woman's mind and treasured it? Appreciated it?

"Because women aren't smart enough to do that."

Agnes jumped up. "Really, mother? I'm not able to figure things out?"

"Of all my female acquaintances, you may be the most qualified to examine a situation and decide your best interests. But, daughter, I know no other with those abilities. If society adopted your preferences, it would leave the rest of us at risk."

"Or perhaps all other women would benefit if I, and others like me, could look after themselves. William's sister-in-law is the graduate of a medical school and yet she may not practice medicine at the hospital because the medical society, all men only, won't let her in."

When mama began to interrupt, she held up her hand. "At first, talking to a female physician seemed as if it would be uncomfortable. But then I realized she has similar experience and has learned from her life or other women." Agnes looked at her mother, trying to make her understand. "If I were having a baby, I would prefer medical help from someone who had given birth to a man who has experienced nothing beyond creating the child."

"Daughter! We do not talk about such things. It is unseemly. It is knowledge no girl needs."

Wrapped up in mathematics and astronomy, she had never had such thoughts in the past. Nor had she considered the liabilities of being a female. "Why? Women die in childbirth every day. It should matter, but how can it, if we can't discuss it? I read the estate books on animal husbandry. I understand what happens generally, between a man and a woman. But my knowledge hasn't caused me to race out and be compromised by the first male I meet. In fact, it has taught me to be more circumspect." Unless it came to William's kisses, which heated her and made her want to hold on to him.

Her mother reached across and patted her hand. "But you are a unique young woman, Agnes. What is true for you is appropriate for other females. It is our responsibility to protect the others from the risk of too much knowledge and too many opportunities to go astray."

In a startling moment of clarity, she realized her frustration with the meeting in her father's study reflected her dissatisfaction with society and the accepted role of women. She didn't agree with her mother that education and information harmed them. It wasn't logical.

Was her disinterest in marriage because of those limits or her? She turned that question over and around and wondered how it would be with a man who appreciated and considered her mind and opinions. Her main example had been her parents' and that was not the least appealing. Could she be happy in a relationship like the duke and duchess shared? William had respected her choices and helped her enlarge her experiences, especially with dancing and kissing. Was he similar to his brother and able to respect her preferences and ideas? That would be a match made in heaven for her. And something to ponder going forward.

Hours later, pacing his sitting room in the Harrisons, William considered what he'd learned. It would be best to discuss his realizations with Allwyn, who had a broader range of experience and contacts, but it was too late for visiting. A baby had transformed their lives, especially the social aspects, which resulted in the young family spending more time together at home.

Finally, William gave up the idea of going to bed and went downstairs. A glass of Port would relax him enough to sleep.

In these circumstances, Agnes would settle into a chair in the library, but he had no desire to go there, even on the chance of seeing her. Libraries had always been uncomfortable for him, for every book shouting his shortcoming. He didn't need to be reminded of his failings and lack of intelligence. They were something he lived with daily. Fortunately, he'd been blessed with a keen memory, which served him well.

Rolling the snifter of Port between his hands, William relaxed on the settee in a salon, his legs sprawled out in front of him. It had been an interesting day, starting out with Harrison's revelations, then finding the body of the man's former paramour, and confirming the earl's opinions of women. Worse was that most of his peers would agree with the man.

Even with this new information, there wasn't any action to take, since the problem was bigger than him. Besides, he had two murders to solve and the safe cracker to find. Those were his priorities right now.

He sipped his port and regarded the well-appointed salon, and his thoughts meandered back to the earl's point of view. What about those who didn't live in such comfort? And the people his sister-in-law attended to in Seven Dials?

All the things Harrison said about women equally applied to England's poor. The work would be different, but the regard and concern would be the same.

The French population had revolted, guillotining peers and royalty almost as soon as they caught them. That hadn't happened in England, at least not yet. But was it far off? When men like Harrison paid a woman for decades to provide sexual congress to him outside of marriage and then banished her and their children, how long could the social order survive?

The longer he sat here, the worse things seemed to be. And he was increasingly powerless to change anything, even if he had a starting place.

Juliette and his brother were making a difference, and Calliope and her friends were working to improve the lot of children. But what about him? What should his role be, if any?

He jumped up and stormed across the room. "That is the damn question."

"What is?" Agnes asked, joining him in the salon.

He watched her cross to him and chastised himself for not leaving but remained rooted in place as she walked to his side. The situation was rife with complications, but he waited for her, unable to tear himself away from this fiercely intelligent woman, who seemed different tonight, in looks and other ways as well.

"You seem... distracted, or perhaps disturbed about something," she noted. "Is there anything I can help with?"

He shook his head, his throat too tight for words. He placed the snifter on the mantle and pulled Agnes to him. Swallowing repeatedly, his voice loosened. "I'm glad you're here."

"I am, as well." She slid her hands under his jacket and around his waist and laid her cheek on his shoulder. "This is where I want to be."

William rubbed large circles on her back with one hand and held her close with the other. His reaction to this woman was a mystery to him but having her in his arms seemed to take his troubles away. His thoughts were no longer complicated or convoluted. Instead, they were calm, and he was relaxed. He would find a way to work towards change. Not today, and not tomorrow, but soon. He would never forget what he had learned and never stop working to implement progress.

"What brings you down here?" he asked her.

"The same as you, sleeplessness." She settled against him. "Some things my mother said, some truths, forced me to think unpleasant thoughts. And once down that road, I couldn't seem to get away from it."

"That's ironic because I'm here for the same reason, except it was your father's words which left me reeling."

"We can talk about it, if you'd like," she offered.

William smiled at her. He had no intention of discussing the earl's opinions and comments about his mistress with Agnes. He wasn't certain if she was aware her father had one or that she had three half-siblings. However, he would not be the man to tell her about it. It was Harrison's family business that he learned while investigating for the earl and would be kept confidential.

"Thank you for your offer, but this is a situation I must mull over on my own."

"Mother said there was much information women need not know, because it was upsetting, unattractive, or painful. But I am tired of living in a glass bubble, part of, yet separate from, the world."

"That is similar to how I've felt, as if I can see what's going on around me but can't change it."

"It's a strange place, isn't it? I'm looking at society through fresh eyes. I didn't understand the rush to marriage by young girls, and then I did. Then I realized how necessary it is in the value it provides to females. Simultaneously, I learned that often the wedded state is nothing more than slavery for women, who are required to do as expected, without complaint or comment."

"I had a similar realization, but my thoughts rambled from there to all sorts of places, none of them positive. Nor conducive to a good night's sleep."

Agnes slid her hand underneath his waistcoat and rubbed his lower back. Although wildly inappropriate, it warmed him.

"It's interesting that we've both realized something important tonight, and it is making it difficult to fall asleep."

"My dear, you are right, but we shouldn't remain here. It would be unconscionable to compromise you, which would take away your choice."

"What if I don't want better?" She trembled.

"On a cool winter evening, standing here with my arms wrapped around you, compromising you, seems like the best option. But tomorrow or the next day, we will see things differently and we won't risk that."

"Can we at least sit together for a little while?"

He leaned back and looked into her eyes and saw a need for something. Perhaps his courageous Agnes needed a friend tonight. That he could give her.

They separated, and he took her hand and led her to the settee, sitting close to her. He placed their clasped hands on his thigh and smiled at her. "Better?"

She nodded. "I wasn't looking for you when I came downstairs, but as soon as I saw you, I knew this was where I should be." She laid her head on his shoulder.

Agnes relaxed against William, knowing they were still in a compromising position, but a rational argument was possible about the two of them on the settee, with the door open, whereas they'd have no recourse if caught kissing. She enjoyed the moment.

He wanted to kiss her, and perhaps more, which wasn't the desire of a friend. But her inexperience in the ways of men's behavior meant she couldn't rely on her intuition.

It was very confusing. Sometimes he seemed to want something more than friendship for them. But then he'd push her away, leaving her hurt and confused.

For the first time in her life, she wished she had a friend to talk to. Another woman might understand the situation better. But she didn't trust any female enough to bring it up.

The females of her acquaintance delighted in making fun of her for her interests, her communication style, and her lack of interest in marriage, and she wouldn't provide them fodder for their gossip.

Which left her mother—a laughable idea. No, she could not ask her these questions. She doubted the answers were in a book, for although printed material abounded about animal husbandry, little had been written about human relationships. In fact, she had never seen a single one. And if she saw such a thing in Hatchards, she would never have the courage to buy it, since she'd have to face the clerk, who would have opinions about her purchase. And could tell everyone about Lady Agnes Harrison's strange taste.

She put her palm on William's chest, over his steadily beating heart. Do married women sit like this? Or perhaps they lay beside their husband, their cheek resting on him. If the latter was true, the rhythm of his heartbeat would be soothing, and likely conducive to a good night's sleep.

William cradled her hand in his, holding it against him. A simple movement, but she felt cherished.

Dare she hope? Could they be more than friends?

He leaned down and kissed the top of her head. "Although I'm comfortable here, it's time we retire. I wouldn't want either or both of us to fall asleep sitting here."

"No, I suppose you're right. Since my mind stopped whirling, perhaps I can rest now. What about you?"

"I must check on my men first. Today has been an extraordinarily busy day, and tomorrow looks to be no better, making sleep necessary."

"Are you getting close to the answer?"

"An investigation is a riddle. I have to find the pieces of the puzzle before I am able to put them together and make my way to the solution. I've discovered many parts, but I'm still missing a couple."

"In other words, you're making progress, but not as quick as you'd like."

"In some ways, you are right, but," he kissed the top of her head again, "in others, you are not."

"Then it's best we retire, and you can be fresh for your problem-solving."

He stood and gently tugged her hand, helping her to her feet. "Exactly. Sleep well, Agnes. I hope to see you at breakfast."

They separated in the hall. She went upstairs, and he walked to the earl's study. She waited until he closed the door behind him.

In her room, she readied herself for bed. When her maid loosened the ties of her corset, she took a deep breath. It was wonderful to breathe deeply again.

Under the covers, she rested her cheek on her stacked hands and looked out the window. The moon shone brightly, and the stars twinkled. On other nights, in these circumstances, she would have donned her robe and gone upstairs to her telescope. But not tonight.

Instead, she remained here and savored the feelings she'd enjoyed with William. Her parents loved her, but he was the first person ever to cherish her.

Could a relationship make her feel any better than right at this moment? She had no idea, but was anxious to find out.

After ensuring the men in the study were wide awake, William returned to his room, while still pondering who killed Shelley and the guard. Did the two deaths tie-in to the break-in or were they unrelated?

Perhaps something was stolen from the safe. It could be anything, but there was no way of telling if he was being honest.

If he had prevaricated about the contents of his safe, it wasn't a leap to conclude it had particular significance for him.

There were many things a man might keep locked up that he wouldn't admit to having. It had to be very important, since he'd acknowledged possessing national secrets, before admitting to its possession. Which meant it was likely personal. But what had such importance that two people were killed over it?

William's train of thought lead him into a bog. Dark, dirty, and hostile. Whatever the situation, he would need clear and undeniable facts before he presented them to anyone, including the earl.

In moments like this, he wished Triple E had the selection and number of informants their predecessor, Bob Murdoch, employed. Tomorrow he would talk to Louis and Mrs. Johnson. He wanted, no, needed, to talk out his thoughts and they could tell him he was losing his mind or was on the right track.

If his hunch was correct, whatever had been stolen would turn this family upside down. He wouldn't do that to anyone without solid proof, but especially Agnes, who deserved the best from him.

The next morning, he sent a message to Louis and Mrs. Johnson, requesting a meeting as early as possible. After a hurried breakfast, taken alone at the Harrison's, he rushed to his brother's home, which housed the agency's office. Both were waiting for him. He settled in the third chair, between them, then fixed his tea while gathering his thoughts, then quickly explained what he discovered about Shelley and her death.

"Have any of our men turned up any additional information about her or the situation?"

Both his brother and their partner shook their heads. "Nothing at all," said Louis.

"That's what I feared," William replied. He looked at his partners. "I had a moment last night where this whole thing unfolded differently and I want to run my thoughts by you, to see if I'm imagining things."

"What are you talking about?" his brother asked.

"Hear me out. Perhaps I am on my way to bedlam. But I need to say these ideas to someone else and discover if they are as ridiculous as I think." They nodded, and he began. "What if Harrison isn't being truthful about the contents of his safe?"

"Are you suggesting there's something even more pressing about national security or what?" Mrs. Johnson asked.

"What if a personal item was taken from the safe and the earl is using the government angle to keep that particular business quiet?"

Her eyes opened wide. "He wouldn't be the first to go to those lengths to protect a secret."

"But what could be that important that Harrison would hire us to identify the person who stole it?"

"That is a good question, and I don't have the answer. But it sends me down some dark paths."

"Me too," added Mrs. Johnson. "Perhaps the man is a spy and his safe held proof of his activities."

Louis nodded. "He's afraid if we find the document, he'll be tried for treason."

"That's a possibility," William said. "I think Harrison is capable of anything that helps him get his way. But I doubt that is what is going on. I've spent a fair bit of time with the man, and in my opinion, he is loyal to a fault, to country and family."

Louis rubbed his temple with one finger and then nodded in agreement. "The man's character is solid. Everyone who knows him, trusts him, and says he's completely reliable, a friend for life."

"I have heard the same," said Mrs. Johnson.

"If I'm right, then the stolen item would turn his reputation on its ear. People would discover it was all a sham." William narrowed his eyes and considered the options of Harrison living a falsehood.

"If your theory is true, little brother, whatever was stolen has to prove the lie."

"It's interesting to me, assuming we are on the right track, that the what and the why of this mess are of equal importance. Knowing either will identify the other. But if we're correct, why is he paying us a fortune to guard the safe when something has already been stolen?" Mrs. Johnson looked from at each of the brothers.

"That's another good question, Mrs. J." William considered what they knew. "Have any of our men found others who are asking questions about Harrison or his safe?"

"No one. And we train them well enough to recognize its significance." There was no doubt in her voice.

"Someone broke into the safe and the earl calls us in but doesn't tell the truth. He says his papers were gone through. Then I suggest a guard for the study. Since nothing was stolen, it seems plausible the thief may return."

"The footman was killed on duty." Louis looked from his brother to their partner and continued. "We assumed he was murdered protecting the safe, but what if that's not true?"

William nodded quickly. "What if he lost his life because he knew too much, either about the robbery or the stolen item?"

The three of them sat in stunned silence.

"That puts a unique twist on this entire case," Louis said.

"Which explains how someone got into a guarded room without being seen. If the murderer was a member of the household, no one would remark on his presence. Servants clean, lay fires, and refill liquor bottles regularly. A servant might have slipped in there, killed the footman, rifled through the safe, and left," William suggested.

"But the villain should have been covered in blood. Surely someone would have seen that."

"I agree, but if the murderer slit the guard's throat from behind, he would have been protected from most of the spray," Mrs. J. said.

"And their livery is black, which would hide most of it."

"But again, we return to a hard spot. Since few of the staff can read, how would they know what to take? If money or jewels were missing, Harrison would have gone to Bow Street. Rather, he chose us, citing issues of national security."

"Which tells me the thief took a document of some sort," Louis said.

Mrs. J. studied the patterns in the carpet. "What if he didn't need to read to steal the desired item?" she asked.

"I'm not sure where you're going with that idea," his brother questioned.

"What if he stole a permit?"

William jumped to his feet in excitement. "You are right. A criminal doesn't have to be literate to recognize the difference between a paper and an official certificate, a formal document, or a penned note. If the thief wanted something specific and he knew what to look for, it would be easy to steal from a pile of legal papers."

"It becomes increasingly complicated, the more we discuss the situation," Louis said, "But I think we're on the right track."

"What is that important and possibly written on a note to cause Harrison to hire us, rather than Bow Street, to kill or have killed one of his staff and perhaps a former mistress, all while lying about the stolen item?"

"When you put it like that, it has to be something personal."

"Could he have another family?" Louis asked.

"He readily admitted he had the same paramour for over twenty years, and they have three children together, two daughters and a son. He doesn't feel any shame or concern about that," William explained. "His wife and daughter have no idea about these people, and we should keep that secret from them."

"Where are they now?" Mrs. J asked.

"Harrison said when the woman, Adelia, became ill, he pensioned her off to Bath.

She nodded. "It is not uncommon for an aristocrat to send an illegitimate progeny to school there."

"Are you certain she and girls are still there?"

William frowned at his brother. "The man we sent to verify the situation and ask some questions of Harrison's former mistress hasn't returned. He could be gone for a week or more. Needless to say, I'm not losing any sleep waiting for what he finds out."

"It's times like these when I recognize the need for trains crossing the country. A trip to Bath would take five hours, maybe six, as opposed to two or three days. If a man departed on the early train, asked his questions, and got good responses, he'd catch the one home and sleep in his own bed that night.

"What can we find out about Shelley? Who knew her or something about her?"

"We have to identify her friends," Louis stated. "Someone must have known her and could tell us about her."

William shrugged. "Seems likely, but I have no idea."

Mrs. J. looked between them and chuckled. "One of you should check the clubs for mention of arrangements, new or old, among the men. Get names if you can. Then I will go to work with that list and find out if any of the women knew Shelley."

"Good plan, if you don't mind questioning them. Eliza would have my head in a basket if she found I spoke to several mistresses."

William laughed. "And it wouldn't take her long to do it, either." He rose and said, "I'm going to talk to people in the theaters to see if they heard anything. The social intersection of actresses with the ton is minimal, but Lord knows many women treading the boards are protected by men of the beau monde."

"That leaves me with the clubs. I'll start asking questions later today." Louis looked at his partner and Mrs. J. and nodded. "I think we're on to something. Good work, little brother. While it seems far-fetched, your idea is the only one that puts all the pieces together reasonably. Once we find those at the center of this question, we can close this case."

CHAPTER FOURTEEN

The next morning, Agnes looked through the eyepiece of her telescope, searching for any change in the sky. She stepped away, heaved an enormous sigh, and made some notes in her notebook. "It is hard to make progress in research, when nothing changes from hour to hour or day-to-day."

She studied her observations for a moment or two, then shook her head. "Now you're talking to yourself. What does that signify?"

Likely that she had been alone too often. Or that she'd enjoyed speaking with William and missed his companionship, since he hadn't shown up today. His guard was downstairs, but he had not yet arrived.

Perhaps she should set aside her study of astronomy for a little while and take up studying human relationships. She had not understood the pleasure of sitting close to someone whose company you enjoyed. The security that came from leaning against him and listening to his heartbeat while knowing it sped up with some simple actions.

This must be another reason that girls of the ton focused their energy and time on marriage.

Perhaps she should start a list. She'd call it 'Reasons to Want to Get Married.' Right now, it would include comfort, pleasure, warmth, excitement, and safety.

That final item just occurred to her. Sitting beside him last night, nothing or no one could hurt her. He wouldn't allow it. An exhilarating realization, even safe in her home. She was certain he would stand between her and anything that might happen.

William took his role as protector seriously—part of what made him such a talented investigator. And a good friend.

Looking from her telescope to the attic door, she remembered his latest visit, where they spoke as friends. Did that conversation reflect his regard for her or was last night closer to the truth between them? How was she to tell?

She needed to make another list. This one, to record the reasons to stay away from men and live your life on your terms. Some early items would be uncertainty, confusion, lack of clarity in communication, and the risk of mistaking the attraction for something more lasting.

Relationships were hard.

Did William feel the same? Perhaps he needed a clear sign that she cared for him. She couldn't run up to him and say, 'I think I'm falling in love with you.' She wasn't brave enough for that, but might she consider the idea differently?

Drawing her bottom lip in with her teeth, she tried to figure out a way to show him the depth of her feelings. Flowers were inappropriate, as were chocolates or some other little treat. They reserved those choices for men.

There had to be some approach to say she wanted to include him in her life, and to demonstrate his importance to her. She ran her hand along the outside of her telescope as she considered and rejected several options. Then she stopped and froze in place.

She had the perfect gift to express her high regard for him and her desire to share more with him. She only required a private moment to give it to him.

Humming, Agnes looked through the eyepiece at the afternoon sky and saw nothing but a few stars. There was no blazing meteor. No comet. No moon.

It reminded her of her life. Commonplace, boring, and tedious.

But now she had a way to fix that situation as soon as the opportunity arose.

She left the attic and hurried to her room and sent for her maid. Guests were expected, as was William. She wanted to look her best tonight, even if it took all afternoon.

When the butler announced dinner, Agnes was ready. Her coiffure was simple elegance, with jeweled pins scattered amidst her tresses. Her gold satin dress had a deep neckline she had previously called indecent. Pearls in the shape of flowers were sewn into matching slippers. And her undergarments were of the finest silk. She remembered arguing with her mother about buying such feminine items, but today she was grateful she'd lost that argument.

This marked the first day of the rest of her life. The best days were ahead of her, and she felt special from the inside out.

Agnes joined her parents and their friends in the salon. Everyone was most complementary, although her mother raised her eyebrows in an unstated question about her apparel. She mixed and mingled and enjoyed the company, despite her disappointment at William's absence.

Eventually, he would return. And she would be waiting for him, ready to show him how much he meant to her.

Dinner was jovial with laughter and enjoyment of those at the table. Was this new, or had she missed such congeniality all these years? After, the women adjourned for tea while the men shared port and cigars. For once, this separation didn't upset her, for if she had been sitting beside William for the meal, she would need a short break to bring her temperature back to normal.

She made small talk about the weather, responded to a question about her current studies, and asked about the families of their callers.

As people departed, she cordially wished them a Merry Christmas and honestly looked forward to seeing them again. Best of all, at no time this evening had she fought with herself to remain in their company. Her telescope seemed far away, and her attention had focused on the guests.

She glanced at the door more than necessary, but she had been waiting for William to arrive. Disappointment had risen several times, but only in a small way. He was solving the mystery around her father's safe. That had to come first. Once resolved, they could assume a more typical relationship and perhaps even a courtship.

E xhausted, William was ready to head home. He had visited more theaters than he cared to count. He had spoken to owners, directors, and actresses. None had heard of Shelley P. It now seemed unlikely that the earl's former mistress had tread the boards.

Despite the lateness of the hour, he had a final stop. This theater wasn't in the best part of London, but close. Inside, he spoke to the director, who was not familiar with the murder victim. But the man directed him to Angela.

"She knows everything about everyone. If she says the woman ain't one of us, then you can make book on that."

William went backstage, searching for his last hope. Stagehands pointed to the far reaches of the theater, deep behind the curtains.

He found an old, bent over female, her steel gray hair scraped into a tight bun at the back of her head, sorting through racks of clothing. This wasn't an actress, but the wardrobe and costume keeper.

"Are you Angela?"

The woman turned to face him. Her eyes squinted. "Wots it to you?"

"I am looking for information about Shelley P. I was told you might know her or about her."

"And if I did, why would I say anything to you?"

"For several reasons," he said, taking some coins from his pocket. "First, I'm willing to reward anyone who can tell me about her. Second, I want to find her family. And third —."

"She's dead and you're the gent wot found her body."

"Exactly. How did you know?"

The old woman cackled. "Like they told you, I knows everything." She stretched out her hand and wiggled her dirty-nailed fingers for the coins and dropped them into a pocket in her skirt.

"You knew Shelley?"

"Not well. But our paths had crossed. She came from my village and looked me up when she got to London. She wasn't," the crone waved her arm to show her surroundings, "one of us. But I introduced her to a couple of women who performed on Drury Lane and they became friends."

"Who are they? Maybe I should speak to them?"

The old biddy shook her head. "No. You'll talk to me. What is it you's wanting to know?"

"We buried Shelley, but I wanted to get word to her family."

"She ain't gots none. At least none she ever spoke of. They sent her away when they found out she was carrying. After arriving in London, and losing the babe, she came to me, then did what any beautiful young woman would do. She got a protector. He was better than tupping in a bordello or on a street corner, but not by much."

"How long had she been here?"

"Two years plus some, as I recall."

"What made him that bad? Did he hit her or hurt her?"

"'Tweren't nothing like that. Mean-spirited bastard. She had to be prepared for his visits every minute. He didn't want her sleeping but waiting for him." She scoffed. "As if anybody can go without sleep forever. He'd come in the middle of the night and if she wasn't dressed, he would yell and make threats and scare her half to death." She spat again. "He enjoyed terrifying her. There was no other reason for his behavior because he kept her for two years."

It was disgusting and, below anyone, never mind a peer who was supposed to uphold the highest standards of society. Why would a man do this except to prove he could? It was unnecessary. There had been glimpses of this nastiness from Harrison, but not directed specifically at one person.

"'Twere interesting that when he broke it off, she called him a bastard. He laughed and said, 'you don't know the half of it.'" The crone shook her head. "Never was sure what he meant by that, although I had my ideas, but it didn't bode well for Shelley."

"Did he give a reason for ending their relationship?"

"Nope," she waved it off. "Told her he had important things to do and wouldn't have time for her." She cackled again. "Made us all laugh, he did. He rarely visited except to torment her and when he did, he couldn't get it up. I thinks he kept a mistress to prove he was a man, as if paying for a woman's keep showed him as something special."

"Are you saying he had her for reasons other than relations?" It seemed silly to ask, but he had to be certain he understood her.

"Yep."

"Did he blame Shelley for his problems?"

"A few times he yelled at her about it, but gradually he stopped trying. He came to the house to torment her or scare her and once he had her crying and shaking, he'd wave her off and tell her he had no patience with emotional women. Then he would leave."

"And he did that regularly?"

"All the time. And often muttered something about showing 'them' who was a bastard."

"Did you have any idea who he referred to?"

She ran her hand over her scalp, smoothing her hair. "None. He never said." She jangled the coins in her pocket. "I had my own ideas about him and his family, but weren't my place to say anything."

He wondered about the old woman's tale because Harrison was an earl. You don't inherit a title and entailed properties if you're a bastard. At least not in England. So he couldn't be referencing himself. Perhaps a son? Was that the secret? But that too was irrelevant.

And how would Triple E find out? That answer, William was certain, would solve this case. And likely two murders.

He handed the crone another coin. "Is there anything else you can tell me about Shelley that might help identify her murderer?"

"I'm wondering if you're interested in her murder or something else?"

"I am looking into a different question, but she is part of it and I do not want to see her death unanswered for." The woman had taken the only avenue open to her for survival, and her 'protector' had made her life a living hell. She deserved justice as much as anyone in this mess.

"That bastard met with some man at her house a few months ago. He sent her upstairs and told her to stay there or he'd send her away. She hid in the hall but didn't hear anything. The next week the same thing happened, only this time she came down the servants' stairs and got close enough to catch a few words."

Shelley's curiosity was likely the cause of her death. "What did they say?"

"Harrison told the other man to take the money and get the hell out of England. He never wanted to see him again."

He'd paid someone off for something. It couldn't be national secrets, or the earl wouldn't have hired Triple E. "Did she hear anything else?"

"No, because she had to hurry to her room. But she noticed from an upstairs window that the man left with a satchel Harrison had brought with him."

Interesting. There were several things that might be in the bag, but bank notes were most likely.

"I just remembered one other thing Shelley mentioned."

"What was that?"

"The men were close in appearance. The visitor looked older and like he'd worked outside most of his life." She played with the coins again. "I told her to be very careful about repeating the things she heard. People aren't always who they seem to be."

William fished out another copper and handed it to her. "You were right. You do know everyone and everything. I can't thank you enough." He gave her his card. "If ever you need anything, or if you remember something else about Shelley, send someone to me. I will be happy to help or provide more coin for good information."

The woman cackled as she looked at it. "Don't understand a word of this gibberish. But I'll keep it."

"Then deliver a message to me, William, at Wolfstone. My brother, the duke, will make sure I get it."

The costumer laughed again and slapped her thigh. "Wait till I tell me friends. I was hobnobbing with the brother of a nobleman. They'll think I've lost my nob." She looked up at him, suddenly serious. "You're a good 'un. If ole Angie can do anything else, just ask."

William walked away, knowing he had made a contact that would serve him for years. Apparently, everybody talked to and around the costume woman. He had come here for information about Shelley, to help him solve her murder. If she was correct, and he believed her, that death and this case were close to being solved.

And he had put the first peg, a very important one, into a network of informants.

William shared the details of his conversation with Mrs. J. and Louis. They agreed it was significant, but weren't sure how it all fit together, given that Harrison was a respected peer with an old title. The other investigators had found nothing new, so they would continue digging around. Perhaps Allwyn could shed some light on Angela's information. Or maybe some context for it. He'd stop there in the morning and question his brother.

They agreed it was now necessary to contact Bob. He knew everything about everybody and might be able to provide additional material to solve this riddle.

In the coach, William concluded that Harrison probably hired them because they were a new agency. The earl promised a big sum of money for the discovery of the person who broke into his safe. That, combined with the prestige of working for a member of the ton, on a project that involved the House of Lords, would yield them enough cachet to keep them in clients for years to come. And since they were starting at this work, he wouldn't expect them to have a network of informants or other ways to discover the truth. He assumed they'd take him at his word and look for a safecracker and a murderer because of national security, when the situation looked much more personal.

Just thinking about the possibility put William in high dudgeon. The ego and the arrogance of the man were beyond belief. The triplets were the sons of a duke, brothers to another, and their mother thought circles around most people. Harrison's assumption that his title and position would protect his secret made William boiling mad.

He stepped out of the hack and slowly walked to the earl's townhouse. His temper had cooled enough, he hoped to meet with Harrison without sharing his opinion with the man. The butler welcomed him inside, then took his coat and hat. What a bloody day. Rage and frustration marked his every breath.

Barely stepping beyond the foyer, Agnes joined him. More truthfully, she floated toward him, like an angel come to visit earth—the woman who soothed his anger and fatigue and cheered him up.

Hands extended, he clasped hers, pulling her close, her eyes mirroring his pleasure at being in her company. "My God, you are extraordinarily beautiful today. A vision to lift the spirits of this poor man." He took one step back and looked her up and down. "I will not let you go out of the house looking like that. Some fellow will sweep you up, throw you in a carriage and race for Gretna Green, just to be in the light of your beauty."

"While that is unlikely, I appreciate the sentiment. Thank you." She studied him for a moment and said, "Are you well? You look exhausted."

"It has been a busy day and the information I collected is confusing, though I'm certain it's accurate."

Agnes patted his chest. "I don't doubt you'll find the remaining pieces and solve this mystery. My father could not have picked a better man for this work."

The truth was likely the opposite.

If he were right, his discoveries about her father's activities would hurt her more than he could bear. He'd be lucky if she ever spoke to him again.

"I didn't mean to embarrass you with my praise about your abilities as an investigator. But there is something important I would like to talk to you about." She looked around and behind her and whispered, "Can we meet in the attic in ten or fifteen minutes?"

He nodded. He intended to enjoy every available minute with this woman, just in case she came to hate him. They would finish this investigation in the next few days, or a week at most. And when the dust settled, Agnes would no longer want to spend time with him. She would feel betrayed and embarrassed and would place the blame for all of it on his shoulders.

He prayed he was wrong.

But this woman adored her father, and anything that affected him would reflect poorly on her. Of that he was certain, despite not being sure where the investigation would end.

He lifted her hands and kissed the back of each. "Go and work with your telescope, Agnes. I will freshen up and join you shortly."

Her face lit with joy at his words. "I'll see you soon." She spun on her heel and raced up the stairs.

William found the decanter of whiskey in the library and poured himself more than a single drink and downed it all at once. It was the only way to numb the pain that was coming when his investigation ended.

Agnes closed her notebook and put it, her ink, and the quill inside her desk. She removed her Christmas gift to William and placed it in the center. Excitement tingled through her. She couldn't wait to see his face when he unwrapped it. It was her invitation to him to share her world, to become one with her as they go forward in their lives.

The words her heart called her to say were stuck in her throat. They were too big a risk and too frightening, but when he saw the depth of her regard, he would draw her close and express his unwavering love for her. And he'd realize they were meant for each other.

Agnes fidgeted with her gift, aligning it with the edges of the desk and making certain it was centered. She then angled it and moved it to one side before changing her mind and moving it to the other. Perhaps she should leave it in a drawer and bring it out when he arrived.

She lifted the book to put it out of sight, then stopped. If the gift sat on her desk when he entered, he'd see it and ask about it. Then she could explain it was for him and why. If things went as she expected and hoped, he would take her in his arms and kiss her as soon as he opened it.

Hearing his footsteps, she slid the tome to the middle and stood waiting, watching the door, for her future to join her.

William walked in, crossed the attic, and came to her side. "As requested, my dear, I'm here. What would you like to talk about?"

He still looked tired and his eyes were bleak, but it was too late to change her mind. But suddenly, her mouth was dry and her carefully prepared speech disappeared. "I... uhm, I...." She grabbed the gift and pulled it towards them. "I got you something." Then she folded her hands in front of her, waiting to see his reaction.

"For me? Why did you do that?"

"Actually, I bought it for you for Christmas, but it means more to me than that, and I wanted to give it to you in private."

"Then best I open it."

He slid it toward him and ripped off the paper. When he saw the book, he burst into laughter. Loud guffaws, as if her gift was the biggest joke he'd ever seen.

She was shocked, and every second of his chortling hurt more deeply. She'd welcomed him into her world, in a way she had never included anyone, and he thought it was funny, hilarious even. Why wouldn't he stop laughing?

Every time he looked at her or the text, he would break into louder, more raucous laughter.

Choking back tears, because she had been wrong about him.

With one finger, he slid it to the middle of the desk and faced her, taking her hands, still smiling widely. "It is a beautiful gift, Agnes," he said, his voice soft. "Thank you very much. Forgive my amusement, but we have more similar tastes than we realized, for I purchased that same book for you."

They'd bought the same thing for each other. At least he wasn't laughing at her gift or her, but the circumstances. The clerk mentioned only having two copies, and here they were. "Oh. I can see where that would be amusing." Although not as funny as he thought it to be.

"Exactly. I was certain you would make great use of this book in your astronomical studies."

"And my plan was that we could read it and learn about the skies together."

Something dark flickered across his eyes, but she couldn't identify the emotion. "I realize it would have to be in the new year, because you're busy right now, but it would be a pleasure to alternate reading about the night sky."

His face blanched, all color fading. "You wanted us to take turns studying this book, in the new year, long after this investigation is completed?" He tapped the cover with his finger. "Why on earth would I want to study it?"

She flinched at his coldness. "I didn't mean that exactly. I meant we could discuss what we learned. As a basis for conversation." His reaction was unexpected and hurtful. She'd never heard him use this derisive tone or inflection.

"For conversation? You thought astronomy would be a good foundation for discussions between us?" He dropped her hands and took a step back.

Why was he being difficult? "You've always seemed interested when looking through my telescope. I assumed you'd want to know more." Although now she wasn't as certain about his enthusiasm. "This," she reached out and slid the book toward him, "has the most current information available."

He straightened away from her. "Did you consider topics such as horse breeding or pugilism or crop rotation?" His voice got louder. "Those are subjects that interest me, and I'd love to discuss them with you."

She put her hand on his, trying to get him to understand. "William, I didn't mean to offend you. I thought this would be something to share, to bring us closer."

He looked at her as if she was a specimen in a laboratory.

She shivered, watching him.

"I think, Lady Agnes, that you misjudge the situation and the depth of my interest in astronomy. While I appreciate your thoughts of me, this gift shows your inability to understand others." He stepped back, gave her a short curt bow, and said, "If you will excuse me, I'm going to speak to your father and explain that it is no longer necessary for me to stay in this house, as I continue looking for the person who broke in and resolve this case. If I don't see you before Christmas, I wish you the happiest of days."

She didn't stop to think but reached out for him. "William, please wait. I don't want you to leave on these terms."

He shook his head, maintaining his distance. "From the bottom of my heart, I wish you nothing but the best."

He stopped and took a deep breath, giving her a cold, steely grin, then turned with his back stiff like one of the Prince's guards and marched out, pulling the attic door carefully closed behind him.

Agnes watched him walk away and consciously locked her knees to stay upright. Only a total misfit would misread the signs of a casual flirtation for something more meaningful.

What nonsense caused her to conclude that a sophisticated man like William Evans would want to have a relationship with her, a spinster, a bluestocking, and a lonely woman?

How had she deluded herself so badly?

She ran her hand up the tube of her telescope and whispered, "Well, old friend, I've made a fool of myself again. But this is the last time. I'll be back in the morning, dressed in work clothes, ready to study the sky with you."

Swiping the tears from her eyes, she returned to her room. She would return to the things she knew best: science, mathematics, and research. They never lied to her or misled her about their intentions. They were constant and reliable, and the only part of the world where she fit in.

She would never make that mistake again. It would take her a while to heal her shame, but work would help.

CHAPTER FIFTEEN

William pulled the door shut behind him, then sank against it. The wounded look in Agnes's eyes broke him. It took every bit of his strength to remain standing when his heart and body wanted to fall to his knees, kiss the hem of her dress, and beg her forgiveness.

The hope in her gaze when she offered him her gift had nearly undone him. She'd taken an enormous risk, for them, and for him. He was more touched than she could imagine.

At first, the book had made him laugh and the more he laughed, the funnier it seemed. But reality hit. For any other person, the book would've been a wonderful present. The perfect invitation to her heart and mind. In the future, it might have led to discussions between them.

But today had piled up on him. The things he was discovering about her father and the risk that such a big secret, whatever it was, presented to this family layered on top of his inability to read were too much. He couldn't trust her with his deepest secret when he was about to expose the one the earl had gone to great lengths to keep.

No, she would think him the worst kind of cad, a man toying with her affections, and she would hold on to that judgement forever. Agnes wasn't a forgive and forget type of person. Not that he deserved forgiveness.

He had been cruel to the only woman he'd ever cared about. It proved to him he was not cut out for marriage or a loving relationship.

He had good reason for his abominable behavior toward her. Best he broke it off now, for there would be no coming back after he exposed her father's perfidy. He wasn't certain of Harrison's crimes, but the man was responsible for at least one death, possibly two, and perhaps the biggest lie ever foisted on crown and country.

William pulled himself together, straightened his shoulders, and hurried down the stairs. The only thing he could do for Agnes was solve the mystery of the safecracker and the motivation behind it as soon as possible. The sooner she learned the truth, the faster she could rebuild her life. He would personally ensure she would be comfortable, study as she chose, and live with dignity.

It was the least he could do.

In his room, he threw his few things into his bag, grabbed it, and walked down the stairs to Harrison's study to tell the man he was no longer staying at the house.

He placed his traveling kit in the hall and joined his employer. "It is unnecessary for me to remain here. My agents will stay to keep watch, but since there's been no activity, it's time I go home."

The earl came to his feet, fingers extended and resting on his desk. "We agreed you would dwell here until you found the miscreant and my study was safe again."

"We both know your documents are not facing any risks. My men will continue to ensure it remains secure. But that does not require my presence. My investigation is better served from outside this house." William studied the older man for a moment, then added, "I am very close to finding the man who broke into your safe and the document he took from it."

Harrison spluttered and coughed. "What are you talking about? I said the documents had been rifled, not that a theft occurred."

"That's not true. Something was removed. I have some ideas about it and what it proves, but I won't say anything until I have it in hand." He squinted at the earl, his gaze hard. "Make no mistake," he warned, "I will find it and present it to the authorities."

"You are a bedlamite!" screamed Harrison. "I have no idea what you think happened here or what is in the supposed document floating out there somewhere, but let me assure you, this is the last case you ever work for anyone in the ton. Everyone will know of your incompetence and your insolence. You can kiss your agency goodbye."

"Do whatever you feel is necessary, for when the results of my investigation are made public, no one will believe a word you say."

"I don't know who you think you're talking to, or what gives you the right to speak to me in this manner, but it ends now. And just to be clear, I'm going to recommend to your eldest brother he cut off your allowance, since you do not respect your elders, or your betters."

"Do as you must." William turned and walked out of the study, closing the door behind him.

His conversation with Harrison proved one thing. The man was hiding something important to him. And he would go to any lengths to keep it hidden.

He took a hack to the office, moved inside, and poured himself a whisky while waiting for Louis to join him.

"What happened? Why are you here?"

"Our client exploded when I told him about the theft from his safe. He threatened to ruin us and me personally, and have Allwyn cut off my funds."

"Obviously, he doesn't realize know our brother."

"His ideas of his importance have expanded beyond reality. As if our duke would pay any regard to an opinion about us."

The brothers laughed, since their eldest sibling rarely paid attention to the opinions of the ton. Their family had always walked their own path.

"Harrison is scared. Cornered animals take desperate chances. Do you have men watching him?" William asked.

Louis nodded. "Maitland is on the job."

"Excellent. And Mrs. J?"

"She left to chat with some of her informants. She felt with the new information, she might knock a few heads together and break out something that matters."

"Smart idea."

The butler interrupted them. "There's a messenger for you, Master Louis."

"Send him in."

"Maybe it's good news from her," William suggested.

Before he got inside, another man arrived, carrying a note.

The first came from Maitland, who said that Harrison had left his home and was in his carriage, traveling away from Mayfair and the House of Lords. He had made no effort to hide his coat of arms, nor did he seem to be in a particular hurry. Their man would follow him and send another message from their destination.

The second message was from Mrs. J., asking William to join her. She had located an informant, but he wasn't talking until he was certain of the client.

"I'll leave you to handle the messages and go to Mrs. J."

He and the messenger jumped on their horses and rode to a tavern. The serving wench directed them upstairs where they found her leaning against a wall, pistol pointed at a skinny, poorly dressed, smelly man.

"Who do you have here?" William asked.

She straightened up and waved her gun at the fellow sitting there. "Calls himself Sammy. Says he's done some work for Harrison."

William crossed the room and stood in front of their prisoner. "You expect us to believe that you're familiar with the earl and have worked for him? Why should we?"

"Because it's the sodding truth," he said. "The old codger paid me a pile of coins to follow some gentry Cove and see where he was staying."

"What fellow?"

"I ain't telling you a damn thing until something's in it for me." He looked at Mrs. J. "She's been waving that pistol around as if I'm to believe she knows how to use it and should be afraid. Not bloody likely."

"I am here. Talk to me."

"What's in it for me? Why should I spill my guts and have her shoot my head off before you leave this room?"

William fought off the urge to slap the fellow because it wouldn't do any good. He handed the man one of his calling cards. He tapped it with his index finger. "This says my name, Lord Evans, and it mentions you can reach me through the Duke of Wolfstone." He grabbed the prisoner by his shirt and lifted him from the chair. "Since he is my brother, and he outranks your customer, the earl, by several steps in Debrett's, it is best if you start talking, or we're going to have a serious problem, as will he. In fact, he might go to Harrison and demand to know what he paid you to do. And while he's doing that, he'll tell the man you came to us with information. Now speak up."

"If your brother does that, I'm as good as dead. Meaning regardless of what happens, my future isn't very bright, unless you've got coin to get me away from here until the dust settles."

William dug around in his pocket and pulled out a handful of coppers and dropped them on the table. The man's eyes grew round and huge. It was unlikely he'd seen this much in one place in his whole life. "There's more, if your information is good enough."

"Better be double that."

He placed a gold coin beside the others. "If it's worth this to me, it is yours. But if you're wasting our time. I'm going to help my partner over there," he dipped his head to Mrs. J, "take shooting practice on parts of your body. Talk."

The man glanced around as if to check if anyone could hear him, then leaned close. He was licking his lips as he stared at the coin.

William flinched at the odor wafting up from the informant.

After swallowing a couple of times, the fellow looked up. "The earl used myself and a friend of mine, a woman, for some tasks he needed done. When he sent a messenger with instructions about another job, I took the coins and did as I was told."

"What did he want you to do?"

"He wanted me to watch the front of his house and follow a certain gent when he departed. I was to report back where he ended up and the direction of the place."

"That's all?"

"Told me if he needed more information, he'd get in touch."

"Who was the gentleman you were following?"

"Never heard the man's name," he replied. "When he left, I was given a signal and followed him to a tavern near the docks. The innkeeper said he had been there for almost a week and had paid for the coming one as well."

"When did this happen?"

"I don't keep track of the days so good, Guv'nor. Six or seven, maybe longer."

That information fit in with Harrison hiring Triple E and asking for help, meaning it might be true. "Can you take us to that tavern?"

"Sure, but it'll cost you."

William leaned over and picked up the coin and put it in his pocket, leaving the two coppers on the table. "Then I guess this will be all you're getting, since the crap you've you've given is useless unless we know where he is staying."

The man frowned at him. "You got a lot of nerve coming in here demanding information and my help. Who the hell do you think you are?"

William took the coin from his pocket and flicked it with his thumb into the air and caught it. Then he did it again. The man couldn't tear his gaze away from the sight of the gold sovereign spinning. He licked his lips and leaned forward, as if he would try to grab it.

"That is not something you want to think about doing, old man," warned William. "If you touch this coin before I give it to you, you'll lose your hand. The choice is yours. Take us to the tavern or collect your coppers and be on your way with Harrison hot after you."

Sammy scooped up the coins and put them in his pocket. "Fine. I'll show ye." he said hurrying to the door.

Mrs. J. stepped in front of it. "We can do this easy or hard." She looked at him and narrowed her eyes. "You nicely follow our friend over there down the stairs and outside with Mr. Evans and I at your back. Or we tie your hands behind you and fashion a loop around the rope to make sure you don't try to get away. The choice is yours."

"You are a damned untrusting bunch, but I'll take the easy way. I ain't done nothing wrong, and I got no reason to run."

Mrs. Johnson tipped her head to the messenger and told him to go first, with Sammy following. "Be sure you understand me," she jabbed the pistol into his back, "Do not try anything funny. One bad move and I will blow a hole right through your middle. We are going downstairs and straight through the tavern. We're not stopping, drinking, or talking to anyone."

"Do as you're told. I don't feel like messing up my suit," William said, as he shot his cuffs. "Let's get out of here."

The trip through the pub was uneventful. Nobody even noticed them. Outside, the messenger grabbed Sammy's upper arm. "Mrs. J.'s pistol is still pointed at your back, although she's dropped the point a mite. Best be careful else you could sing with a high voice from now on."

The man whipped his head around to look at her and then his gaze followed the direction she was pointing her gun. "You mind raising that a bit? It's one thing to get shot in the arse, but another to lose my bits."

"You don't have to worry about either, as long as you do what you're being paid to do, which is to bring us to the inn."

"I know. We'll be there soon enough."

William, Mrs. J., and the messenger kept their eyes peeled for someone coming out of an alley or from behind to rescue their friend. He walked quietly and never tried to escape. Thirty minutes later, he pointed down the street to a tavern called The Scared Rabbit. "That's the place. I followed him from Harrison's and after he went upstairs, the innkeeper told me he'd paid for another week."

"Well, let's see if he's still here," William said. "Since you've been here before, ask if our man is here."

"The man won't remember me. There's nothing about me that would stand out in his memory."

It was doubtful anyone would soon forget Sammy's odor. "You're asking for the information we need."

Inside, there was a set of stairs to the right and, to the left, a public drinking room, which was almost empty. A man with a wide smile on his face met them at the door.

"Say, it's you again. Did you want to speak to our guest this time?" he asked Sammy.

"Yes, we would," answered William. "I think he's a friend from school years ago, but I'd have to see him, to be sure."

"Well, that's a funny thing. He paid in advance for this full week, but packed his trunk and left after you were here," he said, looking at their informant.

"Any idea where he went?"

The innkeeper shook his head. "Can't say for certain, since he didn't mention it."

"Is there something you could tell us that you weren't sure about?"

The tavern keeper wiped the corners of his lips with his thumb and forefinger and looked at him. "It's a right funny thing, but my memory works better when my hand holds a coin or two."

He held up a couple of coppers in his fingertips. "This should help you. But I'm in no mood for games and I have no time to waste. Best you be bloody certain what you say will get me to the fellow who was here."

"Here now! I know where he said he was going, but I can't swear that he is there or was telling the truth about his destination."

"Remember this. If we find him, we won't be back, but if we don't, then we'll return and tear this place apart, looking for hints of where he might have gone." William leaned close to the man's face. "Understand?"

The innkeeper nodded, "Of course." He held his palm out for the coins and said, "I heard him say he was going to that new hotel, the big one, near the palace."

"What's the gent's name?"

"He signed the register as Basil Harrison."

All the air was sucked out of the room. William's brain scrambled to reorder the pieces of this case and, in a single second, they settled into place. This man had broken into Harrison's safe, but not to steal anything. Rather, to take something that belonged to him, probably given to the earl for safekeeping.

"Here now! Harrison is the man what sent me to follow the fellow staying here. You must've got the name wrong."

"No, he signed it right here," the innkeeper said, stabbing a line on the page with his finger. "See?"

William saw only a dancing scribble. He stepped aside and turned to Mrs. Johnson. "Take a look and tell me what you read. I want to be sure I'm not making a mistake."

Confused, she looked from him to the ledger. "Basil Harrison."

He nodded. "Thank you. I wanted to be assured I wasn't seeing things." Turning to the innkeeper, he said, "If your information is accurate and we find this man, I'll be back with another coin for you." Then he shook his finger at Sammy. "I don't trust you any further than I can throw you, but I have no further need for you tonight. However, I can't be sure you'll stay out of my way."

"I have an empty room upstairs. We could lock him in there for a few hours. You'd pay for the whole day, but it would keep him here, for now."

"Good idea," William said. He tossed the man another coin. "When my messenger returns for him, he'll give you more if he's still in there."

"What? You can't leave me here. That's not fair. I did what you asked. You owe me more coins, too."

"Have no fear, gents. One of us will return on the morrow with enough for both of you." He tipped his head to the agent. "Escort Sammy to his room." To the innkeeper, he added, "Keep the door locked. I want him here until tomorrow."

As they were leaving, the tavern keeper said, "Funny how many are interested in that man."

"What do you mean?"

"Another fellow was in here looking for him a bit ago. I told him about the move, too."

As soon as Sammy was closed in his chamber, they left The Scared Rabbit, dashing to London's newest hotel.

Mrs. J. and the messenger remained behind while William went inside to inquire about Harrison. After giving his calling card to the clerk, the young man happily said, "Our guest is in room two zero seven. But he has a man with him now. Funny thing, that. They look enough alike to be brothers."

"I am acquainted with the man visiting my friend. I can't wait to see them both." He motioned to the two waiting in front of the hotel.

The three of them ran up the stairs to the second floor and down the hall.

Ear to the door, William heard the loud voice of one man, his employer, shouting at someone. He turned the knob and hurried inside, praying he wasn't too late.

Holding a gun pointed at a gentleman seated on the couch, surprise marked the earl's face. "What the hell are you doing here?" asked Agnes's father.

"I'm here to make sure you don't spend the rest of your life in Newgate for killing a peer of the realm."

Harrison turned his attention to the fellow in the chair and shook the pistol in his direction. "This man is a charlatan. He isn't a nobleman by any stretch of the imagination. He's an escapee from bedlam who thinks he can convince people I stole his birthright."

"You didn't, but your father did."

The earl spun toward William. "What the hell are you saying? You have some nerve! I hired your useless agency to discover who broke into my safe, and you did nothing. Nothing! I had to find the man responsible for the break-in and track him down myself."

"You found him before I did, but you had better information, didn't you? You had already met your elder brother, Basil Harrison?"

He cocked the pistol. "Shut up, asshole, or I'll put an extra hole in you. I am the Earl of Wellburn and he," Colin swung the gun to the man on the chair, "is an imposter who wants to claim my title and position."

William shook his head. "That's not true. He's the legitimate heir and you're not. Your father, in a moment of drunken desire, married an actress by special license, since she wouldn't agree to be his mistress. But once sober, he knew society would never accept her or her children. When he was done with her, he sent her away, assuming no one would be any the wiser and knowing that many women did not survive that journey. After their departure, he courted a daughter of the ton and wed her. That woman is your mother."

"You're full of shit! Why would you believe his lies?" Colin screamed, spittle spraying the room.

"I don't. I only met him this moment, but you've proven me correct, haven't you?" William studied him. Face beet red. Hands shaking. The man was furious and dangerous. He was capable of anything to preserve his title and position in society.

"What was taken from your safe, Colin? I'm betting it was your father's marriage lines—the ones to his legitimate wife. The one he sent to the colonies."

"What the hell do you know? This colonial comes to my door and wants to talk to me about his father! When he showed me the record, I told him there had to be a mistake."

"You promised to check the church registry where my parents were married, but never did. Instead, you put them in your safe and ignored me, your own sibling."

"You are not a relative of mine, you damn swine. You're nothing but a lowlife from the wilderness across the ocean. No sophistication, a god-awful accent, and a lack of any knowledge of your place in the world."

"But he is your half-brother, isn't he? You share a father." William looked at Basil, still on the chair. "How did you find out about your parents' marriage?"

"It was never a secret. Mother was convinced her husband had died or been injured, else he would have come to us. Even after all those years, she believed in the man. When I got older, I didn't agree, but she considered herself married.

"How did you survive?" William asked him.

"She was a decent, hard-working woman who did her best in a new country. She never looked at another man, even though plenty were interested. Instead, she resumed acting in a company to put food on our table. When the parts for a female her age dried up, she managed the costumes, then made them. I'll never forget her sitting hunched over late at night, sewing by candlelight, until her back ached and her eyes were red."

"She sounds like a remarkable woman," William agreed.

"She was a whore. Father had no choice but to send her away, as far as possible, to make sure there'd be no chance of her returning," Colin screamed, spittle shooting from his mouth.

"He made sure of that, didn't he? He paid for his family's passage and gave her coins to set up housekeeping while he claimed responsibility for finishing some things for his father. Only he never planned to follow her. Instead, he was sending his wife and child away to fend for themselves in a foreign land where they were alone and would have no help." William shook his head in disgust. He saw where this man, the fraudulent earl, got many of his attitudes about women and those outside the peerage. They were abhorrent but passed down through his family.

"I want their marriage lines. Where are they?" Colin screamed at his half-brother.

"You won't hurt him until you have the document, so shut up." William looked at the man in the chair. "I presume they're in a safe place?"

He nodded.

"Why did you keep them? Why not burn them? After all, without the lines, this man had insufficient proof of his claim."

"The doddering fool of a clergyman at St. Giles is the same man who married them, and he remembers the marriage, since it isn't often a peer wed at his disgusting little chapel. Since the bastard refused to show me the register, I couldn't destroy it. I had no choice except to keep them."

"Why didn't he speak up when the banns were read for the wedding to your mother?"

"Apparently the church, at father's urging, sent him on a mission to Africa. The fool had no idea about the second marriage and assumed the countess was the bride from years ago."

"I see. The next step is yours, Colin. Since you don't have the lines, you can't destroy them. And there are three more of us who know the truth. Shelley as well, I'd bet, although she is unable to speak to that anymore, can she, since you took her life?"

"That stupid bitch tried to blackmail me. She'd heard a couple of my comments, seen him," he pointed at Basil, "leave with a satchel that he believed contained the lines and some funds to help him return to the colonies." He shook his head. "The nerve! After her note, I sent a message to tell her to meet me. She planned on getting a paid." He scoffed. "Senseless wench. I instructed her to use the coal door, so no one would see us, and I could give her the coin she wanted." He laughed. "Turns out it's easier to break someone's neck than I thought."

"You were downstairs when I arrived."

"Bad stroke of luck there, but I got out without a problem. Left you to clean up the mess."

"Shelley was in the house both times you met with Basil and figured things out. She asked you to share a bit of the bounty you were keeping from the rightful earl." William studied the man holding the gun. "You also killed the footman."

"So what? I had to make the situation such that I could keep watch on what you were doing."

"He'd been in your employ for a long time."

"It doesn't matter. Besides, who'd believe the likes of you? No one!" Harrison spluttered.

"Except the Duke of Wolfstone. And should something happen to me, he will prove my contentions, even without the official lines, meaning you should be very careful before you take another step."

"The man is not rational," said Basil. "I told him I wasn't interested in the title. He could keep it. I wanted to learn what happened to my father and to confront him if he was still alive. I have a business and a life back home. You can imagine my surprise when I was directed to the study, expecting a man a generation older than myself, but I was met by one of my age, who looked enough like me to be my brother."

"It must have been a shock." William glanced from man to man. "Someone already mentioned how much the two of you look alike. There is no doubt you are brothers."

"Bah. He is nothing similar to me."

"I am aware of your opinion, but that doesn't gainsay his appearance."

Colin mumbled something under his breath and the pistol wavered again.

"You are the one with the firearm. Where do we go from here? You can't kill all of us and we have heard the truth."

"I only have to get rid of him," he pointed to his half-brother, "and my troubles disappear."

"As soon as you shoot him, I will take you to the ground and send you to Newgate."

He watched for a twitch or anything to show the desperate man's next action. "The choice is yours."

Colin looked from Basil to him, then to the two by the door.

"Damnit!" He jammed the pistol against his temple and pulled the trigger.

Silence slammed across the room, an echo of the gunshot.

William stepped back, his mouth open but silent.

The earl jerked away and shuddered at the same time.

"Holy shit!" shouted the messenger.

"Spineless worm," Mrs. J. said.

He was at a loss for words. How would he explain this to Agnes? And how could he protect her?

The sitting room was a mess, her father's body crumpled over the settee. What should he do now? The man known as the earl was dead. He couldn't believe it. He'd seen bodies before, but never the moment of death. Taking a deep breath, he looked around again. There were things that had to be done.

Before anyone moved from their spots, the suite door slammed open, and the hotel manager ran in. "What is going on in here?" He saw the body on the floor, shuddered, then noticed the walls and furniture. "Oh my God."

"Do you have the marriage lines?" William asked Basil, who nodded.

"They're in my bag."

"Get them."

The earl rose and stepped around his half-brother and as much of the mess as possible. A moment later, he returned and handed a paper to him. "Here they are."

Holding the document, he moved away from Harrison's body and gave it to Mrs. J. "Review these for me and then send someone to verify the parish record."

She frowned but took the lines and read them. "The earl married Lilith Woods in St. Giles Parrish in July 1759."

"He sent us to Boston in April, just before my birth in June."

"I see." Using a napkin from the table, William wiped several spots from the front of his jacket and waistcoat.

"We must verify the parish register, of course, but it looks like you are the earl. There will be paperwork and a hearing of some sort, but no problem with the transition of the title and estates." He studied the man for a moment. "Have you given any thought to the former countess and their children? The boys both have solid lives, but the daughter is single and at home."

William watched as Basil looked around the room, his eyes drawn to the crumpled body on the floor. Why would a man with a family do this?

"I explained that I wasn't interested in the title or living in England. I had already started arrangements to return and resume my life." He glanced at the fallen form of a brother he hadn't got to know. "I haven't thought of anything past finding the answers I needed. Are you acquainted with the women?"

William nodded, watching the earl carefully. The shock of this could easily cause an apoplexy, although he seemed strong. Stoic even.

"I assume you'll explain to them what happened today? Please be sure they know I didn't come to take the title. I only wanted to confront my father."

"I will." But his heart was howling in rejection of the task. No matter what he said, telling Agnes and her mother about the situation would rip their hearts out. But he would.

"Thank you. Despite the problems, they are still my family. The only one I have." He shook his head. "I traveled here to find my father and something, maybe a relationship for the future."

William looked at the body, his lip curled in distaste. "Is there anything I can do for you before I leave, Lord Harrison?"

"Nothing. Thank you." He glanced at everyone. "I will move to a different room as soon as possible, but I'm here until this is settled."

Extending a calling card, he said, "I'll be in touch, but in the meantime, if you need a thing, even something small, contact me here." He patted the man on the back. "My brother is the Duke of Wolfstone. With your permission, I will speak to him about this. He can guide you through the paperwork, the hearing, and all the activities that must be done to make it as easy as possible."

"If he wouldn't mind, or even if he could direct me to an appropriate solicitor, I would be forever grateful, since you three are the only ones I know in London, besides him," he said, pointing to his half-brother.

William gave his card to the hotel manager, then told Mrs. J. he wanted to talk to his partner before explaining the situation to the Harrison women.

They had considered the idea of speaking to the oldest son first, but agreed that the widow was a strong woman who should have some role in the decision of how this news was shared with her family.

Taking a deep breath, he stopped at the bottom of the steps. The next conversation was necessary, but he had no idea how to begin and couldn't guess how she would react. There was no easy or kind way to say that her husband had taken his life and everything she thought about their past was based on a lie.

He steeled his spine and stepped up to the door. The butler opened it and quickly informed him that the earl was not in.

"I'm aware of that. I would like to speak to the countess."

The servant searched his face, but finally agreed to see if she was in. A few moments later, he returned. "My lady has a few minutes and will meet with you in her salon."

William took a deep breath and tried to moisten his lips. There was no easy way to deliver the news about the events of today. Perhaps he should have talked to the son first. Maybe he should have brought Calliope with him.

No, they agreed the initial conversation should be with the widow to preserve the confidentiality of the moment, as much as possible. This was on his shoulders.

"Young man, I'm unsure why you want to speak to me. My husband mentioned he fired you and your agency for failure to complete your duties. He also asked you to leave our home. He's not here right now, but you need to talk to him, not me."

William walked across the room and sat in a chair next to her. He looked her in the eye and in a very soft voice, he said, "There is no easy way to say this, but your husband, Colin Harrison, has died."

She closed her eyes and shook her head. "What nonsense are you talking about? My husband left here after lunch. He was hale and healthy."

He twisted his linked hands for a second, then faced the woman whose heart he was about to destroy. She was an innocent victim thrown into turmoil by the actions of a man supposed to protect her. "Your husband took his life earlier this afternoon."

All color leached from the woman's face, then she turned beet red with fury. "How dare you?" she screeched. "You think to come into my home and tell me horrible lies like this for what purpose? My husband won't tolerate this blasphemy and when he returns, you will regret your words."

"He is not returning. I am very sorry for your loss."

"Colin was a decent and God-fearing man. I can't imagine anything that would cause him to take his own life. You must be wrong."

"Your husband discovered that...." William swallowed and took a deep breath and straightened his spine. "That his father's legitimate wife and heir had been sent to the colonies before meeting and marrying Colin's mother. His older half-brother came to London to meet his father and find out why the man never joined them in Boston, as expected."

He stopped for a moment to give her time to take in the information he was sharing and to gauge her reaction.

"But the old earl has been dead for years."

"He had questions he wanted answered but had no idea his other parent had passed."

"But... but if he had a wife in the colonies, he couldn't have married Colin's mother."

"You're right, except the first marriage, to an actress, had been a secret. He realized the folly of his action and sent her, carrying his child, to the colonies, leaving him free to marry a girl acceptable to the ton."

"But someone would have known."

"I have seen the lines and can attest to what they say. I ordered an investigator to the parish of St. Giles to review the register and be certain that the first marriage was recorded." He looked at the crying woman. "I think he married by special license, so there were no banns read and then he sent his wife away. While the pastor was in Africa on a mission, he married again. Who would know?" William took her hand. "Who would look at the east end for the wedding of a peer?" He rubbed the back of her hand. "In all likelihood he told anyone who asked that she was his mistress and then he sent he away."

"Did you say St. Giles? Father Harrison never liked that parish and said the pastor was a demanding man who was hard to work with. Although it wasn't in a good part of the city, he went out of his way to avoid it."

"I think we understand why."

"But if he was married before, his second marriage was invalid," she added, her voice going even softer.

He recognized her moment of truth. It was reflected in the desolation of her eyes and the sagging of her shoulders.

She looked directly at him. "You're telling me my husband was illegitimate."

"Exactly."

The woman sat in silence, watching him, then collapsed in despair. "I am not a countess, but the widow of a bastard." Her gaze bounced around the room. "None of this is ours. It belongs to the other man."

Tears ran over her cheeks, and she slumped against the chair, one hand fisted over her heart. She dabbed at her eyes and wiped her nose with her handkerchief. "That would drive my husband to do this horrid thing. Being the earl is all he knew. It was more than a title to him. It was his life." She sobbed, almost choking. "Losing his position and prestige, made everything meaningless."

William reached over and took one of her hands and rubbed the back of it. "I must work with the process to have your brother-in-law named the earl. He asked me to relay the message that you and Agnes are welcome to remain here. He is in no hurry to change anything, at least until the house and the Exchequer courts recognize him. That will give two of you time to determine your next steps, but I would suggest you meet with him first. It doesn't have to be today or tomorrow, but he is family and none of this is his fault. He came to England wanting to know why his father never joined them in the colonies. His mother's love for her husband never wavered, and he wanted to meet the person who held such an important spot in her heart."

"I will meet with him, but I need time to come to terms with this news."

The salon door slammed open, and Agnes burst into the room. "Mother, the butler told me...." She saw William. "What are you doing here?" She hurried to her mother's side and clasped her hand. "What did you say to make mama cry? Wasn't hurting me enough?"

"Hush, daughter. You do not understand why the man is here or why I'm crying. If you don't mind, I'd rather finish this conversation privately, before you and I speak."

"Mother, this man is not to be trusted. Father was well advised to fire him and his firm and remove him from our house."

"Agnes, please. Master Evans and I are having an important discussion. A private one."

CHAPTER SIXTEEN

Agnes shook her head, resolve strengthening. "No, Mother. This man is not to be trusted. I know him better than you do. I will not abandon you with him to discuss anything, never mind something important. It is best we wait for father's return."

"Daughter, thank you for trying to protect me. You love your father, but this is not the time for your interruption. Please leave us to converse in private."

Agnes pushed a chair close to them and dropped into it, determined to end this conversation, causing this pain. "I cannot allow him to hurt you like this." She turned to him. "Mother is sensitive and has been protected all her life. Anything you have to say will be said in front of me."

"It would be better for her and I to proceed in private."

He had already caused this young woman great suffering, now he was doing the same to her parent. It was necessary, but intolerable. Mrs. Harrison was kind and had never harmed anyone and did not deserve this.

"No. You have proven to be untrustworthy, and I won't allow you to continue to harm mother." She took her mother's hand, stroking it. "It is all right. I intend to tell father every nuance of this conversation. It is beyond the pale that you were horribly upset, but I will remain to be sure our family's best interests are protected." She would not permit this bounder to hurt her family as he did her.

Mrs. Harrison broke into fresh tears and pulled her hand away. "For God's sakes, Agnes, go to the attic and look at your telescope while I finish this conversation." She tried to smile at her. "I am grateful for your care and concern, but I can handle this."

Being treated like a little child hurt more than she could say, but she could not allow William to do any more damage. "No. I'm staying here until father returns."

Her mother shook her head and sighed deeply, squeezing her eyes closed, taking her hand and looking at Agnes. "He took his life this afternoon. He isn't coming home. Now leave us to finish our discussion."

The room ceased to exist for a moment and her heart may have stopped. Eventually, she could breathe again. "What? No! Who told you such rubbish?" That wasn't possible. He would never do such a heinous thing. She glared at William. "Are you spreading such vicious lies to my mother? Father will run you out of town."

"Agnes, these are not fabrications. Lord Evans and I are trying to find the best way out of a difficult situation, and your outburst is not helping. You must control yourself if you're going to stay. If you can't do that, then I insist you leave. The decisions of the next hour or two are too important for your outbursts."

How could anyone, especially her mother, believe such a thing of her father? He was far from perfect, but he'd never hurt them in this way. The stigma of such an action would last for generations and, if nothing else, he cared about his good name and the title. Such a vile act was not possible.

Thoughts swirling, an idea to end the pain, surfaced. "Have you told Peter this nonsense?" she asked him. When he shook his head, she said, her voice calm but cold, "I thought not. He's a man, and a solicitor, and you wouldn't dare spread your lies to him." Including her brother would end this madness and force her mother to see the truth, rather than William's lie.

"As your father's wife... widow, he was kind enough to bring this news to me first, giving me time to come to terms with the death of my husband. I will send a message to Peter shortly but have decisions to make."

Mama was overwhelmed by the nonsense spewed to her. She wasn't thinking clearly because of her emotional reaction. Her father could not do such a thing, but the lie had upset her normally calm mother and turned her inside-out. Someone had to save her before she took irreversible action or caused irreparable harm to the family. "I don't agree." Agnes jumped up and raced out of the room, throwing over her shoulder, "I'm sending a message to Peter right now." She ran down the stairs, determined to put a stop to this. Her brother would end this folly.

"Where is the earl?" she asked the butler.

"He didn't say. Only that he would be out for several hours and planned to return for dinner."

"I need a messenger." She raced into her father's study and grabbed a quill and some paper and wrote, 'Peter, you must come home now. There is a problem here you can solve. More information when you arrive.'

She sanded and sealed the note and gave it to the footman. "Start at my brother's office and if he's not there, find him. Your position depends on him returning here immediately."

Then she lifted her skirts and ran upstairs to the sitting room.

"Are you finished feeding my mother your poison?" she asked him, in a soft, sarcastic tone as she settled between them, an arm around her mother's back. It was one thing to treat her poorly, but mama didn't deserve any of this pain.

William rubbed his neck and winced. "I am sorry I have upset you, Agnes. I thought, because of the nature of the information, that it was better delivered by me than a stranger who might gossip about it." His shoulders were pulled low, then he covered his face with his hands. "I am sorrier than you can imagine."

Yesterday, she would have believed him, but not since she'd seen his true colors. "As if you care about my family. Unfortunately, I don't believe anything you're saying, and I will be relieved when father returns home and puts your lies to rest, then kicks you out of the house for upsetting my mother this way."

"Agnes, please, hush now. There is more going on than you comprehend. When the full story comes out, you are going to feel foolish about your behavior today. Regardless of your opinion of this young man, he is giving you and I and our family a major gift of consideration and kindness by being here." Mother studied her for a minute. "I presume you sent a message to your brother?"

"Yes, he should be here shortly."

"Control of my life has slipped through my fingers." Mama looked at William and sighed. "I've always been aware of the limits of my authority, but I appreciate the chance to have a choice in my future. My daughter has taken that from me and my son will have his way." She rang the bell and ordered a tray. "Since there is no point in continuing until Peter arrives, I'm going to have a cup of tea and order my thoughts."

Agnes had never seen this side of her mother, wanting some control over her destiny. Sadness, or perhaps despair, tainted her mother's voice. A tone she'd never heard before and hoped to never hear again.

William took his cup and stood by the window, looking out. The room slid into a gloomy half-light and needed more candles, but she lacked the energy to bother. The man she thought she had come to know—who seemed to share her interest in the sky—was haloed by the setting sun. She swiped the moisture from her eyes.

Drat these tears.

How could she have been this badly fooled? How did she let someone she knew to be cutting and part of society into her attic and her studies? There was no reason for her good sense to have departed and left her wanting his company and needing his presence. And now, after tearing her heart out, he'd hurt her mother in a way she could never forgive.

The door to the suite flew open, and her staid, steady brother Peter raced inside. "What the hell is going on? Agnes sent me a message of a dire emergency, yet the three of you are calmly drinking tea."

"This man," she pointed to William, "has been filling mother's head with ugly fabrications. You must stop him from hurting her and put the situation to rights."

"What?"

Mother settled into a chair and patted the seat beside her. "Come, sit. There's news to hear and decisions to make." She swiped away the tears and choked back a sob.

"What is wrong? What has happened? Why are you upset?"

"Your father.... I can't.... William, please."

Peter wrapped an arm around his mother's shoulder and looked at the other man.

"I presume you're aware that our agency was hired to investigate a break-in to his safe and find the person who snooped through the documents."

"Yes, he told me. They killed a guard the first night, as I recall."

"There are no leads on his murderer, although I have some ideas."

"What is the relationship between that situation and my mother's tears? Get to the point, man."

"My investigation led me to the conclusion that a document was stolen from your father's safe, which he would not admit."

Peter listened and asked many questions.

Eventually, mama said, "The lines were for your grandfather's first marriage. The legitimate one he hid and then ignored after he sent his wife and child away."

Agnes watched her distraught mother, whose hands were shaking, rub her chest. Her lips trembled if they weren't pressed tightly together.

William's flat voice had dropped off on several occasions while explaining the situation. He pinched the bridge of his nose and looked down, as if he couldn't stand to see their pain. A couple of times in the telling, he'd covered his face with his hands and when he spoke of the moment of her father's death, he scratched at a spot on his coat.

Occasionally, he glanced around, as if uncertain where to look, or unwilling to witness the grief filling the room.

It was smothering. Choking her. Scaring the life out of her. And beyond her comprehension or experience. But as she watched Lord Evans, the penny dropped, and she recognized he was telling the truth.

She was as shocked as if she'd discovered a new star or saw a comet through a weak telescope. Like a shower of falling stars, the picture became clear to her. "The lines proved grandfather was a bigamist and father was the son of that illegal union." She had no idea how the investigator had pieced this together, but taken as a whole, it was the only logical reason he would take his life.

Her father had hired William to find the person who'd removed damning evidence from the safe and kept him nearby to follow his inquiries, even demanding he live in their home. It was no wonder her mother was beside herself, hearing news like this. She owed him an apology.

She looked at him for confirmation. "Correct?"

He breathed deeply and nodded, sincerity warming his gaze. "Yes."

Peter jumped to his feet and put his hands out. "I'm not sure I believe a word of this."

Agnes settled on the other side of her mother, who had broken down into choking, breath-stealing sobs. Wrapping an arm around her shoulder, she offered comfort as best she could.

William leaned forward, his arms on his legs. "Basil Harrison came to the house, hoping to meet his father, your grandfather, but was greeted by Colin, who promised to discover the truth of the matter. He took the marriage lines for his research and put them in the safe. When your uncle realized nothing was being done, either he or someone he hired broke into the study and took them. He wasn't interested in anything else but was determined to keep his only link with his past."

"If supported by the parish registry, that would end everything. Father would lose the title, the properties, and his seat in the House of Lords." Peter looked at his mother, then his sister, and finally, at William. "That would be more than he could tolerate."

Her brother's words were shocking.

"That is why he ended his life in your uncle's hotel suite in front of myself and two other witnesses earlier this afternoon."

"Oh my God. Father's gone?" Peter rubbed his eyes with the palms of his hands. "I can't believe it. I don't doubt what you're saying, but this sounds like a bad dream."

He turned to his mother. "You must not worry about the future." Agnes' thoughts drifted away. His voice was a calm background to the swirling emotions in the salon.

Lies. All of it. Their entire life had been built on fabrications by her grandfather—a man she never liked and who had berated her love of studies when she was a child. An early memory of his derision was interrupted by her brother.

"You and mother shall live with us. We'll be delighted and the children will be thrilled to have their grandmama and auntie close to hand."

"Your uncle mentioned that they can remain here until things are settled. He wanted to meet his father and to discover why he'd never shown up, as promised. He had no desire for the titles or anything else and has said he is returning to his home and business."

"Besides reviewing the marriage lines, how do we know this man is telling the truth?" Peter asked. "I don't mean to disparage his intentions, but I've never met him. He could be a very skilled con artist trying to steal the assets of the title."

"My firm sent an investigator to St. Giles parish to review their register. If both agree, then action to name the new earl will be started. In the meantime, Basil is comfortable where he is and insists he's in no hurry to move into this house."

William looked at them. "You, your uncle, and three people from my firm know the entire story and are sworn to silence. But with the hotel manager having a body in one of his rooms, news of your father's death could spread quickly."

Agnes looked at the others in the room. "We must make decisions about laying father to rest."

Peter nodded. "Legally, since he is still the earl, we could bury him in the family crypt. But," he held up his hand, "it is unseemly to do that only to be forced to move him soon after."

Agnes shuddered. She hadn't thought of that. None of this was his fault. "Father is as much a victim in this as the other gentleman. We need to inter him with dignity and love, somewhere he won't have to be moved." She couldn't imagine his desperation, the terror at losing all he valued.

Everything they had was part of the estate. He owned nothing and the moment the title passed to his half-brother, they could be on the street with nowhere to go.

Choosing to end his own life was horrendous, but he probably felt like it was the lesser evil of the choices in front of him. Or his thinking was confused, as hers had been when she first found her mother crying, that this seemed to be the only choice.

Her damned grandfather. That old reprobate caused all this pain and misery, all because he couldn't face the ton with a wife, an actress, he'd chosen. Instead, he manipulated everything and everyone to keep his dirty secret, and eventually destroyed the lives of those he left behind.

Bastard.

William put up his hand to stop the conversation. "At this moment, your father will be treated as the earl. The Duchess of Wolfstone, Doctor Juliette Evans, runs a clinic. She helped me handle a woman's remains. May I suggest we take him there while you decide? I also think it would be wise to speak to your uncle. He strikes me as a decent sort, although our acquaintance is limited. Perhaps he can help with decisions about the burial."

Peter looked at his mother and then his sister. "You are the wife of Colin Harrison, and the three of us are his legitimate issue. But when news of grandfather's falsity gets out, and it will, we should expect to stand alone as a family. Some of my legal practice will disappear and there is no certainty of Andrew continuing to serve his parish. In fact, the church may strip him of his collar, since he's the son of an illegitimate man."

Their lives were about to be turned upside down. She had spent most of her life isolated from the ton, but this would be worse, for the upper ten thousand would delight in her pain.

Her brother reached over and patted Agnes again. "The next few weeks will be difficult." He looked up at William. "I think I should face this man. It's not that I don't trust you, but I would like to examine the marriage lines for myself."

"I would do the same thing," the agent replied. He pinched his lower lip between his thumb and finger. "We can dispatch a messenger. Today has been exhausting for him, but he wanted to meet you. As a colonial, he likely has no idea of the impact this will have on your family."

"You've sent an investigator to St. Giles. Is that correct?" Peter asked.

"Yes, she is on her way."

"I'm going to send a message to Andrew to return home immediately. He too can verify the parish register for grandfather's first marriage." Her brother shook his head. "Although why an earl should deign to marry in that place is beyond me."

"I think we know why. No one would expect such a thing, nor look at their records."

"Having a man of the church examine it is an excellent idea, Peter." His mother looked at the investigator. "My son might be better able to see anything unusual."

"I'm surprised grandfather didn't have the parish record destroyed."

"I doubt he thought it necessary," William said. "After all, he'd sent his wife and baby to the new world and encouraged the church to send the pastor to Africa on a mission. Who would know about that marriage? That long ago, a young woman and infant rarely survived the journey, and few men of the cloth returned home in good health. It's likely he saw no reason to bring attention to the parish records."

"He was a real bastard," Agnes declared, squeezing her brother's hand. "I'm glad you're here. I've been listening but sometimes miss some of it, but I am confident you are making appropriate choices."

Their decisions were reasonable. She studied William through her lashes and knew she'd wronged him horribly, mostly because she was upset. Needing to make that right, she wiped her eyes, then looked up at him. "I apologize for my earlier outburst. It was unseemly and unfair."

He held up his hand as he watched her. "No apology is necessary. Strong reactions are natural when hearing bad news."

Voice subdued, Agnes said. "Thank you for understanding. But if you will excuse me, my head is swimming with all these details. I need to lie down for a while, lest I get a megrim. If you require me for anything, please rouse me." She looked at her mother, who still sat ramrod straight, no part of her back touching the chair. "What about you? There's nothing more we can do now. Let me walk you to your room."

Her mother's eyes darted up to hers. "Thank you." She rose, leaned on her daughter, and walked out of the salon. The strong woman, who stood tall, was trembling and allowing Agnes to support some of her weight. Would she ever recover from this situation? Or would she lose her remaining parent to this debacle?

Both men watched the women walk away.

"I can't imagine how difficult this must be for your mother." Eyes filled with sympathy, William looked at the man sitting across from him. "Or for any of you."

Peter shook his head and shrugged his shoulders. "While this is very troublesome, the next few months are going to be worse, especially for mama. She is used to the social whirl of town and the season. Losing her friends will hurt in many ways."

"My family is willing to help as much as possible, but the situation is complicated." William rose to his feet. "Perhaps we should send those messages now. The sooner we get the process started, the better."

Peter stood and led the way. "I agree. Father's good liquor is in his study. I'm ready for one and probably two drinks while I craft that note to my brother."

At the doorway, he stopped and looked around. "This epitomized stability and common sense. I knew I wouldn't change a thing in here when I inherited." He took another look at everything, then crossed to the desk and faced William. "This could well be the last time I'm ever in here." He shook his head. "That seems unbelievable, but likely." Then he busied himself retrieving paper, ink, and quills. He pulled the chair up behind him and sat down, taking a quill in hand. "What words do I use to tell my brother that his life is about to be torn apart? That he has to come home and face the music with the rest of his family?"

Lacking an answer to the man's question, William remained silent. "Would you like me to ask Allwyn to attend the meeting between you and your uncle?"

"That's a good idea. But I would prefer to meet my uncle first. Perhaps an hour for we three before your brother joins us?"

"How about ten at the hotel? Then the duke can arrive at eleven."

"That is fine. Thank you." Peter scratched a page of notes, sanded it, and sealed it. "I would feel safer if your men delivered this to Andrew."

William penned his note to Allwyn and then, a second to the new earl and took Peter's. "Someone will be on the road within the hour."

Harrison threw back his scotch, poured another finger in the glass, and swallowed it quickly. He stuck out his hand. "Thank you for everything. By the time this is over, I won't ever be able to repay you."

"I doubt that. If you need me tonight or before our meeting, send a message. I'll be at Wolfstone."

William left him standing facing his father's desk, head bowed. As the butler opened the front door, crystal shattered against the fireplace.

Good for you, Peter.

After returning to Louis', William updated him on all that happened while at the Harrison's. "And we must talk to Basil about Colin's service and burial." He confirmed one of their agents had been sent to see Pastor Andrew.

"I've never seen you this fussy about the details of a case before." His brother held up his hand. "I'm only saying this situation seems to be extra important to you."

"It is. A man took his life and left his family potentially destitute, rather than face the damage caused by his father. HIs act will destroy everything they know."

"And Agnes Harrison is not skilled at handling social situations, difficult or not."

"No, she's not, but she has improved. I don't want this mess to cause her to fall back."

"Your kindness knows no bounds for the lady." Louis laughed. "Are you asking Henry or I to stand as your best man?"

"You're being ridiculous. I haven't time for such nonsense." William waved his sibling off. "The woman can barely tolerate me." He left, jumped on his horse and rode to Wolfstone, muttering to himself about his outrageous brother, making up stupid scenarios and teasing him about them.

Arriving, he called for Juliette and asked her to join him in Allwyn's study.

"You are here, and you look well," she said. "What do you wish to speak to us about?"

"I have a long and complicated story, and I'll need your help to resolve it."

"Is this about your case?"

William nodded. "Yes, the late Colin Harrison."

"What the hell?" Allwyn roared.

"He took his life a few hours ago. We've done our best to keep the information quiet until decisions are made."

"But the man has to be buried on the estate, doesn't he?" Juliette asked.

He repeated the whole sordid tale again. No matter how many times he gave voice to the facts, he still couldn't believe he was caught up in it.

His sister-in-law shuddered. "All this pain because of a title and some property. Now three people are dead."

William explained the rest of the situation and they agreed to help him. "Louis sent a wagon to retrieve Harrison's body. We thought to put him in your cold room overnight until the new earl and his nephew discuss the way forward." He looked at his brother. "Since you are likely aware of the process, I wondered if you could join Basil, Peter Harrison, and I at the hotel tomorrow at eleven? The two men will have met and chatted before you get there. Hopefully, he understands the enormity of what's happened for the family and the future."

Juliette jumped to her feet. "I'll send a message to Pierre and Elise about the remains coming to the clinic. They'll know what to do with him. I'm to the Harrison home to offer my condolences and support to his widow and daughter. Both women need that right now. And you can be assured we will use our rank to help the family as word gets out." She kissed her husband on the cheek and hurried out of his study, calling for her pelisse, bag, and reticule on her way to the door.

Allwyn went to the liquor table and lifted a decanter to his brother. "Care to join me?"

"Definitely. I've earned it today."

The duke poured, then handed a glass to William. "Great job resolving this case. You should be proud of yourself."

"I am glad we know what happened and why. But telling the man's wife, daughter and son was the most difficult thing I have ever done. It's something I pray I never have to do again."

"Delivering bad news to a loved one is much harder than speaking to a stranger. Neither is easy, but the first is beyond comparison."

"Mrs. Harrison and her children are not strangers, but we're not particularly close. Nevertheless, that was difficult." His relationship with Agnes was worse than ever. Between his reaction to her gift and bringing such terrible news to the family, she would only look at him with anger in the future.

"I sensed that you and the daughter were becoming closer."

"There's no possibility of anything between her and I, after I spoke to them this afternoon. I will forever be the reminder of the worst of times to her."

CHAPTER SEVENTEEN

After her nap, Agnes woke up, eyes burning and head pounding, wanting nothing more than to remain abed. She was still reeling from the news. Any of the three, father's suicide, his illegitimacy, and his attempt to keep the title, was enough to knock a person off her stride. But all together, made cocooning under the covers seem like a great idea.

The door opened, and her maid stepped in. "I thought you might wake soon," the girl said. "I brought some cool water and linens for your eyes."

"Thank you, but it's unlikely I'll ever leave this room again."

"That's not true. One day, you'll marry that investigator who's kept you company in the attic."

Agnes snorted. "He has moved out of our home and returned to his own. I doubt I will be seeing him in the future."

"Do you want some dinner? Or some hot chocolate?"

Her stomach revolted at the thought of food. "No, thank you. You can leave the water and linen over there," then she turned on her side, her back to the door and the maid.

Sleep was nearly impossible. Sometimes her headache woke her. Other times it was her tears, but she had a pounding megrim, a sore throat, and swollen, bloodshot eyes.

Unable to bear the thought of remaining in bed for another moment, she rose and rang for toast and tea. Crossing to the window, she moved the drape. The sun shone in a clear, blue sky. She couldn't believe it. Today should have had clouds, snow, and cold temperatures.

She donned her wrapper, slipped into her slippers, and trudged to her mother's room. Without knocking, she entered her private quarters. "What are you doing, mother?" she asked, watching her standing at the table, bent over, pushing around her jewelry.

"I am sorting it. Some of these pieces are included in the entailment. But there are some I brought with me to the marriage or received as gifts after I wed that I will take with me. And this group over here," she pointed to a third pile, "are from your father. Since I don't know if these count as personal or part of the estate, I'm setting them aside."

Agnew walked to her mother's side and rubbed her back. "Have you slept at all?"

"There was no point in trying. Every time I closed my eyes, I came up with a new item or task that must be completed before we leave." She looked around. "Your brother has promised you and I accommodation with his family. It is a most generous offer, and I am very appreciative. But there will not be room for your telescope, nor for your experiments. It is best if you pack it away. We don't know how long we'll remain here, and I'd rather be safe than sorry."

Her mother's words cut to the heart, but she was right. She should feel grateful they had a place to live. But she was uncertain of the value of living if she couldn't study, research, and learn. What would she do with herself all day? How would she pass the time? What would be the point of rising?

These decisions were exhausting. Necessary, but could be made tomorrow. "You have a good start on sorting your jewelry and I will begin to pack up my equipment and supplies. I don't know what to do with the telescope." She held up her hand. "It can't move with me. But I am not acquainted with anyone who would want it either. Inquiries in the community might provide direction."

She reached out. "Come, mother. You must sleep, or you will be in no condition to stand by father during his service. I'll ask your maid to bring some laudanum to help you."

"I do not want that. Nor do I wish to doze. We don't have to worry about standing beside Colin when he's laid to rest, because the church won't bury him since he took his own life. More than likely, he'll be rolled into a pauper's grave, along with all the other bastards of London."

The Church's position on the burial of suicides had not crossed Agnes's mind, but her mother was right. Her father couldn't be buried in the crypt or in the cemetery in the village.

Usually, a family member would lie in state in a salon. "Where is he?"

"The Duchess of Wolfstone stopped by last night. Your father's remains are in a cold room in her clinic, giving us time to decide what to do. She also offered her help and support, however, this turns out. She is a remarkably kind lady, but I explained we don't need anything yet, and said I would send a message if that changed."

Agnes was grateful the Duchess had already made a courtesy call to her mother after learning what had happened from William.

"Your brother and the young man are meeting with your uncle this morning. Later, the duke is joining them. Afterwards, we will have a better idea of how we're going forward."

"That's excellent news. But since decisions are necessary today, I insist you rest, even if you won't sleep. You need to be at your best for the next few days."

Her mother looked at her bed and then at Agnes. "You are right. I will lie down for a while, but promise to wake me when Peter arrives."

After removing her mother's wrapper and settling her under the covers, she felt like a parent attending a sick child.

She stuffed the urge to scream when she faced the piles of jewelry. It was bloody unfair mama had to suffer because her grandfather was a dishonest sack of horse manure, who wouldn't meet his commitments. It wasn't fair.

A piece of paper lying on the floor beyond the bed caught her attention. Her brother's note explained about their meeting and assured his mother that he and William would return to the house as soon as possible.

She raced to her suite, calling for her maid. She was joining them, whether or not they wanted her there. This was hers and mother's future they were discussing, and she demanded a say in that.

Breaking all of society's rules, Agnes made her way to the hotel, knocked, and fidgeted outside the room, waiting for someone to let her in.

Finally, a man opened the door. "May I help you?"

Agnes's breath caught in her lungs. Her uncle looked like her father, especially the shape of his face and his square chin. It was disquieting.

"Miss?"

"I'm sorry. Shock stole my voice for a moment." She stuck out her hand. "I am Agnes Harrison, your niece."

"How lovely to meet you! Please come in." He pulled the door wider and extended his hand, welcoming her inside. "I am Basil, as you probably assumed."

She lifted the heavy black netting covering her to the shoulders. "I understand my brother and a family friend are meeting you at ten this morning. Since I too am affected by these changes, and I assume they forgot to tell me, I came on my own."

He was facing her, a broad smile on his face. "I am glad you did. I am a bachelor and an only child. To discover I have a niece and nephews is a miracle." He extended his hand. "Please take a seat and I will ring for tea."

Before Basil returned to her side, another knock drew his attention. "That must be my other guests." He welcomed both men inside, where Lord Evans performed introductions.

William seemed at ease in the situation, but it wasn't his family falling apart. She would remember his kindness yesterday, despite her attacks. He could have left and let the gossip bring them news of her father's death but had done the kind thing. It was reminiscent of their first waltz when he'd connected music and math for her and made her an acceptable dance partner at ton events.

"I can't believe the resemblance. You could be me twenty or twenty-five years ago," Basil said to his nephew.

"And you look like my grandfather."

"I am very sorry for your father's death. If I had guessed these results, I would have stayed away."

Before the conversation continued, both men noticed Agnes on the settee, watching them.

"What are you doing here, sister? Do you understand the repercussions to your reputation if someone recognized you?" Peter admonished.

"This situation means I have none and there is little, if any, hope for the future. Therefore, at a minimum, I intend to take part in these discussions." She turned to Basil. "Thank you for including me."

Agnes watched her uncle and saw the sensations of overwhelm and shock on his pale face and wide eyes. It was similar to her experiences during her first few conversations with William.

"While I admit a feminine presence is unusual, there's no one here to gainsay my decision to welcome you. I'm sure our decisions will affect you as well." He extended his hand to the men. "Please be seated."

Peter took the seat next to Agnes, while the investigator remained standing, speaking with her uncle.

"There are some significant choices to be made," he said. "The most pressing is Colin's burial. His remains are resting in a medical clinic, but can't stay there for long."

"I assume there is some sort of family cemetery."

"Yes," Peter nodded. "At the estate. But because father took his life, he can't be entombed in sacred ground."

"It is the same in Boston." Basil looked from sister to brother. "The final decision is yours. But it was my arrival that started the chain of events which led to his death. I have no opinion about where he's buried. Whatever meets the needs of his family, and his faith, is agreeable to me. Do what feels right to you."

Peter held his sister's hand, while William and her uncle looked at her brother. "My parents made their home in London most of the year, but father grew up on the estate and I'm sure he would prefer to spend eternity there. Perhaps a spot next to the family cemetery? Gravediggers are rampant in the city, making it a poor choice."

William interjected. "That's a plan. My sister-in-law will prepare him for travel. If you organize a wagon, we can bury him quickly."

Agnes spoke up. "I like the idea of burying father at home. I wonder if Andrew could say some words without creating any difficulty with his bishop or the church?"

Listening to this conversation stole her breath. It wasn't beyond her comprehension, but it hurt to hear these details discussed factually and without emotion. Was this part of the reason women were excluded from these situations? Her mother would not be able to manage this discussion. Perhaps, instead of control, could men be trying to protect them? She'd never considered such an idea, and it gave her pause until she forced her attention back to the room.

Blinking rapidly to stop her tears, she squeezed her brother's hand. She didn't know what she expected, but nothing this difficult. Without becoming a puddle, despite mourning the loss of her father, she would contribute, else the men would set her aside. It took a strong woman to attend a situation like this. This meeting was showing her a new depth to her strength.

"The other thing we must discuss is the assignment of the title to its rightful holder," William announced.

"I don't want it," Basil said. "My life and business are in Boston and I am returning there. I assumed Colin's oldest son would take it."

"English law does not work that way. There are some legal processes to be completed for the change to be formalized, but you are now and, since the death of your father, have been the earl, regardless of your feelings on the matter, or where you live."

"But I choose not to be. Can't I just give it to my nephew? He'd be a better nobleman than I."

"Again, no. You hold it until you die. Then it and the estates will pass to your first-born son. Should you fail to leave an heir, then everything, including the entailments, return to the crown."

"Good God, no!"

"Exactly our sentiments."

"You're telling me I am the earl, like it or not, and if I want to protect the property and my family's title, I have to marry, and sire a male child?"

"That is correct."

"But what about my brother's family? What happens to them?"

Agnes respected the man for asking. For the first time in hours, one of the bands constraining her lungs released a bit.

"That is up to you," William said.

She lifted her teacup, but her hands were trembling too much and she returned it to the table. This was the answer that gave her nightmares and caused mother's lack of sleep.

Basil turned to Agnes and took her free hand. "I suggest that you and your mother remain in residence. I can't see a time when I would need such a grand house, but since I am learning many things today, the future may cause changes."

She sagged against the settee in relief. She had been terrified by the idea of moving. They discussed several more practical items when a knock interrupted the conversation. "That is likely my brother," Lord Evans said, going to the door.

He introduced Allwyn to everyone and mentioned their previous meeting, then moved behind the settee. To her, the new arrival looked more like a hawk than a wolf. He should be Hawkstone. She chuckled softly.

William leaned over to her. "What has amused you?"

"Nothing." This close, she wanted only to lean into him. What was wrong with her? This was the man who betrayed her. And despite his kindness yesterday and how he seemed today, best she never forget that pain.

The duke removed a sheaf of papers from his case and Agnes knew they were moving into the part of the meeting she cared little about. Rising, she said, "Gentlemen, if you will excuse me, I must take my leave. I lack any desire to become familiar with the inner workings of the house or any other political process."

Her brother agreed. "I shall accompany you to the carriage."

Before they moved, William came to her side. "There are many details to be discussed, Peter, and it would probably be best if you remain here. With your permission, I'll escort Agnes downstairs."

Her brother's eyes narrowed as he studied the investigator, looking for something. Finally, he nodded. "Fine, but don't be long."

She looked at William, uncomfortable about being alone with him, and shook her head. "I found my way up here by myself and can return without getting lost. Thank you for your offer of assistance."

He placed her pelisse over her shoulders and waited until she lowered the netting over her face. "Shall we go?" he asked, hand on her back, giving her no additional chance to disagree.

"Is your carriage downstairs?"

She nodded.

"Then all of London knows you're here." Closing the door behind them, he walked to her side.

"Basil seems like a decent man."

"He does. Society will fawn over him as the new earl."

"While they cut my family and I because of the sins of my grandfather."

"I shall try to help with that."

She wasn't sure what he meant, but it didn't matter. They were entering a year of mourning. There would be no balls, soirees, or social calls. By the end of that time, her immediate family would be dead to the upper ten thousand.

William helped Agnes into her carriage and watched it drive away. Deep lines on her face and purple bruises under her eyes said she hadn't slept well. He wanted nothing more than to draw her close and hold her against him and share some of his strength. But that wasn't possible. Her reactions to the events of the last two days were predictable, and he would be lucky if she ever spoke to him again, given how badly he'd hurt her.

His heart stuttered as he watched her drive away. He could do little to change the situation, but he might be helpful to those at the meeting upstairs.

Later that day, they escorted Basil to the townhome in Mayfair. After introductions, the two older people retired to Mrs. Harrison's sitting room, leaving William and Peter to have a drink in the study.

"Where is Agnes?" Her brother asked the butler.

"Miss Harrison is resting and requested not to be disturbed."

"Thank you." Peter turned to William. "Good. She was exhausted this morning."

Before anything more was said, Andrew arrived and was introduced. "I'd like to pay my respects to father."

"He's not here. His remains are being prepared for travel. We can't bury him in London, leaving the estate as our only option."

The youngest son dropped into a chair. "That's a good idea. Now will someone tell me what happened?" He looked from William to Peter. "By the way, I stopped at St. Giles and checked the registry. There is an old entry for Grandfather and a woman I've never heard of. What's that about?"

His brother explained the family history revealed in the last couple of days.

Andrew went to the liquor tray and poured himself a scotch, threw it back and served himself a second. "With such news, I need these," he said, returning to his seat, glass in hand.

"Our uncle says mother and Agnes can remain in the house as long as they want. I've also invited them to reside with us. Either alternative is fine."

"Where will he live?"

"For now, he's remaining at the hotel."

"That's changed," announced Basil from the door as he and the former countess joined them. He crossed the room, extended his hand to Andrew, and introduced himself. Then the pastor wrapped his mother in a hug and held her close.

"You are here just in time. In the morning, the family will form a cavalcade and accompany your father's remains to the estate. He'll be laid to rest next to the cemetery, but outside of it," she said.

"After fencing the plot, I'll have a small crypt built to keep him safe," Basil added.

"Thank you. His suicide complicates everything," Andrew added.

"It does, but we'll honor the man who did no wrong until overwhelmed by his loss. I can't blame him for taking desperate action when he felt he had no choice," Peter said.

"I cannot conduct a service, but I can lead our prayers."

"We were hoping you would say that." The eldest brother turned to William. "I would appreciate if you'd accompany us. You've been an integral part of everything and I respect your opinion."

"Of course. It would be my honor."

"There is other news," Mrs. Harrison said. "After some discussion, Basil and I agreed that he'll move into this house. I'll take another suite and assist as he assumes his duties."

"That was a quick decision. What brought that about?" Peter asked.

"This is Basil's home, and he should live here. Agnes and I are in deep mourning and shan't be in public, but I will manage his household while he settles into the title and takes up the mantle of his responsibilities."

Basil looked at his sister-in-law. "I am most grateful for Odile's assistance. I have no idea how to run this house, nor how to go on in society. She has agreed to help me with both." He smiled at the group. "And I understand we have a scientist in the family, which means she doesn't have to look for space to conduct experiments nor move her telescope to study the stars."

William couldn't argue with the logic. It made sense for Basil to support his female relatives. There was no room for gossip, nor was there any chance for misunderstanding since he must find a wife of childbearing years.

"It sounds like everything is under control. The wagon and I will join you here early in the morning." William said. "My sister-in-law has provided a large quantity of ice for the journey. Given the temperature, Mister Harrison should travel easily."

Agnes should be here, but no matter how much he craved a conversation with her, that was not to be. He understood the risk when he denied their relationship, but it hurt more than he expected. He missed her mind, her voice, and how she felt against him.

T he early morning was cold and clear. Agnes could see her breath as she settled next to her mother in the carriage, wrapping a robe over them and putting her feet on a heated brick. Thankfully, they weren't going far.

Three hours later, the caravan reached the estate, her home for her entire life. It was where she first discovered the beauty of mathematics and became fascinated with the stars when she was supposed to be sleeping.

For the last thirty minutes, Basil had ridden near the carriage, asking questions, and making comments to the two women. When they pulled through the gate to the drive, he took off his hat and wiped his brow. "Are you telling me this is the family seat of the earldom? I can hardly believe it's mine, since I've done nothing to earn it."

On the ride, her mother explained the plans for the future, which meant she could continue her studies. "He insisted I keep the jewelry I received as gifts," her mother said, "which is more than kind." Only the pieces that were entailed would go to his future countess.

Agnes was glad to get out of the carriage, despite the cold. She needed to move around after sitting so long. And since she couldn't sleep any more, she'd broke her fast early this morning, and hunger was making itself known.

Her oldest brother dismounted and stood beside their uncle. "You will earn every acre and pence, as you take up responsibilities in the House of Lords, for your tenants and your future family. Then you must find a wife and sire an heir and a spare, to ensure the smooth transition of the title."

Andrew agreed. "First, let's go inside and warm up. After introducing the staff, and giving them time to pay their respects, we'll lay father to rest."

On the wide steps leading into the house, the servants stood in a half-circle, waiting for them. Snow crunched beneath his feet as Peter walked to face them at the foot of the stairs. He thanked them for their service to his family and introduced the new earl.

Her uncle made appropriate comments to each person, assuring them positions were secure and that nothing would change. He indicated the wagon carrying her father and offered the opportunity for each of them to pay their final respects before the burial.

A black ribboned wreath hung on the door and all the Christmas decorations were gone. As the family made their way inside, William stepped beside her and extended his arm. She glanced up at him and whispered, "Thank you."

While everyone moved into the salon for tea and drinks, Agnes went upstairs to check on her smaller telescope, which was also in the attic.

While still making adjustments, the door opened and William walked in. "How did you find me? Or even know how to get here?"

"Your mother noticed I was looking for you and provided directions over Peter's dissent."

"Really?"

He nodded. "She said something about mending things." He crossed the room. "How are you? I can't imagine how difficult this must be for you or your family, but you've been silent about the whole thing."

She wasn't sure how to answer him. A week ago, she would have thrown her arms around him and shared her feelings. But not anymore. She no longer trusted him.

"I'm fine," she shrugged. "As much as anyone who's discovered their illegitimate father committed suicide."

"Juliette says that whatever reaction you're having is normal. That when we lose someone, it is common to experience a range of emotions, from one extreme to the other. There is no right way to grieve, there is just yours, and it's all that matters."

"Please thank her for her words of wisdom. I will keep them in mind. And repeat that, in this moment, I'm fine."

He pointed to her telescope. "I am glad you came up to look at the sky. It says that some of the old Agnes is still there." His gaze was warm and caring, except she knew better.

Despite his perfidy, she was glad he checked on her, but lest he think all was forgotten and forgiven, she put up her hand to keep him at a distance. "There is only this one, betrayed by a friend and her father, because they weren't honest."

She stared at him for a moment, a new idea in mind. "When you rejected my gift, did you know about my father's transgressions? Were you distancing yourself from the shame it would bring?" She could hear the hysteria in her voice, but couldn't seem to stop the words from tumbling out. "Perhaps the wonderful William Evans could accompany a smart social misfit, but as the untitled daughter of an illegitimate man that became too much for you to bear."

He dropped his head and took a deep breath. "I knew something was amiss in our investigation, but I swear," he lifted his right hand, "on my honor, I had no idea of what was really going on."

"How can I believe you?"

"This is the truth. I was in your father's employ to find the person who went through his safe. I found some of his comments about those events unsettling. They certainly didn't justify the murder of a servant. But I knew little more than that."

"What else did you know?"

"It doesn't matter. We are here to bury him. Let's give him the dignity of a quiet day."

"Well, it's all out now, isn't it? There's nothing to hide."

"Dammit, Agnes. Do not push me. Some things are better left unspoken."

"What are you keeping from me? There must be something you're not saying. What is it? Tell me right this minute, if you have a shred of respect for me."

He sighed heavily. "It would be inappropriate for me to discuss anything more."

She nearly lunged at him. "Well, isn't that convenient? There's more bad news, but you can't say. I'll have to take you at your word, but we both know how much that is worth."

"My investigation is confidential and I won't discuss it." He dropped his gaze, then said, "I can see now that coming up here to check on you was a mistake. I'll excuse myself and return to the others." He left, not bothering to close the door behind him.

The open door told her he did not need a barrier to stay away from her. He could leave without concern. Not that she minded. She shook her head. She didn't mind in the least. Whatever she'd thought was between was obviously a figment of her imagination and best left in the dust, just as she dropped a hypothesis that had been proven incorrect.

But what had he known and when? What other secrets did her father have? What else could there be? Maybe William had noticed more in her father's safe than he let on. She would watch him, because he would betray his silence in some way. It was only a matter of time.

Mind made up, Agnes left the attic, closing the door behind her. She joined the others in the salon and then they moved into the dining room for lunch, where the candleholders were wrapped in black ribbon and the white linen tablecloth had a black runner down the middle.

Attentive of the hour, after their meal, they accompanied her father to his burial site and placed the box containing his body in the open grave.

Her brother, without his clerical collar, asked them to pray with him. Then Peter handed out hymnals from the chapel and invited everyone to join him in father's favorite hymn, Amazing Grace.

Sharing the books, they flipped through the pages, looking for the song. William declined, insisting the family have theirs first. Determined to watch him, she moved closer and held hers, allowing both to follow, but he never looked down. Instead, he stared straight ahead, eyes closed, lips pressed together.

For a moment, his presence strengthened her, but then she remembered his behavior and frigid words. She had apologized for lashing out, but he remained cold. Even his visit to the attic had been difficult.

After a couple of moments, her mother sang the first line and everyone joined in, except him.

After nudging him with her elbow, he looked at her and then down to where her fingers followed the words, to show where they were. He shook his head and glanced at the sky.

What was the man's problem? No one in this group had a stellar singing voice. He had been all that was respectful to her father and the situation, but he wouldn't sing a hymn as they covered the coffin. It made no sense. And it was insulting.

She remained graveside with her mother after everyone left. While walking away, William looked back over his shoulder and shook his head. Going home, she'd have time to consider his actions and see if she could figure out his secrets.

CHAPTER EIGHTEEN

Their trip to London was uneventful. Through the window of the carriage, Agnes studied William and considered his behavior since the investigation started. Her opinion about him had changed dramatically as they became acquainted, and his kisses had given her a new experience. But then he'd refused to sing at the service, while standing in silence at the graveside.

The next morning, the men were in her father's study. The safe had been opened, and its contents spread across the desk.

"Do you mind if I join you?" Agnes asked.

"Of course not. Have a seat," her uncle responded.

She sat across from William, her gaze drawn to him.

They were reviewing the documents. Everyone except him followed the same routine: they read a bit on the first page, then scanned the following pages, stopping to study a line or paragraph.

It seemed he was doing the same thing, but sometimes his eyes were closed for more than a blink. Other times, he looked over one too quickly to read a single word.

Later, when they discussed what to do with the documents, William added nothing new from his stack. Instead, he listened to the others and made suggestions that pulled their preferences together.

They agreed to ignore the information her father was reviewing for the House of Lords. And yet, when commenting on something else, he tapped that sheaf of papers. After returning the documents to the safe and closing it, then realized they had missed one stack. Her uncle spun the dial, placed those, and closed it again.

"How did you know the combination?" Agnes asked.

"The first time I was here, your father and I had an extensive conversation, including our birthdates. He used his birthday when he opened it to set their marriage lines inside. When it became apparent he wasn't doing anything about the situation, I came to the house late one night, through that window," pointing to the front of the room, "and retrieved my document." He looked around at everyone. "Breaking in was wrong, but this was the only record I had of my parents' wedding, and I was determined to keep it." He scratched his chin and said, "I'm surprised he didn't burn it, given his reaction."

"That did no good, because the record remained at St. Giles. It is likely father would have visited that parish when the pastor was away, to avoid bringing attention to his search. Without a reason to go there before Christmas, he was biding his time." Peter shook his head. "It is beyond belief to calmly discuss father's motivation for an illegal act. I never thought to see the day."

"Uncle Basil, where was the guard the night you broke in?" Agnes asked.

"The room was empty."

She turned to William. "But there was a footman in here. He was murdered."

He nodded. "That's correct."

"But the document was already missing."

"It is my opinion that your father hired me to find the marriage lines without telling me about them. He explained that certain documents in his safe had to do with national security and therefore the safecracker had to be found and brought to justice. His stated concern was that someone had read them to determine what information the country had collected." William looked away and then back at her. "He was a respected member of the house, and I had no reason to doubt him."

"Did you review any of the papers in his safe?" Agnes asked, wondering if that's why he hadn't reviewed them today.

"No. As soon as your father mentioned their confidential nature, I kept my distance."

William had read none of them.

"You are more disciplined than I, for my curiosity would drive me to discover the information in them."

"Mine was focused on solving an investigation. I did not need to be aware of the contents of the documents, but who wanted them."

His answer sounded superb, but something was missing.

Agnes' life seemed to revolve around her questions, which never stopped coming at him. That damn songbook had been unexpected, as had been her reaction. He'd felt her gaze on him the entire trip back to London. And this morning was more of the same.

"Has your curiosity extended to finding the murderer of the guard?" Agnes asked.

"While any death is sad, father's passing has taken precedence. Unfortunately, we may never discover who took the life of that footman," Peter said to her.

Watching her brother, her eyes narrowed. "You believe father killed him."

William turned to face her more fully. "We lack proof of anything to do with that man's death. Lacking sufficient information, there can be no further investigation. Our case is closed, leaving certain situations without solutions."

"What are the ones wanting answers?" she asked.

"I discovered several things while working on your father's behalf, which may be related to your grandfather's bigamy or not. Because of that, your brother and I agreed to leave them be."

"I dislike unanswered questions."

That made her a gifted scientist, but a tough woman to appease when she wanted clarity. It was part of the reason he had to keep his distance.

As tempting as she was, it would take no time at all, and she'd figure out his failing and hate him for it. Agnes, with her great mind, would have no patience for a dummy like him.

After lunch, Allwyn arrived to take the documents pertaining to the House of Lords and deliver them to the appropriate people. He also provided the papers to name the new earl.

When Basil signed the first document, the duke said, "This must be witnessed." Everyone looked at William, but he shook his head. "My brother's signature has more meaning than mine. He should sign."

He would not be a witness to something he hadn't read.

After Wolfstone left, the Harrison men began discussing the duties of the earldom. With no desire to sit in on that conversation, William excused himself. He wandered around the house, then went upstairs to check the sky through Agnes's telescope. It would be his last chance to see the details of the heavenly vista, which had filled him with awe. Since Alice was with her mother, the attic would be empty.

Two steps past the door, Agnes stood behind her desk. "What are you doing here?"

"I could ask the same of you. How is your mother?"

"She is resting. The heavens take my mind off things. And you?"

"The men are discussing family things. I remain nearby in case I'm needed later. With nothing else to do, I thought to study the sky."

She moved away from her telescope. "Enjoy."

"Thank you." He stepped around her, breathing in the warm scent of her cologne, then looked into the eyepiece. "It's amazing, isn't it?"

"There's a picture in here, if you'd like to see it." She tapped the cover of the red leather-bound book in a stack on the far edge of the table.

"I wouldn't trouble you." He wanted to enjoy his last look at the sky through a magnificent instrument, without spoiling the moment. He didn't want her opening the tome they had argued over, nor did he wish to look at it. The woman was too smart by half and if he gave her the opportunity, she'd figure out his shame. Heaven help him if that happened. He could hear the derision in her voice as she taunted him, which would tear him to pieces and hurt their investigation agency beyond repair. He would do everything in his power to avoid that.

She slid it to him and opened it. "Here it is, right here," she said, pointing to a diagram.

Without a choice, William looked at the page and then through the eyepiece and back at the picture again. "It's close, isn't it?"

"It is. And here are the names of the stars in this position at night."

He didn't glance at the list. The words would jump around and mean nothing. "Thanks, but I'll pass. I'd never remember all of them."

"Are you sure? I can't imagine looking at them without identifying them." She was watching him, much as she'd study a star through her lens.

He sighed. The woman was persistent in everything. In the bedroom, it would be exciting, but standing here, it annoyed him.

"That's because it's your passion, whereas for me, this is a casual interest."

"Really? I thought you cared more than that."

Depend on her to pick up on his reaction to seeing the sky in this detail. "Hmmm." He added nothing more, for Agnes would take his words and run with them. "I should return to the study in case I'm needed," he said, straightening away from the eyepiece.

"Perhaps they'll need you to review documents again."

William spun around to face her. "What are you talking about? We went through the papers in the safe." He had made it through that painful exercise with no one the wiser and did not want to repeat it.

"Agreed, but you didn't read any of them, did you?" She looked him in the eye. "You wouldn't glance at the hymn when we buried father."

"Since I can't carry a tune in a bucket, I don't sing. It has nothing to do with the words."

She snapped her fingers. "That's why you over-reacted when I gave you this book for Christmas. You can't read!"

"What drivel are you talking about? Everyone can read."

"Except you. Why not, William?"

"This is a ridiculous conversation and I have work to do." He circled around her.

Agnes put her hand on his arm and stepped in front of him, blocking his path. "Read something for me."

Fear pressed his lips together and fisted his hands against his legs. This was his worst nightmare come to life. He shook his head. "You are not my tutor nor my professor. Please excuse me, I must return downstairs."

"No."

Damned woman. He needed to distract her. He cupped her shoulders and pulled her close. "I'd rather kiss you than read to you." She closed her eyes and leaned toward him, and he claimed her.

Her lips were soft and when he tilted his head for better access, she opened up, inviting him in. Her taste was an aphrodisiac, igniting a fire that threatened to burn out of control. He softened his lips and gentled the kiss. Then he pulled away from her.

"Now I must return to the study," he said, savoring her flavor.

She held on to him. "Why won't you be honest with me, William? I trusted you, and you helped me, starting with hearing numbers instead of notes, when I dance. I've shown you my passion for the sky. And you know all my family's secrets, but you won't trust me with this one. Why not?"

"Because, it's not—."

She remained in front of him, hands on his arms. "Please do not insult my intelligence by denying the truth. You have fascinated me all this time. I watched you and can't think of a single incident where you read anything. You have an excellent memory and use it to cover up the facts, but that doesn't make it less of a lie."

"Agnes, let it go. You are fighting shadows. I am an adult man with a business and a rewarding life, none of which would be possible if I couldn't read."

"Despite this, you are successful, and no one will hear any different from me. But this is me. The woman who took the biggest risk ever and invited you into my private world, with a book, no less. I trusted you, and I'm asking you to give me the same respect."

He looked into her eyes and saw determination. His heart sank. She would not let this go and as soon as she discovered the truth, she'd send him away as a dumb oaf, just like his tutors and many others, before he learned to hide his deficiency.

But she was right. He knew all her secrets and fair was fair. He took a deep breath, closed his eyes, and exhaled. "It's not that I can't read, Agnes. But rather that the letters won't stand still long enough for me to make sense of them."

"What does that mean?" she asked, her voice soft.

He pulled the big red book over to them and opened it in the middle. "I am told that people see straight rows of characters, going from left to right."

"Yes, that is printed on the page."

"But that's not true for me. When I look at this, every letter is moving, usually up and down. There is no order to the movement, nor is there any pattern. I've tried everything possible to fix the problem with no success." Emptiness swamped him after his admission, but a small taste of freedom lurked, as well.

Was his honesty worth it? How long until her lip curled and her nose wrinkled and she flinched away from him?

"Have you used a piece of paper to cover the lines below the one you're reading?"

He nodded. "Many times."

"Have you put something black over the page, except for a single line?"

"Yes. When the letters move, they disappear against the dark card."

"All of them? Every time?"

He agreed. "Always."

"That is most interesting. Why were you reticent to tell me about it?"

William scratched his forehead. "You lack patience for people you deem stupid. What do you call a man who cannot read? Every derogatory term has been hurled at me my whole life. I couldn't stand it coming from you."

"This quirk of your vision has nothing to do with your intelligence. It is a failing of your eyes. Do spectacles help?"

"No, they don't. In fact, they make it worse." Depend on Agnes to ask questions trying to solve the problem.

"How strange." She shook her head, then slipped her hands around his neck. "If I could kiss it better, I would, but this is beyond kisses, nor is it about how smart you are. Rather, it is a physical obstacle. Some people have poor vision and must wear spectacles. Unfortunately, they won't help you. It's not very different from seeing nothing in the sky until a focused telescope is available. The stars appear to twinkle but don't. These are like your situation. Although yours is not discussed, it is likely common."

Relief swamped him, nearly buckling his knees. He blinked a couple of times, then took a deep breath and chucked her under the chin. "Depend on you to view my problem as relating to astronomy, rather than my intelligence."

"There is nothing wrong with your brain, except for your lack of trust in me." Guileless, she looked into his eyes.

"There is another thing you should know, since we're being honest about my shortcomings."

"You have more than one? What's that?"

"I bought the same book for you for Christmas."

Head thrown back, she laughed out loud. "You're admitting that part of your reaction was because I spoiled your surprise."

He smiled at her. "Perhaps."

"Admit it, I caught you unexpectedly, and you reacted."

"There was more to it, Agnes. I had just begun to consider other things to do with the break in to your father's safe. I assumed you would hate me for bringing any of those possibilities to light."

She shrugged. "It's a fair opinion. I was furious when you told mother her husband was dead."

He grinned. "I noticed."

"I don't feel that way any longer. As the story came out, I concluded father probably murdered the footman, to make it appear as if another break-in had occurred."

He held her close. "That was my conclusion, although I have no proof."

"What other secret are you keeping?"

He shook his head. "You never give up, do you?"

"No, I don't."

"Promise me you won't be angry because of my conclusions."

"I'll do my best."

"Initially, I wondered if there was something of a personal nature in your father's safe. Perhaps a note from a mistress that he didn't want to become public. Or a blackmail threat." He rubbed her back, holding her close. "He assured me his long-term paramour and their children were in Bath, where she could take the waters for her health."

More secrets about their family, although these would likely remain hidden. Such situations were sadly common in society and it was unlikely she'd ever meet these people.

"There was another woman, but he severed their connection early in December."

"None of this is unusual. Most men of the ton have mistresses."

"Of course. But it's rare that the latest mistress turns up dead after I started my investigation."

"Why would you think that had anything to do with my father?"

"Because he'd said to her that he was a bigger bastard than she realized, the day before he sent her packing."

She grimaced, wrinkling her nose. "That cannot be a coincidence."

"My thoughts exactly."

"I'm not sure what your mother knows about your father's other life, so we'll remain silent about these discoveries. I can't swear they have anything to do with the later events, and I will not speculate or guess about what happened."

She stretched on her toes and kissed him quickly. "I love that about you. You are careful about what you say and the words you use. It is a trait I must learn and practice."

"Unless it comes to trying to protect you. I apologize, Agnes. I should have credited your strength to handle the news, but it was ugly and had enormous repercussions."

"Now I understand why you said what you did. But I am not blameless either. I jumped to conclusions, and they were wrong. How I spoke to you and behaved in mother's study resembled a two-year-old reacting to being told no. A part of me knew you wouldn't lie to mother, but I still accused you of that very thing. It was unfair of me. You deserved better."

He kissed her eyelids and held her against him. "Let's put these events behind us, sweetheart. They came out of a difficult situation, the likes of which we'll never see again. I'd rather focus on the positive things. How you feel in my arms when we're dancing. Or the excitement on your face when you're explaining something about astronomy or science to me. Or your pleasure when chatting with Juliette and realized that women can step out of the norm and live their own lives.

Agnes relaxed against him, and he tightened his hold on her, needing her close. Shocked silent after telling her he couldn't read—saying the words out loud to someone outside of his family. It was an enormous risk, but she was trustworthy. He needn't rely on the reciprocal secrets they held, but, rather, their trust in each other.

"Where do we go from here?" she asked.

He had been considering the same thing, but it seemed inappropriate to bring it up. Depend on Agnes to get to the point. "I think for the next three months, while you're in deep mourning, nothing changes. If your uncle and mother approve, we will spend as much time together as possible, either here or at Wolfstone. Then, when it's appropriate, we can be married."

Her gaze fixed on his. "Is that your version of a proposal?" she asked, her brows arched, and her chin dipped down.

Apparently, his sweetheart had a romantic side, like many other women. "No. But it is my plan, if you're agreeable. I want no more secrets, Agnes, and I will endeavor to be as plainspoken as possible."

"I love that idea. Let us both be open and honest with each other. It is the only way to keep our marriage happy and content."

"But let's remember in those rare times when things are not perfect, making up is wonderful."

"Agreed." She stretched up and pressed her lips to his, her tongue sliding along the seam and dipping into his mouth.

He was a lucky man, for his Agnes was not afraid to ask for what she wanted. And she could take all that he could give.

Regretfully, he ended their kiss. "Come, sweetheart. We'd best return downstairs. I don't want to add any more difficulties to your family."

She nodded. "I agree. We must be circumspect. For now."

CHAPTER NINETEEN

The next three months were as difficult as everyone in the family feared. The ton would have given them the cut direct, except the new earl wouldn't tolerate it. He insisted on holding meetings in his study and often had his sister-in-law pour tea for them.

"Another one?" Agnes asked her uncle as a man stormed out of the house.

"Unfortunately, yes. He had the nerve to suggest that allowing Odile to maintain her home here was not done and I should insist both of you find other accommodation as soon as possible."

"What did you say to him?"

"I told him the Duke of Wolfstone, and I discussed my living arrangements and we agreed it was the best for all concerned."

"Is that true?"

"Yes. You and your mother are at no fault in this situation. You are victims of your father's choices, as am I. We will go forward as a family, and anyone who doesn't like it can stay away. I am not that enamored of the season, the marriage mart, and the constant gossip, that I can't live without it."

Agnes squeezed his arm. "Have I told you that you are a decent man?"

"It never hurts to remind an old fellow about his good points, niece. It keeps us from forgetting them." He grinned at her. "Is your suitor visiting today?"

Her cheeks warmed at her uncle's reference to William. Although he'd been busy with several cases, he made sure she was aware he was thinking of her. Most days he came to the house, and they looked at the sky together, but on those days he wasn't able to stop, he sent posies, a book from Hatchards, or a treat his mother's cook prepared. Nary a day passed that he didn't show his thoughts about her.

His actions warmed her heart and made her soft and mushy inside. Her feelings grew stronger and deeper. This must be the love written about by poets and novelists, for she would do anything to keep it alive.

That afternoon, William joined her in the attic, took her in his arms and kissed her. When he pulled back, she had to catch her breath. "That was a nice hello."

"I'm glad you approve. Do you know what day it is today, my dear?"

She stopped to think. "It's Wednesday, isn't it?"

"Yes, but it is also three months and a day since your father passed."

"I knew it was coming, and I've been working, hoping not to drown in my sadness."

Holding her hand, he dropped to one knee. "Agnes Harrison, will you do me the great honor of becoming my wife?" He took a small box from his pocket and opened it. "I saw this stone, and it reminded me of you," he said, showing her a blue sapphire with a star in the middle. "The stars brought us together and as long as they shine, we shall be happy."

For a moment, the beauty of the setting stole her breath. "Oh, William," she exclaimed, clasping her hands tightly. "It's perfect."

He slid it on her finger and kissed it. "Since engagement rings aren't common, if you'd prefer to keep this for our wedding, I understand. But it was meant for you."

"Yes, yes, and yes. I can't wait to marry you. I am thrilled with my engagement ring, and will wear it from now on." She pulled him to his feet and into a hug, holding him close. "Thank you for finding the perfect stone for me." Leaning away, she glanced at it again. "It could not be better."

He took a tiny step back from her. "Mother thought a small family wedding in three months would be appropriate. But of course, the final decision is up to you and your mama."

She nodded in agreement. "Thank you for your concern about her opinion. I appreciate your care for her feelings. And that isn't too long to wait. However, if you'd shown up with a special license for the weekend, I would've agreed with you, too."

He stepped close again, claiming her lips, then kissed the tip of her nose. "By the way, I spoke to both your brother and your uncle, and they approved our courtship, and Peter is working on the marriage settlements."

"My only request is our home comes with an attic for my telescope to look at the stars."

"Allwyn has insisted on providing a residence. He says it is his responsibility as the duke and eldest brother. In many families, they would ask a son to manage a property, but since Triple E Investigations is in London, he knows I'm staying here. And we need to remain close to your mother."

"That is very generous of him. Does he have a place in mind?"

"No. He told me he wouldn't do all the hard work. You and I have to find a house of our own. Which means," he tapped her on the end of the nose, "finding the proper attic will be up to you."

She captured and held his gaze. "I never dreamed life could be this grand or overflowing with joy, but here I am."

With warmth spreading throughout her and her heartbeat racing, Agnes took William's hand and followed him downstairs, stopping on every landing to share a kiss.

Her mother was in her sitting room, completing some correspondence.

"We have some news," she said.

Mama came to her, taking her hand. She looked from the ring to Agnes and up to William. "I cannot put into words how delighted I am for both of you. I wish you every happiness." She hugged them. "Young lady, I want to remind you I knew this was the man for you when the two of you met. And although you pooh-poohed my comments. I saw no reason to change my mind. You are good together because you bring out the best in each other."

"Thank you."

"We thought to wait for three months to wed. And we would prefer a small service, with immediate family only," William explained.

"Lovely. A June wedding."

After a few minutes of chatting and planning, they went to her uncle's study. The man had surprised everyone as he picked up the pieces of legislation in the House of Lords. And with her brother, Peter, they had increased the finances of the earldom, after selling Basil's business interests in Boston.

Agnes knocked, then opened the door. "Excuse us, Uncle, but we have an announcement."

He smiled and crossed to them, shaking William's hand and hugging her. "I didn't think it would take long after he and I spoke yesterday. Congratulations to both of you."

From behind them, Peter said, "Is this the expected disclosure of impending nuptials?"

Another round of well-wishes followed. William explained their preference for a small wedding.

"Basil, you have been everything possibly kind and generous, and I would be honored if you would walk me down the aisle."

"I never imagined myself doing such a thing as a lifelong bachelor. Nothing would please me more."

Her fiance looked at the clock and then at each of the men who would soon be relatives. "If you will excuse us, I told mother to expect two extra for lunch today. I'm expecting the whole family in attendance, which makes it easier to share our announcement."

After more hugs and congratulations, the couple climbed into the carriage and were off.

William reached over and closed both curtains. "Finally, we're alone." He lifted Agnes to his lap. "Now I can have my wicked way with you," and he began ravishing her mouth.

He pulled away to catch his breath. "Your scent drives me to distraction. One whiff and I want to drag you to a private place," he said, nibbling on her earlobe.

"I wouldn't fight you very hard if you did that." She slid her fingers into the hair at his neck and added, "I might not resist at all."

"We have a lifetime to make love, sweetheart. I will not risk your good name by having a child any sooner than nine months after we wed. As painful as abstinence is, it's the better choice."

"But since there's no peril to kissing, less talk and more action, please."

It wasn't long until the carriage slowed and made the turn into the Wolfstone drive. "We've arrived," William announced.

"Oh, my goodness. I must look a mess." She straightened her neckline and reached up to tidy her hair.

"Let me tuck this strand into place and straighten your hat. I can't do anything about the flush on your cheeks or your red lips, but otherwise, all is well."

"I'm hoping your mama agrees with you because I don't want our marriage to start off poorly with her."

"Fear not. Pay attention when she and my grandmother talk. You will soon understand my family and their values."

Inside, all five of his siblings and their spouses and children, and his mother and Grandma Welther, were enjoying a glass of wine in the salon.

The moment he and Agnes crossed the threshold, everyone turned to them, applauded, and rose to welcome them. Hugs, handshakes, and toasts were the order of the day. The women gathered on one side of the room, discussing wedding plans while the men were on the other, talking about the future.

"I guess this means you owe me a boon," Louis reminded him.

"One we agreed on, not some silly thing meant to embarrass me or my bride."

"I wouldn't hurt Agnes like that, but you, however, are fair game."

He groaned, knowing his older brother would make him feel foolish.

"It won't be that bad, I promise."

William slapped his brother's back. "Best not be, or I'll refuse to pay."

He looked around. "I can't thank all of you enough. I do not know how the Harrisons would've managed without all of you standing beside them."

They fell silent, fascinated by the floor, the women, or even the doorway.

"That's what family does, little brother. Always." Allwyn said.

Looking at his wife in the midst of the women of his female relatives, he was more grateful for their support than he could say. And he and Agnes would pass on those same values to their children.

EPILOGUE

William waited in the ballroom of the Harrison's home for Agnes to join him in front of friends and family and pledge their troth to each other before God and her brother Andrew, who had agreed to perform the ceremony.

Walking beside her uncle Basil, his bride walked to him. She was stunning in an ice blue silk gown was diamonds attached to the bodice. The stones twinkled with every movement, reminding him of an early morning sky. It was the perfect choice for her.

They exchanged vows and her brother Andrew proclaimed, "I now pronounce you man and wife. You may kiss your bride."

He did, leaning her back over his arm and showing her and their family how much she meant to him.

They were toasted and feted until late afternoon, when they left. A short carriage ride later and they arrived at their new home, several doors down from Louis.

He carried her across the threshold and up to their room. Her mother's cook had prepared a wedding feast for them and placed it in the master suite. Champagne was on ice and candles cast a golden glow.

"This is beautiful. I must remember to thank mother for her consideration." She smiled at him. "But it is unfortunate we will eat it cold." She turned and loosened his cravat. "We have other appetites to feed."

He couldn't agree more.

If you enjoyed this book and would like to help other readers discover it, please leave a review on my Amazon page:

Or you can go here

Watch for the next release in this series, Philip, Her Portrait of Love, available soon at this link

They were unsuited to each other. He was a recluse who hid in his loft and painted, while she was in the middle of the social whirl.

Lady Jane Sutton craves a change. Despite her extroverted personality, the impulsive young woman struggles to feign interest in ton events after three interminable seasons. But when she gets caught kissing a handsome family friend in the library, she quickly agrees to pretend the faux pas never happened.

Lord Philip Evans can sense a chance for success. Finally receiving support from his brother in his artistic pursuits, the quiet youngest son hopes his sweet embrace with the subject of his latest commission won't make the work awkward. But as he traces the lines of her face on paper, he's charmed to discover that her beauty is perfectly matched by her loyal and independent nature.

As Jane finds unexpected joy in their budding relationship, she gives in to worry and rashly heads to his apartment when he uncharacteristically misses a sitting. And when the couple is discovered in a compromising situation for a second time, Philip knows the only honorable choice is to offer her marriage.

Can they blend their differing views and paint a happily ever after?

Philip, Her Portrait of Love is the fourth book in The Duke's Brothers Regency romance series. If you like heroines who defy society, delightful dialogue, and dark mysteries, then you'll adore this vibrant courtship.

W ould you like a free novella? ***Wedding the Spare*** is available here: or use this QR code:

A second son, desperate to forge his own way in life. An innocent debutante forced into marriage. But will his family destroy both their dreams?

Gregory Sutton is a second son, with no prospects and no hope. Until his father arranges a marriage to a woman who will provide the funds for his freedom. When they meet, he discovers a shy, quiet young woman who fulfills his every dream - one his toxic family will traumatize and terrify.

Lady Patience has no choice in her marriage; the contracts are signed and she is marrying a stranger. But she decides to meet her fate with grace, for the sake of their future. But their first meeting is marred by his older brother's drunken violence.

When Patience disappears, Gregory fears his brother has kidnapped her to get even with him. And though Patience has fallen in love with her soft-spoken, gentle fiance, she is terrified to share the family home with his brother, who left her to die.

Can these two gentle souls overcome the risks from his brother and find their happy ever after?

Wedding the Spare is the emotional prequel to the London Railroad Society, a Regency Romance series. If you like trusting women, determined men and a love story that defies their circumstances, you'll love this story.

Get your free copy now!

THE END

L̲ouise Behiel is a coach and therapist, and in another life, a diversity specialist, and an accountant. A feminist, mother, and grandmother, she has three children and six grandchildren who delight and inspire her.

Louise delights in examining the realities of today under the light of historical times, for she believes that people have always been the same – they just weren't as open about it.

Visit her website at louisebehiel.com

Thank you for taking the time to read *William, Her Guiding Star!* I know your time is precious. I hope you enjoyed reading this book, as much as I enjoyed writing it.

This is book 3 of the series, *The Duke's Brothers*, which follows and is set in the same world as another series, The London Railroad Society, as well as *The Dowager Duchess,* the love story of Patience Sutton, Jane's friend in this novel.

Books in both series can be read on their own, but your reading pleasure may be enhanced by reading them in order.

Cheers,

Louise

www.ingramcontent.com/pod-product-compliance
Lightning Source LLC
Chambersburg PA
CBHW060627260626
47161CB00008B/2824